SHORT
STACK

Reed Farrel Coleman

Acknowledgements

I would like to thank Marjorie Tucker for everything she does for me as a friend, reader, and all-around good person. She was kind enough to read the contents of this collection for typos and errors missed during their first go arounds.

Big thanks to Erin Mitchell for putting this together in all its various forms and for her sage advice.

Thanks to my son Dylan for the cover art. It is based on an old sketch of me. He loves me enough to make sure the cover image now looks like I would like to look instead of how I look.

Much appreciation to the editors who took chances by publishing my early short stories and to editors who later on solicited my contributions. I love the hell out of writing short stories and without your encouragement I'm not sure I would have kept trying.

Introduction

"If you want to be poor, be a writer. If you want to be destitute, write poetry."

Anyone who has heard me give a talk has also heard me discuss how I grew up in an angry family and that we communicated through yelling. When everyone yells, no one hears. While I don't think anyone knows for sure why they are inflicted (I use the word intentionally) with a particular calling, I'd like to think I began writing poetry as a way to be heard above the din. Apparently, it worked. My poetry began appearing in school publications by the time I was in the eighth grade. By the time I finished high school I was the editor of the school's literary magazine. At college, I worked as an editorial assistant on the literary journal in which some of my work appeared. And I began to get published in independent literary journals and magazines. I studied poetry with David Lehman and had the pleasure of sitting in on classes taught by Allen Ginsberg and John Ashbery. But the truth is I never thought my

poetry would amount to much. My plan, such as I had one, was to take a "regular" job and keep writing and publishing poetry. That's what happened.

In the mid-1980s, a few years after I met my wife in a poetry class at the New School in Manhattan, I took a night class back at Brooklyn College. The only class that fit my schedule was American Detective Fiction. Funny thing is, I never read crime fiction. To me, crime fiction were those cheesy books on my dad's nightstand with the lurid covers of half-dressed woman holding guns. Boy, did I get that wrong. After reading *The Continental Op, Farewell, My Lovely,* and *The Maltese Falcon,* I went to my wife and in an act of utter insanity, told her I wanted to quit my good paying job, with perks that included free trips to Europe, in order to write detective novels. Twenty-nine published novels later ... Who could have predicted it? Not me.

While I can guess where my poetry came from and I can point to the exact moment I chose to leave the everyday world to become a crime fiction writer, it's a little bit more mysterious when it comes to my short stories. My guess is I was deeply affected by episodes of *The Twilight Zone.* I was always amazed, even as a kid, at the ability of the show's writers to tell what seemed to be punchy, intense narratives with big payoffs in such a condensed amount of time. I'd also read all of Poe's short stories and burned through lots of sci fi short story collections. And many of the short stories I'd read in college made quite an impression, yet I didn't attempt to write a short story until I'd published several novels.

Short stories are a different beast. A novel is the night sky full of stars. A short story is a road flare. A novel can be about a thousand things. A short story is about one thing. It's difficult moving from a world where one has the freedom to explore broader issues to a world in which every single word has to matter a lot. While my first stories weren't very good, they made me a better writer. And I can say without reservation that every short story I

have ever written has made me a better novel writer. Somewhere along the line, though, a strange thing happened—I became pretty good at short stories and my affection for them has grown over the years. So much so that six or seven of my stories will appear in various publications over the next several months. Stories that range from the tale of a crazed junkie written in second person present to a tale of a crime-solving talking cat named Murray. My short story "The Terminal" (not included in this collection) is a thousand words long and, I believe, the shortest piece of fiction ever nominated for an Edgar Award. Alas, I didn't win.

My favorite anecdote about a short story of mine goes like this. One day several years ago I received a phone call from Sarah Cortez, a writer I had never met before. She said she was coediting *Indian Country Noir* for Akashic Books and wondered if I might be interested in contributing a story. I was honored to be asked but confessed that I was confused as to why she would be asking a Jewish boy from Brooklyn with an Irish name who wrote hard-boiled detective novels to contribute a story about Native Americans. She was honest in saying that they were on deadline and they needed one or two more stories to complete the collection. She said Johnny Temple, the Akashic publisher, had suggested asking me because I had done a few stories in other Noir series books and that I was reliable and quick.

I agreed, saying I wanted to write about the Poospatuck Indian Reservation on Long Island. Although the reservation was only seventy acres in size, the Unkechaug Tribe who lived there suffered from many of the same problems that plagued the larger Western tribes on their vast reservations.

Sarah's response: "No, we already have too many stories about Eastern tribes.

"My wife is part Chippewa ... how about a story set on Michigan's Upper Peninsula?"

Sarah's response: "No, Lawrence Block is already doing that."

"Well, Sarah, how about you just tell me where you need me to set the story, pick a tribe, and let me deal with it."

A week or so later I sent Sarah the story originally titled "Chief", the tale of a washed-up Hollywood actor who looked the part of a classic Indian but who had been cut off from his Pima roots. Eventually the story was renamed "Another Role" and was included in the collection. Neither the collection nor my story garnered much attention. A year later, however, the story was sold to Audible.com and the person in charge of the project told me to pick an actor, any actor I would like, to read the story. "Dream big, Reed," she said. I did. I chose Liev Schreiber.

Six months, a year, went by. I had totally forgotten about the story when I received an email with an audio file attached from the project manager at Audible. I listened, but it wasn't Liev Schreiber's voice I heard reading my story. It was Cheech Marin's! That's right, Cheech of Cheech and Chong. And you know what? He was fantastic. I couldn't believe it. The story is still available on Audible.com if you want to purchase it, but you can read it here first.

Reed Farrel Coleman
October, 2018

Stories

Crime Fiction

Baby Pigeons

Have you ever seen baby pigeons? From the anthology
UNLOADED.

Fuckup: He's such a fuckup.
Fuck up: Please don't fuck up.

Look either of 'em up in Webster's and you'd understand Tommy Dushane. Tommy, as they liked to say in the Gravesend neighborhood he'd grown up in, was a royal fucking fuckup. With him it went beyond the anatomical, biological, or psychological. It was downright metaphysical, though he would have been hard pressed to pronounce the word let alone define it. He was a buffoon wrapped in a flag. His neck was red, his collar blue, and his skin a trashy white. These days he lived in a place that

1

gave shitholes a bad name: a rickety firetrap of an illegal apartment in Central Islip that began its existence as a tool shed. Not even the illegals who had fairly overrun CI, Brentwood, and North Bay Shore would've lived in that shitbox.

To be a real fuckup, though, was to understand highs and lows. Fuckups weren't losers. Losers go down for the count and never get up off the mat. They live out their lives, such as they were, below the radar screen. That wasn't Tommy. Nuh-uh. Tommy knew highs, several of them, a countless number. Whether it was a bad choice, an ill-timed word, or a stupid bet, he always self-destructed. Always. One of his old friends used to say that Tommy Douchebag could fuck up finding a genie in a bottle. When Tommy went down, he went down in flames. It got so he developed a sixth sense about it, like how animals know when an earthquake is coming. As Tommy stumbled down the aisles of the 3:14 to Ronkonkoma, blue hard hat in hand, he got that feeling. The big fuckup was at hand.

It was odd how you never saw the Tommy Dushanes of the world on their way into Manhattan, only on the trains back to Long Island from Penn Station. It was like how you never see baby pigeons. It was kinda like those fuckers just appeared whole, all grown up and ready to shit on your head. The trick was that the construction guys took the pre-dawn trains into the city, so it left the stockbrokers to ponder the baby pigeon problem of where the construction workers had come from. Although their wardrobe was strictly Dickies and Carhartt, their shoes steel-toed Red Wings, they did not lack for quiet desperation. Some sat wondering where the money for their kids' college tuition would come from. Some would fall off scaffolds tomorrow or the tomorrow after that or ... Some would die of cancer. And some would happily hold their great-grandchildren in their arms.

Tommy didn't believe in silent despair. Good thing, too. He might've drowned in it. No, he was one of those guys who put his faith in Budweiser. In Anheuser-Busch he trusted. He had finished a six pack by the time the train had reached Bethpage and had bummed a seventh off a fellow hardhat. Never much for introspection, he didn't bother ascribing today's accelerated consumption of alcohol to that gnawing fuck up feeling in his belly. Nah, it was nothing a hot shower—his landlord let him use the basement bathroom for an extra ten bucks a month—and a few cups of coffee wouldn't fix. But right at the moment all he was worried about was finding a place to unload the seven cans worth of excess fluid.

"For fuck's sake!" he screamed loud enough for the whole car to hear. Tommy slammed a wind-chapped hand into the locked bathroom door. "What the fuck you lookin' at?" he slurred, pointing at a Wall Street type who had turned to see what the commotion was about. "Fuck you and fuck this!"

Tommy stepped into the next car and the car after that one. The handle to the bathroom in that car had been removed and replaced with a steel plate.

"How the fuck am I s'pposed to get in there?"

"Use a can opener, ya prick!"

Tommy didn't exactly recognize the voice, but it had a vague familiarity. The vagueness only enhanced by the seven beers and the distraction of a bursting bladder. But he smiled at the man who had just called him a prick, showing his chipped front teeth

"Hey, man," Tommy said as if the guy was his favorite uncle. He didn't have a favorite uncle, but if he had one, he would have greeted him like this. "What's the good word?"

The guy smiled back at Tommy, but not like an imaginary favorite uncle. No, it was more the smile of a shark. He knew

Tommy didn't quite remember him and that was all to the good ... Well, except for Tommy.

"Come on, I'll show you a car where the bathroom's working."

Riding the elevator up to the 27th floor of the Carillion Park West, Picassa—her "stage" name—stared intently at the cleanly shaven nape of the elevator operator's neck. For his part, the elevator operator stared at her ample cleavage reflected in the mirror-lined car. As she stared she wondered about the night ahead, what preliminaries the client had in store before the matter at hand. A show? Christ, she hoped not. She'd already sat through that inane *Finding Neverland* and the incomprehensible *The Incident of the Dog in the Nighttime* so often she knew the stage blocking better than the understudies. She never understood why they insisted on Broadway. Half of her clients didn't understand six words of English. And the words they knew other than hello were usually: fuck, blow job, tits, and anal.

Would dinner ensue at Masa or Eleven Madison Park followed by drinks at the Algonquin or some hot rooftop bar where they could behold the skyline? Or would the client skip the prelims and go for the old suck, hump, and run? Sometimes she could tell what the night ahead held in store by what she was told to wear. Not tonight, though. Tonight could go either way. The instructions were to dress for an evening out, but not in anything with too many buttons or clasps.

The elevator slowed. A quaint, old fashioned bell chimed.

"Twenty-seven. Your floor, ma'am," the operator said, turning to have a direct view of her cleavage. He was unable to hide the smile at the corner of his mouth.

Although it was just the two of them in the large elevator car, she brushed her breasts against him as she exited. His smile grew wider still.

Stepping out of the car, the doors closing behind her, Picassa turned left as she had been instructed to do. She was now to walk down two flights and go to room 2512. Clients, she thought, could be such children. Some were just desperate to be seen with beautiful Anglo women. Some were so fearful about blackmail, about their business rivals using proof of their dalliances against them. It was bad enough she had to fuck some of them, but she especially disliked it when they made her jump through hoops to do it.

Presumably, she could have been horse-faced and dressed like a char woman as long as she could follow instructions and had breasts, lips, and a functional vagina. Checking her makeup in the hall mirror and smoothing her strapless indigo gown, she decided she more than met those prerequisites. She added a spray of perfume to her cleavage, blew herself a kiss, and walked to the stairwell door. She pushed it open.

Clients my ass! From the day she had gone into the life, she had been schooled to think of these men as clients. Never johns. Never.

If you think of them as johns, then you will think of yourself as a whore. We do not employ whores.

Those words went round and round in her head as the stairwell door slammed shut at her back. But playing pretend, regardless of profitability, had a limited shelf life. Just lately they were all johns to her, these little Asian men with their big bankrolls and eager yellow cocks. She kept telling herself she could make it a few more months, that just a few thousand more was all she needed to stake her. She could get Tommy Jr. back from her mom and get the fuck out. Out of the business. Out of New York. Out of the same

atmosphere as that jerk off who'd knocked her up and fucked up her life.

"Shit!" she whispered to no one, noticing the light was out on the landing below. Stairs of any kind were treacherous enough, decked out as she was in a form fitting gown and nosebleed stilettos. Picassa hitched up her gown with her left hand, the same hand that held her matching clutch, and took a firm hold on the cool banister with her right.

Almost fully to the dark landing, she heard a man's breathing. She froze. She let go of her gown and the rail in order to reach for the canister of pepper spray she carried in her clutch. She stumbled forward to the landing and in reaching reflexively back for the railing to catch herself, the clutch and spray vanished into the vacuum of the dark stairwell. The man in the shadows seemed to sense her fear and to reassure her, jingling his room key. She exhaled and an audible sigh of relief escaped her lips. She noticed she was panting and felt the sting of sweat against her freshly shaven underarms.

"Konichiwa, Ichiro-san," she said in perfect Japanese. It hadn't been easy for a girl from Gravesend, Brooklyn to master the proper inflection. She waited for Ichiro-san's reply.

His response was universal. A strong hand shot out of the dark, grabbed a handful of her hair, and forced her to her knees. She was a little unnerved by this, but not because it had never happened before. On the contrary, she knew that sometimes they enjoyed a little danger or wanted to play out some long-held masturbation fantasy. She had once doubled her fee for letting a Saudi prince watch one of his wives go down on her in a private box at the Met. He said it was a wife, but for all she knew, the woman might've been another escort. Probably was because she was awfully good at it and Picassa hadn't had to fake her orgasm.

No, there was something else about this client. His hands were too big and powerful, his palm too rough and calloused. But maybe not. His pants were expensively made and when she reached for him through the open zipper, she felt that his boxers were silken. From that point on it was automatic. She made the proper coos and sighs and placed him in her mouth. Then she showed off by taking him all the way, deeply into the back of her throat, keeping him there for quite some time. They all liked that and it usually earned her extra gratuities. Many of them would ask her to spend the night afterwards, no matter the expense, so that she might reprise the performance over and over again. Men were such uncomplicated animals.

It was only when her client's thighs stiffened and his back arched that the unease fell over her again. It was too late now. He yanked on her hair so hard her eyes teared up. It was done. Again, she made the proper ego building coos and sighs. But as she tried to stand, he held her down, pulling her hair harder, tugging her head back. Then in a flash, it came to her.

"Show me your room key!" she said, even as some of her hair pulled away from her scalp.

He showed it to her and laughed. Although the Carillion Park West was a grand old hotel, it had gone keyless last year.

Her eyes got wide with fear, her heart pounding so hard she might have been able to see her chest vibrate had there been enough light. He pulled her up off her knees, keeping her head tilted back. She opened her mouth to scream, tried to scream, but she felt a slight breeze, heard a swishing sound, felt a pinch in her neck. She gasped for air. She grabbed for her throat. Her heaving chest was warm and soaking wet, yet she was desperately cold inside. She was losing consciousness when he finally let go of her hair. She pitched forward, gravity and inertia pulling her body down. There was a

dull thud when her near-lifeless body smacked onto the concrete
landing below. Outside the door, in the hallway, she heard a man
bitching to his wife about a grown man having to go see a silly play
about Peter Pan. If she wasn't already dead, Picassa might've
laughed.

After his new friend, Bobby—he said his name was Bobby—had
showed Tommy where there was a working bathroom, they'd sat
together for the remainder of the ride to Central Islip. Bobby was a
helluva guy. He was from Gravesend, too, the old neighborhood in
Brooklyn. Tommy was relieved to find out where he recognized
Bobby from.

"I'm a few years older," Bobby said, "but we used to see each
other around like on Avenue X sometimes or by Spumoni Gardens."

"Yeah, yeah, sure," Tommy said, still feeling the buzz from
all the beers.

"Hey, Tommy, let's you and me go have a drink for old
times' sake and maybe get something to eat. On me, of course."

Tommy Dushane was a fuckup, but he wasn't a stupid one.
He was also a poor one because even though he had a good paying
job, he was into every guy who put money on the street. He bet on
everything that was bet-able and lost on everything you could lose
on. He owed so much vig that he would never live long enough to
see the light of day. That's why he lived all the fuck the way out here
and in a shitbox the size of a half bathroom.

"Free meal. Free booze. Hell, yeah."

Now Tommy was a fucked-up fuckup, maybe drunker than
he had ever been and still been semi-conscious. He didn't really
recognize where Bobby had taken him, though he figured it was
somewhere near the railroad tracks. He didn't guess he would
recognize much of anything in the state he was in, but so what?

Bobby was cool. He'd treated him all night, brought him to a bar, bought him a few Jack Daniels, a cheeseburger and fries, and another JD for dessert. After that he'd given Tommy cash to go buy them a bottle of whatever he wanted at a liquor store on Suffolk Avenue.

They'd polished off the bottle of JD, sitting together on the grounds of the old college, north of the new minor league baseball stadium. They'd talked a lot about Gravesend and some of the people they knew in common. Talked about the girls they had fucked. Tommy had gone on about one in particular: Pattie Petrocelli. Talked about how she was the hottest girl in the neighborhood even when she was young.

"Man, I was fucking her since she was twelve. Taught her how to suck cock so that no one ever did it no better. Wasn't nothing I didn't teach her," Tommy bragged. "I taught her how to do it all, man. And I mean all."

"Come on, Tommy," Bobby said after Tommy had described a particularly interesting encounter with Pattie P. in the boys' bathroom at Lafayette High School. "Let's walk some of this shit off."

That was before. They had walked for what seemed like forever and Bobby had been really quiet. Tommy just figured that the booze had finally gotten to Bobby. Shit, they'd had enough to drown a freakin' elephant.

"This is good here," Bobby said, stopping in place.

"Good for what, huh?" Tommy slurred.

Bobby didn't answer. He just kind of smiled like he had on the train. Then he said, "I thought you woulda remembered me by now, Tommy Douchebag."

"Hey, man, there's no need to—"

He didn't finish the sentence because Bobby's left fist connected with Tommy's gut so hard he puked. When Tommy was done puking, Bobby grabbed Tommy by the hair, stood him up and broke his jaw with another left. Tommy was writhing in pain at Bobby's feet, making tortured squeals and screams. Bobby checked his watch and yanked Tommy by his jacket collar past some bushes, up some stairs, and onto an overpass.

"Still don't remember me?" Bobby asked again, putting his fist into Tommy's rib cage so hard that many of his ribs snapped. "You should. You sure remember a lot about my sister, Pattie."

Tommy's eyes got wide as he remembered Bobby. But Pattie's big brother was named Nick and he had been in prison when ... Oh shit!

Bobby saw the look in Tommy's eyes and knew Tommy knew. A train whistle blew in the distance, maybe a mile or two away from the overpass.

"That's right, Tommy Douchebag."

Bobby stopped talking while he proceeded to beat Tommy into unconsciousness. Then he lifted Tommy up over the railing and dropped him right in front of the oncoming train. Bobby, Nick actually, watched as the train shredded Tommy Dushane into little pieces of fuck up beneath its wheels.

As he made his way down the steps, he noticed a bunch of sleeping pigeons on a horizontal metal beam on the underside of the overpass. He shook his head and wondered why you never saw baby pigeons, ever.

Another Role

Originally titled Chief. *More about this story in the Introduction.*
From INDIAN COUNTRY NOIR.

It wasn't Harry Garson's fault he didn't speak a word of Navajo or Apache or Ute or Hopi or whatever the fuck kind of Indian he was. He didn't know and he didn't give a shit. Never had and he wasn't about to start caring now. Not that he was barking about his genetics, mind you. His classic Indian looks—the rich bronze skin, dark and distant eyes, high cheek bones, proudly bent nose, granite jaw, downturned mouth—had landed him over a hundred and fifty roles, large and small, in A, B, and C oaters dating back to 1938's "Forked River, Forked Tongue". As he advanced in years, his classic features, once those of the stereotypical proud brave—"Makeup and costume, c'mon, get over here and get some fucking war paint and feathers on Harry. He's got a wagon train to ambush.

We're losing the light, goddammit!"—had morphed into those of the sage chief. The distant eyes were now achingly sad, the brow above them knitted and furrowed. His cheeks had gone hollow and his angular jaw was now crooked thanks to a bar fight with Lock Martin—Klaatu barada nickto. Yes, that Lock Martin, all 7' 1" of the guy who played Gort in *The Day the Earth Stood Still*—at Musso and Frank in '53. Word was that Harry was getting the better of it until the normally gentle giant introduced the leg of a barstool to Harry's chops.

"Harry, you're turning my *kishkas* inside out," said movie agent Irv Rothenberg when he visited his client in the hospital."Who picks a fight with a guy bigger than Mount Shasta, for chrissakes? Lock is a sweetheart. What did you say to him to set him off like that?"

"I said Patricia Neal told me he had a small *shwantz*," Harry said, waving his right pinky at his agent. "Big man, little pecker." Harry even managed a laugh, though his mouth was wired shut.

"*Oy gevalt*, you're killing me, Harry!"

Harry was blessed—Irv would say cursed—with the genuine gift of gab, which he could use for good—like talking his way into a part or into a starlet's bed—or for bad, a la Lock Martin. He also had a facility for doing impersonations. When he was on the set with John Ford, Duke Wayne used to pay Harry to call up the second unit director and give him all manner of insane orders in Ford's voice. It got so bad that Ford had to start giving special code words to his staff so that they could recognize him and not the schmuck pretending to be him. The irony for Harry was that he didn't get his first speaking part until 1956's *Red Scout* and then his only line was, "Blue horse soldier with yellow hair like waves, across running river." Not exactly the stuff of Shakespeare, but the speaking parts came more frequently after that and by the mid-60s, Harry Garson

had landed a regular role as Smells Like Bearstein, Chief of the Sosoomee Tribe, on the short-lived series *Crazy Cavalry*. By the late 60s, as Westerns fell out of favor and parts for aging chief-types with a flair for the spoken word grew scarce, Harry settled into an angry semi-retirement. The few big roles Harry auditioned for in the late 60s and 70s, he lost to Chief Dan George. That really got to him going, especially when reruns of *Little Big Man* and *The Outlaw Josey Wales* played on the movie channels.

"That fucking Canadian prick!" Harry would bark at the screen and imitate Chief Dan George's quiet, monotone delivery. "Every eighteen-year-old in this country ran to goddamn Canada to avoid the draft and this is who we got in exchange? I bet they had to write out his lines in pictographs, the senile old bastard."

He was a charmer, Harry, but he had the bitterness in him too, and it began to overtake him as the years passed and the parts — those in the movies and those on his body — shriveled up. Those weren't the only things shriveling up either. He had never been good with money, especially when it was plentiful. Although he denied it until the day he died, Randy "The Crooning Cowpoke" Butterworth of B movie and early TV fame, was known to have once told Harry he was "... the only redskin who acts like a kike, speaks like Olivier, and spends like a nigger." By the summer of '83, Harry Garson was about tapped out. Fourteen years since his last meaningful paying gig, he was living on fast food and five-buck-a-blow-job drug whores in a SRO hotel in downtown LA. Then the phone rang in the hall outside his room and that all changed.

"Chief, the phone's for y'all!" It was Marissa LaTerre, the black drag queen from two doors down. "Come on, y'ole redskin, you. Man on the phone got me all wet with that sexy voice a his."

"Wet!" Harry said. "What, he make you piss your pants?"

Harry, long used to being called Chief, pulled the door open to behold the slender, 6'4" man with dark coffee skin and features as delicate as a first kiss. Without her makeup, lamé outfits, and wig, Marissa was just plain old Morris Terry, formerly of Camden, New Jersey and myriad points in between.

"He says it's about a part, Chief," Morris cooed like a teenage girl, but it simply didn't work without the feminine accoutrements. Frankly, delicate features notwithstanding, his golf ball-sized Adam's apple and towering stature made it a tough sell to begin with. "Y'all think if I do him, there'll be a part in it for Marissa?"

Harry didn't answer, pushing his way past Morris-Marissa and to the payphone, its receiver dangling in mid-air.

"Yeah," he barked. "Who is this?"

"Harry Garson, is that you?"

"Last time I checked. Who is this?"

"Dylan Rothenberg, Irv's kid."

"Irv's kid?" Harry was drawing a blank.

"Your old agent, I'm his youngest boy. Remember me? You used to come to my birthday parties when I was little. I've got home movies. You gave me my first cigarette and first sip of scotch."

"Sure. Sure. I remember you. You were the blond-haired kid with the blue eyes. You looked like your *shiksa*-goddess mother. What was her name ... Kitt, right? Kitt was her name. Christ, she was hot."

"And you're still the picture of tact and diplomacy, I see."

"Sorry, kid."

"No worries, Harry. She still speaks fondly of you as well."

Harry wisely shifted gears, remembering he'd once nailed Kitt Rothenberg after a movie premier Irv was too sick to attend. "So what's this about a part? You following in your old man's footsteps?"

"God no, I teach physics at Hofstra University on Long Island. Someone tracked me down because of my dad having been your agent. I still have some friends and contacts back home who found you for me."

"So you found me, kid. Now what?"

"You got a pen and a piece of paper?"

He knew he didn't, but Harry unconsciously patted his pockets.

"Here, honey, you looking for these?" It was Morris, who'd been watching the whole time, handing Harry a little yellow note pad and a pencil. "You can thank me later." Morris blew Harry a kiss.

They made quite the couple, strolling down Sunset: Harry, stoop-shouldered in his pink Salvation Army leisure suit and the now 6' 7" Marissa in her heels, khaki mini-skirt, fishnets, and green chiffon blouse. Harry didn't like acknowledging it, but age and too many Maker's Marks had rendered his once steel trap memory rusty and full of holes. Lines, no problem. He could remember reams of dialogue like when he played Geronimo in *Mission Apache* or the rebel brave Eyes Like Knife in the cult favorite *Hunting Ground*. He tested himself, running lines with his ersatz escort before they left for the audition.

Harry's trouble was with figures and his once trusty sense of direction. His navigation system was shot and he couldn't recall phone numbers for shit, not that he was recently in need of that facility. What Harry needed was someone's help getting him to the address on Sunset and it wasn't like he had thousands of eager candidates from which to choose. He supposed he might've gone stag and taken a taxi, but that meant he'd have to pay cab fare in both directions. In turn, that meant he would have to sacrifice a few

meals this week. He'd had to do that a lot lately. When he weighed the unlikely prospect of getting the part and a paycheck versus lost Big Macs, Whoppers, and Potato World cheese fries—his favorites— Harry decided Marissa's company and help was worth the four bus fares.

"Will you slow up, goddamnit!" he growled at Marissa. "You take longer strides than a fucking giraffe!"

"I didn't know giraffes took long strides when they were fucking, Chief."

"Funny lady."

"Streisand already got that part."

"You're so tall, they could have made a disaster movie about you in the Seventies: 'Towering Transvestite'."

"Steve McQueen and Paul Newman can climb all over me whenever they want. Here we are," Marissa said, looking up at the non-descript building wedged between a dry cleaner and an abandoned music store.

The interior of the building was even less impressive than its exterior. Harry had seen furrier putting greens than the threadbare carpet that lined the lobby floor. Come to think of it, he'd seen cleaner putting greens and putting greens were half dirt. It wasn't encouraging and all he could think about as he and Marissa rode the creaking elevator up to the fourth floor were the burgers and cheese fries he'd sacrificed to pay for the bus fares. Still, when the elevator jerked to a stop at four, Harry took his traditional deep breaths and mentally flicked up his on switch. Irv Rothenberg had always said that no one auditioned like Harry.

"I got stars in my stable, sure," Irv once told a junior associate, "but Harry Garson is the guy who bought my house and paid for my first son's bar mitzvah. He's automatic, like a given in geometry. He gets the audition, he gets the part." Problem was that

after "Crazy Cavalry" Harry couldn't get many auditions. Charm is less charming on a typecast actor with a bad off-screen rep and too many years on his bones.

Suite 403

The Rights Agency, LLC.

"This is the place," Marissa said, reading Harry's chicken scratch off the sheet of yellow paper. "The Rights Agency."

Now this was better, Harry thought. The carpeting in the fourth-floor hallway was clean and, while the pile didn't exactly tickle your shins, it was at least soft under your shoes. And he liked that the company name was painted in gold and black on the door the way people with class did it in the old days. No cheap plastic piece of shit sign or gold-plated tin placard. Class. Harry appreciated class.

"You going to wait for me here or downstairs?" he asked.

"No way, Chief, nuh uh. I didn't take y'all to the church just to get jilted at the altar."

Harry thought about arguing the point, but he knew better than to use up his limited energy on futile arguments. He knocked, turned the knob, and strode in, his escort looming behind him. The eyes on the two well-dressed men inside the office got big as dinner plates at the sight of Marissa LaTerre. Harry had expected nothing less. Helen Keller, he thought, would've gotten big eyes at the presence of the power forward drag queen, especially dressed up in that outfit.

"I'm Harry Garson," he said, walking up to the older of the two men and slid his ancient black and white head shot and CV across the top of the fancy etched glass desktop.

"Paul Spiegelman," the man said, shaking Harry's hand. His eyes were still on Marissa. "This is my partner, Mel Abbott." Spiegelman nodded his head at the man at the adjoining desk.

17

Abbott, about thirty and twenty years younger than his partner, stood and shook Harry's hand.

"And this is ..." Abbott said, gesturing at Marissa.

"My agent, Marissa LaTerre," Harry said, immediately regretting it. He was more nervous than he suspected he would be and the words just came out.

The partners managed not to roll their eyes at that. There was a second round of handshakes. Both Spiegelman and Abbott took silent note that LaTerre's right hand more swallowed their own hands than grasped them.

"Let's get down to business, shall we?" Spiegelman said, gesturing at the two red leather chairs facing the desks.

Spiegelman was a fit fifty. Compact and thin with probing hazel eyes that looked through Elvis Costello glasses, an angular jawline, a sharp nose and a crooked but ingratiating smile. He was dressed in a gray light wool pinstripe suit and his accessories were all silk and gold. To Harry, Paul Spiegelman smelled of Yale Law School and twenty years at a New York firm, a big New York firm. He was definitely a lawyer or a money man. In the business, they were sometimes one in the same. Mel Abbott, on the other hand, was a Hollywood hyena, all lean and hungry looks. Harry would have to keep an eye out for him.

"The part," Harry said, unable to contain himself any longer. "What about the part? Where are my lines?"

"Lines?" Abbott asked, seemingly confused. Spiegelman waved a calming hand at his partner.

"I'm afraid you misunderstand, Harry. This isn't that kind of part."

"Christ, I knew it!" He jumped out of his chair. "What is this? Listen I—"

"Harry, Harry, please ... sit down. Relax. Let me explain." Spiegelman kept his voice even and reassuring. But what Harry found most reassuring were the two bundles of crisp, rubber-banded bills the older partner was pushing across the top of his desk. "That's ten thousand dollars there, Harry."

Now it was Marissa LaTerre's eyes that got big. Harry's weren't exactly squinty either. It was all Harry Garson could do not to reach out and snatch the money. Instead, he sat back down and tried not drooling over the notions of what he could do with that much cash. And visions of cheese fries and hookers, a lot of hookers, danced in his head ...

Marissa decided to take her role as agent to heart. "So what are you gentlemen speaking about here for my client?"

"It's more theater than film work, though it's a little bit of both frankly," Abbott said.

"We want Harry to play the part of an Indian," Spiegelman added. "We need him and only him for the part and this ten grand is only a down payment."

Suddenly, the buzz all came back into Harry's bones and he was rushing harder than a junkie who'd just gotten fixed with the purest skag on Earth. He was barely thinking of the money anymore. It was about the role. He was so juiced by the thought of being in front of the cameras again, he nearly broke into one of those stupid war dances he'd done in fifteen movies and on almost every episode of "Crazy Cavalry".

"But I'm still not hearing what the role is exactly for Harry," Marissa persisted.

"Harry, do you think you can stay in character for a long period of time?"

"No problem, Mr. Abbott. I worked for some directors who demanded we stay in character for the whole shoot. It was a pain in the balls, but I did it. I'm a professional."

"See, Mel, I told you Harry was our man," Spiegelman spoke up. He then launched into a long stroking session, naming several of Harry's movie roles and commenting on just how well Harry Garson had done this or that. "And even in your comedic roles, you always stood out. My favorite was in the 'Bismarck Goes West' episode on CC. Your timing was great when you did the line about the Goodyear Blimp."

Harry chuckled. "Yeah, the trooper asks Bearstein how his future will be and I say, 'It will be a good year ...' Then I look up and yell, 'blimp.' And there's Bismarck and his Siamese kitten Cleo flying overhead in a zeppelin."

Now they were all laughing. All except Marissa. "I'll ask this one more time," she said. "What is the role?"

"Fair enough," Spiegelman said. "Look, we've been hired to make training films for Native American tribes looking to set up gaming establishments on reservation lands. It's about time the indigenous peoples of this country made some profits off the lands the government ceded to them. It's a difficult and arcane process, as you might imagine, and it just makes sense to the lawyers who do this kind of work to have a tool they can use to train the tribes."

"Okay," Marissa said, "that's better, but—"

Spiegelman held up his palms like traffic cop to stop her. "I understand your concerns. Here's the deal. Harry will have to relocate to the Tucson, Arizona area and live as ..." he looked down at a sheet of paper, "Ben Hart, the long-lost son of an elder of the Tohono O'odham tribe, they're a Pima people. Actually, you'd be part of a subgroup of theirs, but we can discuss that all later. We will have film crews following you and have you mic'd whenever you

leave your house. We will supply you with paperwork, references, etc. and we will walk you through the process of dealing with government agencies and the tribes themselves. But you absolutely must remain in character during this whole period. When you go out to a store or to a diner or go to the bathroom, you go as Ben Hart. Do you understand that, Harry?"

"Who's Harry? I'm Ben Hart the long-lost son of a tribal elder of the Tohono O'odham," he said, perfectly mimicking Spiegelman's pronunciation. "When do we get going?"

"Well ..." Mel Abbott hesitated, "first you're gonna have to go through some schooling while you're in LA. We need you to get very familiar with the role and then we'll send you down to Tucson. It won't be a cakewalk, this will be—"

"Stop being such a worrier, Mel. Harry—I mean, Ben Hart is up to it. Right Chief?"

"No problem."

"Very well then," Paul Spiegelman said, pushing one of the money piles toward Harry and pulling the other one back. "Here's half as an advance. When you complete your education for the role up here, you'll get the second half. I trust you, but our clients need some guarantees, you understand."

"Well, I don't!" Marissa stood up and walked over to Mel Abbott's desk. She knew he was the more easily intimidated of the two and, at 6'7", she was pretty intimidating. "What about a little thing called a contract?"

Abbott's mouth moved silently as he fumbled for an answer. The hyena was looking mighty scared. Harry was enjoying it all and thought Marissa LaTerre born to the role of agent. An image of Irv Rothenberg in fishnets, a mini skirt, and high heels flashed through his mind and Harry shuddered. One of Kitt followed quickly thereafter and Harry almost got hard. Almost.

"Contract. You want a contract?" Spiegelman asked. "You got one. We'll have one drawn up, but first we had to see if Harry would take the part. It's only reasonable, no?"

Harry said sure, sure. Marissa was still skeptical. Harry took the money and shoved it in his jacket pocket.

"Now, Harry," Mel said, "don't disappear on us with that five grand."

Harry was really starting to dislike Mel. Most people, he guessed, would dislike Mel. "Listen, mister, I'm a professional. I was never late on set in one hundred and fifty plus movies. I never called in sick or injured, ever. As hard up as I am, I'm not going anywhere."

Spiegelman chided his partner. "Mel, I keep telling you, Harry Garson is a pro. Besides, he knows the five large is *bubkes* compared to what he'll make for the whole shoot."

"And speaking of that ..." Marissa chimed in. "What are we talking about for the whole gig?"

"Minimum of fifty grand less the ten up front. Depends how long the shoot goes. Anything over a month, Harry will receive five grand a week. The clock on the shoot starts ticking once he lands at the airport in Tucson. One month from that day, the five grand per kicks in. Once the shoot spills over into the next week, five grand will be pro-rated. How does that sound to everyone?"

"Wonderful," Harry said. "When can we sign the papers and get started?"

Mel answered. "It'll take a day or two to draw up the contract, then we'll have them messengered over to your hotel and you can have the signed copies sent back here."

Marissa kept at it. "And you have no issue with a lawyer looking the contracts over?"

"None at all," said Spiegelman. "Contracts are meant to protect both parties. For now, Harry, go home and enjoy yourself a little. It's going to be tough work once we get rolling." He stood and offered his hand to Harry and Marissa. "Mel and I have to get things started on our end, so please excuse us. I think this is going to work out very nicely. Very nicely indeed."

In the elevator on the way back down, Harry Garson peeled off five crisp hundred dollar bills and handed them to his new agent. "You should give up the drag queen routine, kid. You're a natural as an agent."

"Harry, I can't take this."

"Take it. Take it!" he insisted, shoving the money through the low-buttoned chiffon blouse and into Marissa's thickly foamed bra. "You earned it. Besides, you heard Spiegelman. I'm looking at home run city here."

"About that, I—"

"Forget it. When the contracts come, we'll worry about it."

"But—"

"No buts. Come on, I'm treating for a cab."

Paul Spiegelman and Mel Abbott stood silently, watching out their office window as Harry Garson and his drag queen agent stood on Sunset trying to flag down a cab. It was almost as if they wouldn't speak until the oddest of odd couples was completely out of sight. Of course they understood that no one, not even people in the hallway outside their door, could hear their conversation. Still, they waited. When a cab finally pulled to the curb out front, gobbled up the two riders, and sped off, Spiegelman and Abbott sighed with relief. The older of the two began whistling "We're In The Money", but all Mel could do was pace.

"Why the fuck did he have to bring that fucking African queen with him? He—she's gonna fuck everything up."

"Mel, will you calm down, for goodness sakes? You're going to give yourself a stroke."

"Calm down he says. How can I calm down? You know what's at stake here?"

"I know, Mel. I know."

"I told you we should have sent a car to pick him up. I told you."

"If we sent a car for him, he would have gotten suspicious. Harry's dumb and hungry, but he's not stupid. He knows the business. He knows that someone who hasn't worked in nearly fifteen years doesn't get picked up in a limo for an audition. That would have queered the deal right there."

"Stooping to puns now, Paul?"

Spiegelman thought about that for a second, snickered quietly and said, "Huh?"

"Never mind. So what are we gonna do about Sheena Queen of the Jungle?"

"Go round up Joey Potholes for me. Tell him I need to see him here. In the meantime, I've got Harry Garson's contract to write up."

At 4:27 AM the next morning Marissa LaTerre stumbled out of Midnight Cruiser, an afterhours club frequented by freaks, geeks, and the beautiful people alike. She'd had a hell of a night, giving head in a back room to a pretty boy British film star and having the favor returned by the film star's fifteen-year-old date. She'd also managed to spend every dime of her agent's fee and then some.

A tall, elegantly thin man with pocked skin and fish eyes leaned against the front fender of a Lincoln Town Car. He watched

Marissa come out of the club and turn in his direction. He'd made sure to shoot out the streetlamp under which he'd parked the stolen Lincoln. When Marissa got close to the back bumper of the car, the thin man pulled open the rear passenger side door.

"For you, Miss LaTerre," he said. "Compliments of Harry Garson."

If she hadn't had so much coke and Dom in her system, Marissa might have listened to the alarm bells her street-smart former self, Morris Terry, was ringing as loudly as he could. But even then, it wouldn't have mattered. It was already half past too late. She couldn't have known that every stitch of clothing, every piece of jewelry, every wig and false eyelash, everything she owned was in the trunk of the stolen car and that she would soon be keeping her possessions company. She couldn't have known that the desk clerk at the hotel had been paid off to check her out and box up all of her worldly goods. It was only when she felt the ring of cold metal press against the back of her skull as she entered the car that Marissa finally heard Morris' alarm bells. With a flash, a snap, and a wisp of smoke, Marissa collapsed in a heap across the backseat.

Harry Garson loved Tucson. He'd shot on location in Arizona about thirty times but being here on his own and getting to step outside his own persona was a revelation. After the first few days wearing the Nagra recorder taped to his body, he'd learned to forget about them and since he never knew where the film crew was, it was as if they weren't there at all. Somehow, he felt, for the first time in his life, at home. In the past, on movie shoots, he'd always been a part of the crew and his exploration of the area tended to be of the area's bars and brothels. Sure, there were a few times he and some of the other actors had taken their horses out into the surrounding mountains and desert when the day's shoot didn't involve Indian or battle

sequences, but that too wound up being about someone having a few bottles and getting *shickered*. That's what Irv said the Yiddish word was for getting drunk.

Irv. These days, Harry found himself thinking a lot about his old agent. It was only with Irv that he ever spoke about his Indian roots and his puzzlements over how he'd come to be raised by the sweet but clueless Garson family in northern Wisconsin. He knew his adoptive parents had been Lutheran missionaries, but they never spoke too much about it. They never spoke much about anything. What he remembered most about his childhood was the silence of it.

"I never felt a part of the life there," he confided to Irv.

"Look, we're all members of a tribe. "

"Yeah, Irv, but what tribe?"

Irv just shrugged his shoulders. In his seventy-five plus years, it had been his one and only conversation on the subject. Now when Irv crossed his mind, Harry's thoughts inevitably turned to Marissa LaTerre. He was still pretty pissed at the fruit cake for abandoning him like she had and without a word. He tried figuring out why she'd done it and turned her back on the ten percent he would have given her, but it was a waste of time and energy. Who could figure out someone like that? They couldn't even figure themselves out, Harry reasoned. Besides, the contracts had been signed; Harry having paid a c-note to a disbarred lawyer from the hotel to give the documents the once over and to make sure they were in order. He'd done his studying up on Tucson and the Pima. For instance, he knew that Ira Hayes, one of the guys who held up the American flag at Iwo Jima, was a Pima Indian. That the name Tucson is taken from a Spanish bastardization of the O'odham name Cuk Son, meaning at the base of the black hill. He'd been an apt pupil and the second five grand installment had been paid in full in cash.

They'd flown him down to Tucson first class and set him up in a neat little adobe bungalow in the foothills of the Santa Catalina Mountains. When the cab dropped him off, Harry found a 1980 Ford F150 pickup in the driveway with the keys in the ignition. It had been ten years since he'd driven, but with a little practice it all came right back to him. It was wonderful to be behind the wheel again, to feel in control of something other than his bodily functions. Driving, he thought, was like humping: it felt great no matter how rusty you were at it. He'd been supplied with property department ID of the best quality in the name of Ben Hart.

Once or twice a week, he'd get documents of one sort or another delivered to the bungalow and those deliveries were inevitably followed by phone instructions. They were usually about driving over to some federal office building or municipal building in this county or that. He'd driven along the Salt, Gila, Yaqui, and Sonora Rivers. He'd visited with tribal elders and councils and filed papers of every kind with every kind of bureaucrat—black-skinned, red-skinned, white-skinned, and just about every shade of skin in between—and stood in more lines than at the department of motor vehicles. He liked to laugh to himself that they were eventually going to ask for a urine sample, have him read an eye chart, and then give him some goddamn road test. No wonder they needed training films. This shit was confusing and stupifyingly boring. He could only imagine how much more boring it would have been had he actually had to read all the crap he was signing and filing.

Still, it was worth it to Harry. Most days were his to do with as he pleased as long as he stayed in character. That was pretty easy for him to do as he was a virtual stranger in Tucson. Even when his role didn't require him to do so, he'd take long drives in all directions. And that was another amazing thing about coming back to the Tucson area; Harry had somehow recovered his once

impeccable sense of direction. Even when it let him down and he got lost, Harry looked at it as an opportunity to explore. Sometimes he'd head out at the dawn of the day and sometimes at dusk. The scenery and the landscapes were breathtaking, almost otherworldly. It was as if his eyes were reborn and could now see what he had missed or ignored during his many acting gigs. Duke Wayne once told him that if you live in the desert long enough, brown becomes just another shade of green. Only now did Harry see the truth of that. More than anything, he'd come to love the rich redness of the rock and soil, a shade not so different from the color of his skin as a young man. There was something comforting about it. From the moment he landed, Harry knew he fit here. He just didn't know how.

There was a knock on the door and Mel Abbott shouted, "Come!"

"These have to be them," Paul Spiegelman said, rubbing his palms together.

The office door pushed back. A stocky Hispanic man in blue spandex bicycle shorts, a wet Los Lobos t-shirt, a backpack, and a helmet stepped into the office and laid a fat envelope on Mel's desk. "Sign here." He pointed at the receipt.

The pen shook in Mel's right hand. It took him so long to put his name down, it was like he was etching it rather than signing it.

"Sometime today would be nice, *jefe*," the messenger said, staring at his watch.

Spiegelman smiled. Not Mel.

"Here." Abbott shoved the receipt at the messenger. "What's the matter, you afraid you'll be late for your date with your *chica*?"

The messenger snatched the receipt, balled a copy of it, and threw it in Mel's face. "I don't know about my *chica*, but your mama

she don't like me to be late. She dries up quick these days." He took his time leaving the office, not exactly fearing for his life.

"Can you believe that motherfucker?" Mel asked. It was only after Spiegelman stopped laughing that his partner understood. "Very funny, Paul. Very funny."

"Just shut up and give me the package."

When he opened the envelope, Spiegelman started whistling "We're In the Money".

"What should I do with all these fucking audio tapes we got from Harry?"

"Toss 'em. I can't believe he still thinks he's being followed around by a camera crew. You gotta love actors!" he said, then went back to whistling.

Mel was already dialing Joey Potholes's number.

There was a knock at Harry's door. He dreaded answering it. Not only because it was barely daylight, but because it had been five days since he had received his last package of documents or a phone call. An actor, even one as old as dirt who hadn't worked for a decade and a half, knew when a shoot was winding down and this shoot was definitely winding down. He hadn't wanted to think about it, but it couldn't be avoided any longer. The truth was that as much as he felt he belonged in Tucson, Harry wouldn't be able to afford to relocate here. Sure, it was all great now, but in the end it was an illusion, no more real than any of the other movies he'd been a part of. The house, the pickup, his groceries, the utilities, his cable TV bill were all being paid for by the folks who cast him in the role. And as many cheese fries as fifty grand would buy him, it wouldn't go very far if he were responsible for the things the film people were footing at the moment. No, it was back to burgers, LA, and cheap hotels for Harry. Who knew, he thought, maybe when he got back

Marissa LaTerre would be back too and together they could rekindle Harry's career.

But when Harry reluctantly pulled open the heavy, hand carved front door, it wasn't a UPS or Federal Express man that greeted him.

"Can I help you?" he said to the impassive young Indian woman who stared at him across the threshold. She was quite pretty, with almond eyes, a broad nose, full lips and a head of the blackest hair. In tight, faded jeans, a light denim blouse, and cowboy boots, she was dressed as many of the young women dressed in Tucson.

"My great grandmother would like to speak with you. She's in my truck." The woman turned and pointed to a beat up old Chevy in the dirt driveway next to Harry's Ford.

"What's your name?"

"Rebecca. Please come. She is very old and it is very hot in the truck."

Harry followed Rebecca to the truck and there in the front seat sat a frail, ancient woman with hair as gray as her great granddaughter's was black. Her deep brown leathery skin was wrinkled and heavily lined. She looked familiar to him. He remembered seeing her, but not where or when. It might have been on his trip to the Gila River compound or maybe it was when he was standing on one of those endless lines in some county or federal office. As he was about to find out, it was less important that he remembered her than she remembered him. When Harry stepped up to the door, the woman held an old black and white photo out to him.

"Isaac Hart," she said. "Your father."

Looking at it, Harry nearly fainted. At thirty, Harry would have been the spitting image of the man in the photograph.

Mel Abbott and Paul Spiegelman sat across the table from the man who had acted as the buffer between them and the mining company. He was the man who had availed them of Joey "Pothole's" services and who had supplied them with the expense cash they needed to pull off the scam. He said his name was Walter Hogan. Con men themselves, neither Abbott or Spiegelman—neither of whom were actually named Abbott or Spiegelman—believed him.

"Do you have the package?" Walter asked.

Mel's lip twitched. "I might ask you the same question."

Walter placed an attaché case on the table, flipped open the latches, pulled the lid open, and spun the case around.

"Five hundred large," Walter said. When Mel went to reach for a pile of bills, Walter slammed the attaché closed. "This isn't the time to get sloppy or foolish. What we're going to do, fan a stack by your ear like some moron in a movie or did you want to show off to the waitress?"

"Sorry."

"And the other half?" Paul piped up.

"When the documents check out. Then you'll get your percentage when the client starts pulling copper out of the ground. Now, don't make me ask again. The package."

As Paul Spiegelman slid the fat envelope across the table to Walter, Walter relaxed his grip on the attaché case and smiled.

"You sure everything's here?"

"Everything," Mel said.

"Everything," Paul chimed in. "Everything: a copy of the original birth certificate, the dummy contracts he signed, the original adoption papers, copy of the father's will, the deed on the house in Tucson in Ben Hart's name, a copy of the truck registration and insurance in his name, the tribal papers acknowledging Ben Hart's

31

rightful heritage, the land deed that his father held on the acres your guys are going to mine. And, of course, the coup de grace: Ben Hart's will, which we wrote and he signed without a second look. In it, as per your instructions, he bequeaths all his assets to Robert T. Ramsland. A friend of yours, I imagine, who will no doubt turn right around and sell it to Francoeur Mineral and Mining."

"A fair assumption," Walter agreed. "How did you get this guy to do all this?"

"Shit, Walter, we even got the idiot to make us co-signers on his bank accounts, so we can draw out his money and give it back to you once he's dead. Actors are the easiest marks in the world! Jesus, they're so fucking narcissistic. Stroke 'em a little and they lay down like a two-buck whore. He probably never read one of the documents. Besides, for him, it was just a gig, a role."

"Keep it." Walter said.

"Keep what?"

"The money in bank account as a tip for a job well done." He actually shook both men's hands. "Good work, boys. Now I'm going to leave. Give me a ten-minute head start and then enjoy the rest of your lives!"

Neither Mel nor Paul could figure out how they'd run out of gas this far short of Phoenix. They had filled up just before meeting with Walter outside of Palm Springs, but it was a moot point now. Help was here in the shape of a Jeep pulling up behind their car. The tall, elegantly thin man with pocked skin shot Paul in the heart as he stepped out of the car. He put a second shot in the dying man's head as insurance. Mel ran. Joey didn't waste his time chasing him. He was heading straight for the two holes Joey had pre-dug for them in the desert. First thing he did was put the attaché case into the Jeep.

Now Harry Garson finally understood why he fit. He'd been born here and was of the Pima people, but he wouldn't be of them for very much longer if he didn't get a handle on what was going on. It occurred to him that Marissa LaTerre had probably not taken off of her own free will and that she had more than likely come to the end of the road prematurely and violently. Harry spent the rest of the morning and afternoon visiting as many of the offices he had visited in the last few weeks trying to see and/or collect copies of the documents he'd signed and blindly filed without taking a second look. And once he had gathered as much of the paperwork as he could, he made two last stops.

As he drove back to the bungalow, a bungalow he was shocked to discover he owned free and clear, in a pickup truck he also owned free and clear, Harry ignored the thick envelope on the seat next to him and kept staring at the photograph of his biological father. Even after more than seventy-five years of life, it was an amazing feeling to fit in and to belong, to know your place in the world. Maybe all those years made it that much sweeter. Rebecca and the ancient woman, Isaac Hart's youngest sister and Harry's great aunt, explained that his father had fallen deeply in love with a teacher at the Indian school and had made her pregnant. He wanted to marry her, but she refused. She had the baby but disappeared a few weeks later. He always hoped of finding her and the child he named Ben.

"He worked hard to purchase many acres of land off tribal territory, so he could prove his worth to the teacher when she returned or he found her," Rebecca explained. "He never found her and she never returned, but in your father's will he left the land for you and your children. Until you returned, it was to be kept by the family. We were not allowed to sell it or use it. I have been told this story since I was a child. For your father to have bought white land

when he did has been a source of great pride for us, but I have always thought it was only a story." It was no story and the proof of that was there on the seat next to Harry.

It was dusk when Harry got back up to the little adobe house in the foothills, a place he had come to love. He also loved how the light of the vanishing sun lit up the sky with streaks of orange and purple, gold and blue. And although his eyesight wasn't great in the falling darkness without his glasses, he caught sight of the Jeep parked across the road from his house. If he hadn't been looking for a strange vehicle, he probably wouldn't have spotted it, but after what he'd learned today, he expected it to be there. He rolled to the side of the road, reached into the envelope and pulled out one particular document. He took his deep breaths, flicked up his famous on switch, put the truck back in gear, and pulled onto the dirt driveway. When he got out of the Ford, Harry held the document out in front of him like a shield. He had had it all planned, the words he was going to say to save himself. Yet, now out of the truck, he decided not to speak. Harry Garson was an old man, too old to be fully transformed into Ben Hart at this late date. He had been a caterpillar too long to suddenly grow new wings and fly. Belonging, being Ben Hart, son of Isaac Hart, even for only a few hours, had answered all the important questions that he'd kept locked up inside all these years. All he hoped for was that the end wouldn't hurt too much when it came. It didn't.

The elegantly thin man with the pock-marked skin and cold fish eyes, stood in the trashed living room and dialed the untraceable number Walter had given him. He had been thorough, making sure it looked like his target had walked in on a robbery, surprised the thief, and was shot to death in the process. Joey had even used a .45

on the old man, not the kind of weapon a professional killer would generally use.

"You're fucked," Joey said when Walter finally picked up.

"How's that?"

Joey explained about the document the old Indian held in his hand when he got out of the truck. "He was holding a piece of paper in his hand, so what?"

"It's a last will and testament," the assassin said, "a brand new one, dated today."

"Shit!"

"Shit is right. He left the land to the tribe and some woman named Rebecca to do with as they please. I don't know how he managed it, but the will was witnessed by the Mayor of Tucson and a tribal elder. He's got a Polaroid of the signing stapled to the will. You're fucked."

"You said that already."

"My money?"

"You did your job. It'll be in your account in the morning."

There was a click on the other end of the line.

As Joey left, he took one last look at his victim to make sure everything was just so. And as he did, he thought he recognized the old Indian from a TV show he watched as a kid.

"Bearstein!" he whispered to himself. "Sorry, Chief."

Due Diligence

From WALL STREET NOIR.

Trisha Tanglewood didn't bother scanning the safety card slipped into the seat pouch in front of her nor did she bother listening to the flight attendant's sonorous rendering of William Shakespeare's least known work, *Much Ado About Floatation Devices.*

> *Whether 'tis nobler, at the captain's behest,*
> *to use the fetid fabric seat cush*
> *Or plumb the icy depths with the yellow plastic vest*
> *placed thusly beneath one's tush ...*

Her disdain was neither an expression of fatalism nor boredom, but of familiarity. Miss Tanglewood knew more about commercial

aircraft than most human beings who didn't actually design them for a living. It was a safe bet she knew more about the 737-700 than the pilot at the controls of the updated Boeing, certainly more than the cabin crew.

"Excuse me ... Kathy," she read the flight attendant's winged name tag. "Can you tell me are these engines GE CFM56-7B26s or 27s?"

A blank stare washed over Kathy's face. Trisha might just as well have asked her for the gross national product of Burkina Faso.

"I'll make sure to ask the pilot," Kathy said, recovering nicely. "Enjoy the flight."

It was silly, she knew, harassing flight attendants this way, but it comforted her.

Ladies and gentlemen, this is Captain Saunders on the flight deck. Just wanted to let you know we'll be taking off in just a couple of minutes here. We'll be cruising at an altitude of thirty-six thousand feet at a speed of approximately five-hundred and fifty miles per hour. The weather's pretty clear between hear and Tegucigalpa, so we anticipate a fairly smooth flight. If there's anything we can do to make your trip more enjoyable, please let one of the cabin staff know. Once we get to cruising altitude, I'll be back on with you. Until then, enjoy the ride. Flight attendants, please prepare the cabin for departure.

"You seem to know a lot about planes," said the man to her immediate right.

Trisha was taken aback. Usually prepared for anything, she was caught off guard by his remark. She hadn't been herself just lately. No, that was a lie. In spite of the aura of self-confidence and competence she projected, Trisha had, since her dad's death eleven

months ago, functioned in a state of psychological vertigo. An executive at Sikorsky had once described piloting a helicopter as trying to balance yourself on a basketball on one leg while playing the piano. Until her dad's death, she hadn't quite gotten the analogy. These days, she understood it perfectly.

"I said, you seem to know an awful lot about planes," he repeated.

Fighting her vertigo the only way she knew how, with a sort of single-minded focus on the task at hand, Trisha had barely noticed any of the other passengers. She took a moment now to study the man in the next seat. He was forty-ish, ruggedly handsome, with a square chin and lined face; a refugee from Marlboro Country. He had a mouthful of straight white teeth and shiny, silver-gray hair like her late father. She noticed too that he had the armrest between them in a death grip and that his speckled blue eyes darted nervously to the tarmac then back inside the cabin.

"You're right, I do indeed," she said. "There's not a lot to worry about, so try and relax."

"You a pilot or something?"

Trisha laughed. "Or something."

"What's that mean?"

"I work for Paisley Shutter. We're an investment banking firm."

"Investment bank, huh? Sounds more like a bad 60s' design idea."

"Cute. Can I use that line?"

"Feel free. I'm Pete Dutton, by the way." He removed his hand from the armrest and offered it to her.

"Trisha Tanglewood." She briefly shook his hand. He had firm grip and a surprisingly dry palm.

"Pleasure to meet you, Trisha." He tipped an invisible hat.

"Yes, a pleasure."

"So, how's it you know so much about planes?"

"Sorry, we did get a little sidetracked there. At Paisley Shutter I was Chief Analyst for the manufacturing sector of the commercial aircraft industry. It has been both my occupation and preoccupation for the past seven years."

"Really?"

"Really. If you'd like to discuss the relative merits of this aircraft as opposed to, let's say, the Airbus A320 or why some airlines prefer Pratt & Whitney power plants over GE or Rolls Royce, just let me know."

"No thanks. Too much knowledge makes me even more unsettled," Pete said, trying to smile and failing. "I already have enough trouble thinking of jets as gas tanks with wings."

"Well, that's essentially correct; wings and seats."

"Great. You're a real comfort."

As if on cue, the pilot wound up the turbofans and the jet began its urgent rumbling down the tarmac. Then they were off, gradually leaving Miami behind and beneath them. Trisha could see the near panic in Pete's face as the servos repositioned the flaps and the bottom seemed to drop out of the starboard side of the aircraft, the captain turning west into the setting sun. In her own way, she was equally unsteady, maybe more so.

She had gotten what she thought she had wanted, a kick up the ladder. No longer could she hide herself in the shadow of tail fins or rotor blades. Trisha had been forced out of her paradoxically cozy titanium, aluminum, and carbon fiber womb. Manufacturing was her gig now, all of it, everything from baby bottles to ball bearings, from farm equipment to pharmaceuticals. The days of simple, seamless trips to Seattle and Toulouse were no more. She

was far less familiar with her new arena, an arena with a distinctly third world flavor.

Trisha knew she was good at managing herself and her career. She was more than good, she was superior, and had handled her small team quite deftly. Problem was, the team had grown exponentially. And as much money as was at stake in aircraft manufacturing, it was penny-ante compared to the whole manufacturing shebang. Shebang, she thought, what a silly word, but her dad had used it all the time. He was just full of quaint phrases and quiet cowboy wisdom. Even now she had trouble accepting he was gone. Other than her job, he had been all she had. He would have been so proud of her. Remembering him, his crooked smile, his rough and tumble looks, the day he gave her her first saddle, Trisha looked past Pete Dutton and out the window into the deepening night. Yet she found her eyes drifting toward Pete's decreasingly tense face.

He seemed an interesting man, polite and confident enough to show vulnerability. She could count on one finger the number of male colleagues who would have dared display fear in front of her. On The Street, fear equated to weakness and weakness to death. Meanwhile, they were, like her, sometimes nearly consumed by their fears and insecurities.

> *Ladies and gentlemen, the captain has turned off the seatbelt sign, so you're free to move about the cabin. However, when you are in your seat, we'd like it if you could keep your seatbelts on. The captain has also indicated that you may use all approved electronic devices, such as laptops ..."*

Trisha already had her tray table down, her Dell out of its case and booting up before the flight attendant had gotten past the

first sentence of her announcement. She called up the file marked MM/ZIPS/H.1. Six months earlier Paisley Shutter had been retained by Mega-Mart, Inc., one of the world's largest big box retailers, to look into the feasibility of acquiring PriceStar, Inc. PriceStar was an undercapitalized, debt heavy, second rung player in the retail business, but the one big asset PriceStar possessed was its offshore textile plants. Their profit margin on their in-house clothing lines was the envy of the industry. And now that takeover talks had progressed from flirtation to third base, Trisha was going down to Honduras to make sure all the numbers that her team had given her checked out.

She not only owed due diligence to Mega-Mart, but to herself. Partnerships at Paisley Shutter didn't exactly get handed out like Halloween candy, especially not to women. In fact, Trisha Tanglewood was the first woman under the age of forty to have even sniffed a partnership. Some of her male colleagues had warned her off making the trip at all. They were all full of sage advice and playful chiding, but she understood the old boy code better than they suspected. Her taking this trip not only made her look good. It made them look bad, worse than bad, lazy. Like her dad used to say, "If the crows're gonna caw anyhow, you might as well give 'em a reason." Fuck 'em! was the way they said it on The Street.

"Christ, how do you deal with all those figures?" Pete spoke up, peering at the laptop's screen. "Gimme anything more than three digits either side of the decimal point and I'm befuddled."

Almost reflexively, Trisha slammed her laptop closed. She did it with such force that passengers from surrounding rows snapped their heads about to see what had happened.

"Goodness, I'm sorry," Pete said. "Didn't mean to peek."

"It's okay," she lied.

"No it's not, Trisha. That was rude of me. My momma schooled me better than that." He pressed the call button.

"What are you–" Trisha started to ask when the flight attendant arrived.

"I'm sorry to bother you," Pete said, "but is there an empty seat somewhere. The lady wants to do her work and I'm afraid I'm disturbing her."

"That's not necessary," Trisha assured her. "I'm fine."

"Well, I suppose that's a good thing," said the flight attendant, "because we're fresh out of empty seats. Will there be anything else? No? Good, enjoy the rest of your flight."

There was a moment of awkward silence before Pete stood up and moved to the front of the cabin. Trisha felt like a fool. Even without the added burdens of grief and vertigo, paranoia was a requisite feature of the successful Wall Street personality. That was the oddity inherent in the world of high finance, things that were considered certifiable and unhealthy by the rest of the world were encouraged, even celebrated. Caution was for losers. Paranoia was the breakfast of champions.

What had happened, Trisha wondered staring out at the stars, to the little girl who'd won all those blue ribbons for her trick riding back home in Wyoming. Once, the two most important things in the world to her were her dad and Dancer. Dancer was a beautiful roan, the most graceful animal on God's earth. Dancer's death had been her first encounter with grief. Trisha's mom had died when she was too little to remember. Everyone who mattered was gone. She suddenly found little solace in her new title and took little comfort in her paranoia.

"I hope you'll accept this in the spirit of forgiveness with which it's given," Pete said, catching her off guard once again. He carried two plastic glasses filled with champagne.

"Where did you–"

"Ssshhhh!" He winked, sitting back down. "It's a little secret."

"But how?"

"I make this flight twice a month. There's an acquaintance of mine in first class. Let's just say he and I and the flight attendants reached a mutual agreement. Cheers."

They both drank. Trisha found her face forming a smile. It had recently been an unfamiliar feeling.

"I'm sorry for overreacting," she said. "Paranoia's an occupational hazard."

"No, the fault was mine. Let's stop apologizing. Deal?"

"Deal."

They shook on it. Trisha held onto his hand a little longer this time. This silly encounter was the first relief she'd had in months. She even felt a bit of a tingle. This man had that rare quality of both relaxing and exciting her.

"What do you do, Pete?"

"I'm sort of in HR."

"Human resources. For a financial concern?" she asked almost hopefully.

"Oh, no, no, nothing like that. I set up American firms, usually small family shops, with foreigners who fit their very special needs. I handle the paperwork, transport, housing, all of it. That's why I'm in Honduras so frequently."

"A headhunter."

"Of sorts, but it's a little more complex than that."

"Interesting?"

"Challenging's more like it. So, not to bring up a potentially sore subject, but what were all those numbers about?" he asked, sounding a bit sheepish.

Trisha felt the usual surge of paranoia but beat it back. "Well, I can't really discuss the specifics, but I can give you a brief overview."

"Shoot."

She liked that. Her daddy used to say shoot.

"The long and short of it is that we have a client who is seriously interested in purchasing a smaller competitor. We've been retained to make assessments and recommendations as to the value of the competitor's assets and the most financially advantageous method of acquiring the company."

"M&A?"

"Human resources, huh?" She eyed him skeptically. "You seem to understand this type of transaction just fine."

"Sorry, I line my bird's cage with the Wall Street Journal and sometimes when I'm cleaning up, I catch a phrase or two."

"Sure."

"Okay, so I didn't just brush the hay out of my hair. You can't blame a fella for chatting up a pretty woman. Besides, though you look all business and seem to have the world at arm's length, there's a real sadness in your eyes that's hard for me to resist."

Trisha Tanglewood was utterly flustered. She felt transparent, exposed. Although her life in New York was filled with activity and people, the people in it were more like specters.

Everyone was so rootless, empty, in danger of spinning off into space. Home was where the money was. That could be Hong Kong, Tokyo, the fifth rung of Hell. Only the security guards, the mail room kids, the secretaries from the boroughs seemed the least bit grounded. And the men ... There were plenty of men, but it was always so complicated, even orgasms were a matter for negotiation. Wall Street men were such children, constantly showing off the size

of their dicks by proxy. She was sick of all their finest this or most expensive that.

The scariest part was, it had taken a stranger on a plane to recognize the sadness in her. Sure, there had been the somber condolences, the "Take as much time as you need" speech from the senior partner and the Let-me-know-if-there's-anything-I-can-dos from her colleagues. But it was all pro forma, it was just what one did, like mucking the stalls at day's end. And here was this total stranger who just knew.

"My daddy died about a year ago," she found herself confessing in her spontaneously recovered Laramie accent. "My momma died when I was little, so it was just me and him forever."

"Sorry doesn't quite say it, does it? Listen, I'm gonna be in Tegucigalpa for about a week. It's a city I know, to use a cliché, like the back of my hand. Why don't you let me show it to you or at least take you to dinner? I'd like to hear about your daddy, if you wouldn't mind sharing."

No! "Dinner would be lovely," Trisha thought she heard herself say. "But I've got to go north for a day or two and then– "

"I understand," Pete saved her from the awkward explanation. "You've got to spend time with your people. Due diligence, right?"

"Another one of those bird cage phrases, I suppose."

"What can I say? My African Grey has a healthy appetite. Here," he took out a card and scrawled a number across the back. "You can reach me at this number directly anytime. This way there's no pressure and if you change your mind, at least we had a pleasant flight together."

His wasn't so much a business card as a calling card. There was his name, a Miami phone number, and a cryptic email address on heavy beige stock. No company name, no snail mail address, no

title. Trisha studied the card, hesitating, wondering if she should
return the courtesy. He noticed her hesitancy.

He let her off the hook again. "No card necessary.
Remember, no pressure."

After two more glasses of champagne, Pete Dutton drifted off
into sleep. For her part, Trisha went back to her work, occasionally
twirling Pete's card in her fingers and smiling. Yes, he reminded her
of her daddy, but there was something else about him, something
sweet and comfortable, but also a little bit dangerous. She liked it.
The boys on The Street all fancied themselves masters of the
universe but disarmed of their Pings and squash rackets they were a
relatively impotent bunch. Impotent was about the last word she
could think of to describe Pete Dutton. When she put his card away
on final approach to Toncontín International, Trisha noticed she was
more than a little wet.

If anyone wanted to see where all those textile jobs from Georgia,
North Carolina, and South Carolina had migrated to, they'd just
have to hop a plane from Tegucigalpa to San Pedro Sula in the
northwest of Honduras. That's where PriceStar, Inc. had their main
textile plants or *maquilas*, as the locals called them. It was also where
Trisha Tanglewood was forced to spend the first two days of her
stay. But PriceStar was only one of the players that had set up shop
in the free trade zones. Christ, the whole country was one big free
trade zone. Everyone from Oshkosh B'Gosh to Maidenform to
Hanes to Wrangler had factories in San Pedro Sula. Some, like
PriceStar, also had smaller *maquilas* in the Tegucigalpa area.

The list of American companies that operated textile plants in
Honduras was long, but by no means exclusive. The range and
number of Asian manufacturers who had sent many of their home-
grown jobs to permanent summer camp in Central America did not

escape Trisha's notice. She passed more than a few Korean, Taiwanese, and Japanese factories as her driver made his way to PriceStar. She didn't think twice about the impact the loss of jobs had on the people in their homelands nor on the people of Honduras. It was simply smart business.

If she didn't know better, Trisha would have thought San Pedro Sula was the patron saint of time warps. There seemed to be shackles on the hands of the clocks, the hours dragging as she suffered through her two days with her team and the PriceStar, Inc. reps. She found herself thinking that maybe her colleagues in New York had been right. Climates may change as one approaches the equator, but numbers add up just the same. By 3:00 PM on her first day, Trisha was almost regretting making a show of her meticulousness.

As a matter of courtesy and protocol, she strolled the factory floor with the Honduran operations manager, a PriceStar exec, and a Paisley Shutter analyst named Ellis Quantrill. Although part of Trisha's team, she wasn't terribly fond of Quantrill. Just thirty, WASP-ishly handsome and bred for success, he fancied himself such a shark. He made no secret of his desire to go very far very fast and at any cost ... any cost to others. She'd seen his type before, the eaglet hatched first that pushes its brother out of the nest. What Ellis hadn't learned quite yet was that there was always a bigger eaglet. Always!

Their relationship hadn't started out badly, but the antagonism had seeped in over the past few months. First, Ellis had tried to be the teacher's pet. Then he'd tried to make himself indispensable to Trisha by revealing all the inside info he'd picked from his peers at the firm. Neither approached got him very far, but the real trouble started after he'd tried coming onto Trisha at the golf outing last May. He kissed her hard on the mouth behind the clubhouse at the country club in Armonk. Trisha just laughed. She'd

have done better to slap him. That was the peculiar thing about Ellis' type, they'd eat dogshit to get ahead, but not if anyone was watching. Personal embarrassment was intolerable. From that ill-fated kiss forward, Ellis Quantrill had put Trisha Tanglewood in his crosshairs. She knew it. He knew she knew it.

The factory was clean and modern with all the latest machinery, but the production area was still terribly noisy. There was a lot of broad hand-gesturing, head shaking, and very little speaking. At one point during the tour, Ellis tapped Trisha on the shoulder and shepherded her into an empty break room.

"Noisy, isn't it?" he said.

"What is it, Ellis?" Trisha enjoyed being curt with him.

"I just wanted to take a minute to talk. This isn't the kind of thing I could say in front of the rest of the team or in front of the Hondurans."

Christ, she thought, was this yet another one of his ploys to curry favor? Was he going to profess his love? That would be a novel approach given their recent friction.

"So talk."

"Look, Trisha, I know we haven't been on good terms lately. I've been a complete ass since the golf outing and ... well, I have something planned for you tonight, so please don't make alternate plans. Okay?"

"I shudder to think what you've got planned for me, Ellis."

"I know I haven't earned it, but I'm asking you to trust me this once."

"All right. What time?"

"There'll be a car waiting for you at the hotel at seven." He picked his ear protection off the table. "Come on, we better get back to the grand tour."

While she wasn't about to tuck Ellis Quantrill under her wing to suckle, she had to confess that the evening began as quite a bit of fun. The entire Paisley Shutter team that had worked so hard on the MegaMart-PriceStar Project had been assembled in an Asian restaurant that featured a mix of Thai, Korean, and Japanese foods. A bizarre setting in the midst of northwest Honduras for sure, but seemingly par for the course in the topsy-turvy world of third world manufacturing. The team presented Trisha with a classic Mont Blanc fountain pen, an exquisite Piaget watch, and a beautifully framed picture of her as a teenage girl atop Dancer. No one would tell her where they'd gotten the photo, but she didn't really care. A lot of sake, champagne and local beer passed through everyone's lips. And Ellis made sure not to be too present. Trisha caught glimpses of him every now and again, but he really was hanging back, showing newfound restraint.

As things were winding down, the men in the group did the Cuban cigar and port thing, while the women gathered around Trisha to give her the lowdown on where to shop and what restaurants to go to when she got back to Tegucigalpa. Trisha found herself engaged by the conversation and felt almost her old self. It was the longest time she'd gone without thinking of her dad in months. Pete Dutton had put a crack in the dam and now it seemed to be breaking.

"But there's one thing," Pam Richter, a junior analyst, said, her voice turning suddenly serious. "When you're in Tegucigalpa or anywhere in the country, you don't want to–"

"Oh, Pam, don't spoil the evening with this," chided Maggie Wilson, a thirty-year Paisley Shutter vet. "It's nonsense and the boss is only going to be here a few days."

"No, go ahead Pam," Trisha demanded.

"It's not safe for American women to walk the streets alone in certain parts of the cities, especially after dark."

"Why only American women?" Trisha asked.

"Baby thieves!" Pam blurted.

"What?"

"It's sort of a Central American urban legend. You know, like the one back home about a couple who kidnap a toddler in a Toys "R" Us and are found in the bathroom changing the kids clothing and coloring its hair. The Baby Thieves is even bigger here and in Guatemala."

"I've never heard that. I only know the one about the poodle in the microwave," Trisha admitted.

"Well, boss, down here their myths and legends are a bit more ... um, radical. Here the legend goes that rich American women come to this part of the world, choose babies, have the mothers executed and ship the babies back to the States to raise as their own."

"God that's horrible."

"It's a load of crap," Maggie said. "Whenever the government feels threatened or the economy takes a hit, they spread these rumors around. The good old U.S.A. still makes one hell of a scapegoat. And it's not like our government hasn't screwed with these folks down here. The trouble is, the rumor persists, especially in the poorest areas, long after it's served its purpose."

"That's why it's not safe," Pam said, and reading the expression on Trisha's face, added, "I'm sorry to have mentioned it. I–"

"That's okay, Pam. I appreciate it. I think we better call it a night."

But it really wasn't all right. Pam's story had brought all of her vertigo and sadness rushing back in. The alcohol only made it

worse. And the photo of her atop Dancer, something which only an hour before had brought her incredible joy, now reminded her only of the man who had taken the picture, her dad.

When Trisha looked up, she saw Ellis Quantrill standing about ten feet away. He raised his cognac to her, a mischievous smile on his face. Had he been listening? No, she thought, it was just the booze, the regrets, and the paranoia.

Back at the hotel, she took a long hot bath. For some reason her thoughts kept drifting to Pete Dutton and her fingers to her pussy. She masturbated over and over again, anything to wipe away the sadness. She imagined any number of ways Pete Dutton might have her or she him. Her orgasms were as intense as if the sex were real instead of imagined. It scared her a little. She found she liked being scared, that it heightened her climax. Still, she resisted the urge to call Pete.

Her resistance continued even after her plane touched back down in Tegucigalpa thirty-six hours later. Trisha had the driver take her straight to the hotel. The sky was beautifully clear blue, but the streets of the capital city spread out before her like a soft blur. Noises mixed with colors, colors with indistinct shapes, shapes with shadows. She couldn't seem to focus on any one thing. It wasn't all Pete Dutton either, she realized. She found herself missing her old job, missing her dad, missing Tom Skilling, the boy she'd first let slip his hand beneath the elastic band of her panties in his car on the side of the road just outside Laramie. The world came back into focus when she opened her hotel suite door.

There on the desk sat a spectacular arrangement of orchids and a single white rose in a handcrafted enamel vase. The card read:

No pressure

Pete

Trisha, never a woman to long for a protector, longed for one now. She was weary, in need of comfort and distraction. She took out Pete's card and made the call.

Oddly, Trisha found she could focus for the first time since boarding the plane at Miami. The PriceStar *maquila* on the outskirts of Tegucigalpa was a much smaller proposition than the one in San Pedro Sula. Both the PriceStar execs and the people on her team noticed the change, but neither was necessarily happy about it. The woman who had sat so quietly during their sessions at the big plant was now spitting out questions like a Gatling gun. And if the answers didn't come as rapidly in return, she did not hide her displeasure. Even she recognized she was being hard on everyone, but she was enjoying the high of her own adrenaline.

The morning smelled of spilled champagne, orchids and sex. Pete's flavor still lingered in her mouth with grace notes of herself. And she was sore, gloriously sore. Peter had been everything she had imagined, more. He really did seem to be able to see right through her, to read her. Somehow, he had known exactly how far to push things and when to draw back. The real surprise, however, had been her. She had let go for the first time in years, fighting the habit of holding back her screams as a negotiating ploy. Dinner had been great, what she could remember of it. Actually, she remembered very little of it. Last night hadn't been about the food.

Pete was gone. There was no surprise in that. He had warned her he had early business, but that he would take her to dinner again tonight, if that's what she wanted. If she wanted! At the moment, it was all she wanted. Stepping into the shower, she ignored the soreness as if to prove the point. When she left the suite, Trisha placed a twenty-dollar bill in an envelope for the chambermaid. Given the state of the bedroom, the woman would surely earn it.

Walking past the reception desk, the clerk got her attention.

"Miss Tanglewood, *por favor*. We have a message for you," he said, handing her a note.

The note was in English, but very cryptic:

If you want to see how PriceStar makes such profits, come see the real factories.

There was an address. Trisha showed the address to the clerk. He did not try to hide his worry.

"This is not a place for a ..." he searched for the word.

"Woman," she offered, perturbed.

"For anyone, but especially for an American. It is a slum, a ghetto. Very dangerous. Very dangerous."

"Okay. Thank you."

Trisha gathered her thoughts. She had been somewhat suspicious all along about how PriceStar, which chronically underperformed in almost all other segments of the market, had managed to outperform even its bigger, better competitors. There were rumors that all of the big retailers resorted to unsavory practices, especially in their specialty textile lines, but PriceStar had checked out, and no one on her team had even hinted at PriceStar using under age or slave labor. Yet, this note had to be investigated. That's what due diligence was all about. She couldn't very well ask one of PriceStar's execs to show her nor could she ask someone on the Paisley Shutter team. Trisha wasn't about to give anyone, especially Ellis Quantrill, a chance to shred and cover-up. She called the only person in Honduras she could trust.

"They're called *cuarterias*," Peter Dutton explained, driving his rented Jetta through the narrow streets. "It means rows in English. They're these long tracts of wooden buildings with tile roofs, dirt floors and connected rooms. Usually six or seven people to a room."

"Oh my god."

"It's rough, but they're good people. We'll be okay."

"Why did the desk clerk warn me that this was a bad place for Americans?"

"Well, there's the obvious reason. Money. They're good people, but they're sometimes desperate too."

"And the baby thieves myth," she said.

"Yes, that too. It's bullshit, pardon my French, but these are poor people with no education."

"I understand."

"Can we change the subject?" he asked.

"Please."

"Last night was ..."

"Yeah, I know, Pete. For me too. I've never felt like that before."

She could see his face redden a little. That made her smile.

"Here we are," Pete said, rolling to a stop. "You ready?"

"Let's go."

Before they got five feet, Trisha stopped and pointed at the noisy gas generator right outside the door they were about to enter.

"What's this for?" she wondered.

"You'll see soon enough."

Pete Dutton had tried to warn her she might not like what she was about to see, but words were just inadequate to the task. Inside, ten girls– the youngest about eight years, the oldest about fourteen– dressed in filthy, frayed frocks, were ankle-tethered with leather straps to sewing machine tables. Most of the girls kept their heads down, unfazed by the man and woman who had come through the door. One girl, a bony, twelve-year-old with a hare-lip and the most haunting brown eyes Trisha had ever seen, was too curious to resist. This did not go unpunished. A squat man with a

cloudy left eye, who stank of alcohol even above the smell of urine, snapped a switch across the hare-lipped girl's hands.

Pete reached out for Trisha, locking his hand on her forearm. "Don't!" he said. "Let me

handle this."

Dutton called the man over and whispered something to him. Cloudy Eye grunted. But when Pete slipped a twenty-dollar bill in his hand, he smiled like an old dog with a mouth full of rotten teeth and walked outside.

"We have five minutes."

"Her!" Trisha said, pointing to the hare-lipped girl.

That evening the sex was more intense, if less satisfying. Trisha had gotten so mind- numbingly drunk, that she barely remembered asking Pete to hit her, hit her hard as he rode her from behind. In fact, it was only when she looked in the dressing mirror and noticed the palm-shaped bruises on her flanks that she recalled her demanding that he hurt her. She brushed her fingers across the bruises. The pain had been only a temporary fix. The weather outside had changed to reflect her mood. The skies were eclipse dark and biblical amounts of rain threatened to bury the city. Trisha would gladly have applauded as the water rose over her head.

"Something's come up," she said to Susan Blum, her assistant in New York. "I'm taking the day to handle some loose ends. I'll call everyone here. By tomorrow, we should be back on track." She lied.

Even as she spoke, Trisha could not get her head around what the hare-lipped girl had told her and Pete. Her name was Linda and she was, as Trisha guessed, twelve. She was the eldest of six children, the daughter of a whore who had no idea who the fathers were of any of her children. Recently, her mother had gotten

very sick. So about three months ago, the whore had "sold" her eldest child into pseudo slavery. She worked fourteen-hour days and made a few *lempira* per piece. None of the clothes she sewed had labels, but yes, a man from PriceStar came sometimes to talk to Jorge, the cloudy-eyed overseer who sometimes made the girls fuck him.

"I am a smart girl," Linda said through Pete. "I may be ugly, but I hear things, see things."

But Trisha had no proof. She could not stop a multi-billion-dollar deal based on the word of an abused twelve-year-old Honduran girl. She needed something real, something tangible, something to bring to the firm. Even then, she wasn't quite sure it would do any good. These sorts of deals have a kind of self-sustaining inertia, especially this late in the process. Trisha had explained as much to Linda.

"Okay," said the little girl. "I understand. You come to my house tomorrow night and I will bring your proof. Other girls, too, to tell their stories."

Trisha had reached into her bag to give money to Linda.

"No! No! Not now!" she shouted in English. Then in Spanish to Pete, "Jorge will just take it. Bring it tomorrow night. Bring some money for all the girls."

When she clutched Trisha's hand and kissed her fingers, it changed her forever.

The rain had gone from biblical to drizzle. Pete picked her up in front of the hotel at nine. Trisha got in the backseat. There was someone in the front with Pete. He was a bulldog-faced fellow of thirty with red skin, thick arms, and flat affect.

"This is Paolo," Pete said. "He works for me. He'll have your back. He speaks perfect English. Right Paolo?"

"Very perfect. The best," he said in an accent-less monotone.

"What about you? Aren't you–"

"I wish I could, but I've got business of my own to handle. And besides, the two of us in that area at night ... We'd attract too much of a crowd. The wrong kind of crowd. You'll be much safer with Paolo. Trust me. No one is apt to fuck with him. Isn't that right, Paolo?"

"They wouldn't dare."

"Please, please, Pete forget your business. I'm scared out of my mind. I'll do anything if you come with me. I'll do anything ..."

"Okay," he said.

They drove into the mountains that surrounded the city. Trisha was numb, frightened about getting into a situation over which she would have very little control, but remained silent. When Pete turned off the main road and into a neighborhood of *cuarterias*, it was hard for Trisha to know if these were the same slums she had been to the previous day. Places, times, dates ... It was all starting to run together into an indistinguishable blur.

"It's right over there," Pete said, pointing to a shabby door as he rolled by. "I'm going to leave you and Paolo off at the end of the row. I'll be back for you in ..." He checked his watch. "Half an hour, tops." He reached over the seat and squeezed Trisha's hand reassuringly. "You'll be fine. Paolo will see to that. Right, Paolo?"

"I'll take good care of the lady."

"Good," Pete said. "I'll be right back in this spot in a half hour."

Paolo and Trisha got out of the Jetta. Pete beckoned Trisha to his rolled down window. She knew he wanted her to kiss him, which she did with little enthusiasm, the rain pelting her cheeks. He smiled at her when their lips parted. There was, she thought, something disquieting about his smile. Then, as she watched his

taillights disappear, Trisha shook it off. It was her own discomfort, she thought, projected onto Pete.

"Let's go," Paolo urged, placing his meaty hand around her bicep.

Paolo didn't bother knocking and just pushed back the shabby door to the hare-lipped girl's house. The inside was lit by a string of bare bulbs. The tamped down dirt floor was not muddy but was dark with moisture. The room was crowded and noisy and smelled of a sickening mixture of wet garbage and feces.

Linda sat on a crude bench, a young baby wrapped in a blanket cradled in her twig-like arms. There were children of varying ages all over the place, the older ones staring at Trisha and the big man at her side. The younger ones cried or played, happily ignoring the strangers. There were adults too, mostly haggard old women, probably not nearly as old as they looked. There were a few younger women too, but no one, in Trisha's estimation, who looked like the whore who had sold her child into a life of slavery and rape.

"Ask her where her mother is," Trisha told Paolo.

He did as she requested and translated the answer. "She's out sucking strangers' cocks for some lempira."

Some of the women laughed. Trisha failed to see the humor.

"Okay, ask her if these are the girls and women who will talk about PriceStar."

"Yes," Linda answered herself.

Again some of the women laughed. Again Trisha failed to see the joke.

"You have the money?" Linda asked in perfect English.

Trisha removed an envelope which contained five hundred American dollars in twenty-dollar bills.

"Let me see it, touch it," Linda said in Spanish. Paolo translated.

Trisha Tanglewood slowly removed the cash from the envelope and placed it in Linda's bony left hand. Linda showed the money to the baby in her arms and cooed something in the child's ear. Then, when she was done, she looked up at Trisha. On the hare-lipped girl's face was a cruel, almost feral smile. It made Trisha's blood run cold. She could feel herself blanch, feel the strength run out of her through the soles of her shoes and seep slowly into the shifting wet earth under her feel. All the individual sounds in the little room became a muted ringing in her ears. A wave of nausea slammed into her and she nearly fainted.

Linda's malformed lips and darting tongue shaped words which Trisha's eyes read but could not understand. They repeated the words again and again. She was shouting them. Now everyone was shaking their fists at Trisha, shouting, but the shouts just blended into the ringing. Somehow Trisha found the strength to ask Paolo. "What are they saying? What are they saying?

Paolo turned to look Trisha right in the face. His flat affect seemed to vanish, replaced by a broad mirthful smile. "Baby thief. They're calling you baby thief. Run!" he screamed. "Run!"

In a quieter but not dissimilar *cuarteria* no more than a thousand yards away from where Trisha Tanglewood was now running for her life, Peter Dutton was taking cover and comfort in the house of a sixteen-year-old whore. He found her disappointing. Even at sixteen she was so experienced as to be robotic but let her finish what she had started. He needed at least another five or ten minutes. By nature, he wasn't much for regrets, yet he had really enjoyed fucking the broad from New York. What she lacked in expertise, she made up for with enthusiasm. A shame, he thought, to waste that kind of talent.

When he finally came, he yanked the Honduran girl by the hair to make sure she swallowed. He couldn't abide spitters. He zipped up and threw two twenty-dollar bills onto the damp earthen floor. She smiled at him with more feeling than she'd displayed the whole time she'd had him in her mouth, but he'd already turned to leave.

The skies had opened up once again and as he closed the driver's side door, Pete could hear the cries of Baby Thief! Baby Thief! spreading through the slum like an airborne virus. Not a soul noticed as he drove off into the blackness.

She had gotten a pretty good lead on the mob. Trisha didn't ride anymore, but she kept herself in great shape. Unfortunately, a big lead when you have no idea of where you're going or the terrain or what lurks around the next dark corner is of limited value. Suddenly, a searing pain tore through her left shoulder. A rock! Shit, they're throwing stones. They're going to stone me to death! Trisha picked up her pace, but it did little good. The next rock caught her square in the jaw. Only her instinct for self-preservation and adrenaline kept her legs moving and then, only for a few more steps. She toppled over face first into the mud.

She was transported to the netherworld between consciousness and coma. Things she heard, things she felt, all seemed like they were happening to someone else. She could sense her body move with each kick, but the pain was so remote. Above her, buried in the clouds, she heard the roar of an ascending jet. What kind of aircraft, the type of power plant, she could not distinguish. It suddenly occurred to her that the flight attendant, Kathy, had never gotten back to her with the answer to her question. It's funny what you think about. Then something bounced violently against her skull and the world turned a silent shade of black.

A few hours later, Peter Dutton met with Ellis Quantrill at a prearranged spot on the road to Toncontín Airport.

"Is it done?" Quantrill wanted to know.

"Like you wanted, painful and nasty. It's going to be hard to identify her. I got the call a few minutes ago from my man confirming it."

"Excellent. That's the other forty grand plus expenses," Quantrill said, handing over a sleek leather attaché case.

"Boy, that chick must've really pissed you off."

"I don't think that's any of your affair. Now, I've got to go and act shocked and grieved. Goodbye, Peter."

Of course, Peter was no more his name than was Linda the name of the hare-lipped girl.

"Remember," he called out to Quantrill as he retreated to his car, "if anything should happen to me in the near future, I've seen to it that you'll go in a manner far worse than Miss Tanglewood. My colleagues will make it last much much longer."

"Are these sorts threats really necessary?"

"Due diligence, Ellis. Due diligence."

Jump

Originally published on the Akashic Books website.

Skeleton umbrella. Coney Island crucifix. Tilyou's Eiffel Tower. Steeplechase shrine. Icon. Landmark: looming, impotent, mocking, futile, naked, moot, regal, red, and ridiculous. Soaring twenty-six stories above the beach and boardwalk, passersby genuflecting at its feet, the Parachute Jump was all of these and none of these and more. Never less. Never. All you had to do was ask Richie.

Richie Rabinowitz spent his free waking hours on an invisible tether attached to the Parachute Jump. Sometimes he paced the boardwalk in front of it. Sometimes he sat on a bench beneath it, but he could not escape it. It was his obsession, always had been. Richie didn't mind tethers so much. His life was defined by them. In the womb the cord that tethered him to his mother had wrapped around his

neck so tight that it squeezed the oxygen right out of his head. Brains with it, the doctors said.

Every day after his school, from the time he was ten, Richie came to be near the Jump. On weekends, he would shower, eat breakfast, grab some juice boxes, make himself peanut butter and jelly sandwiches, bag them, and run the boardwalk from his apartment in Brighton Beach to the Jump. He liked it best in the winter, when he could be mostly alone with his obsession. He didn't mind the cold. The colder it was, the more alone time he had. But it was spring now. He hated spring, especially after Passover and Easter came. That's when people came back, and he had to share. By summer he adjusted, but he hated the spring.

This spring was different, though, because he had started to notice things. He noticed girls. He noticed them a lot, all sorts of stuff about them, like how they smelled different than boys. He liked how their hair looked on them, and their breasts. He liked their breasts. He really really liked their breasts, not the way he liked the Jump. Not like that. Nothing was like that. The breasts he liked most were on the girl he liked most, Karen Klingman. He didn't understand why he liked her so much. She had always been mean to him. She was the first kid in their building to call him Richie the Retard, but somehow that didn't seem to matter now.

It was really late. Almost no one was on the boardwalk and Richie was getting sleepy. Then he heard girls' voices carried on the breeze. Richie's heart thumped in his chest when he saw that it was Karen and her girlfriends coming his way. Seeing her did that to him lately, but he was also scared because he'd gotten in trouble for telling Karen about how much he liked her and what parts of her he liked the most. That happened to him sometimes, him saying stuff he shouldn't. Mrs. Klingman had told his parents and they went

crazy. His dad yelled and his mom just cried. He hated it when his mom cried, and she cried a lot.

"Hey, Richie," Karen whispered in his ear. She was so close to him he could taste her in the air, wisps of her blond hair brushing his cheeks. "Do you wanna touch my tits? It's okay." He didn't have time to answer because Karen grabbed his hand and put it on her right breast. "Ummmm," she sighed, squeezing his hand over her breast. Her girlfriends giggled. She took his hand away.

He stirred inside like he did sometimes when no one was around, but he didn't speak.

"If you climb the Jump, Richie," she was in his ear again, touching it with her lips, "I'll let you touch them under my shirt. You can lick them." She kissed his ear, bit the lobe a little.

When he hesitated, Karen took his hand again and put it under her halter. When he felt her nipple, he shook. She pointed up.

Forty minutes later Richie had climbed his Everest, the winds buffeting him as he slid along the red steel to the rim of the Jump, where the parachutes used to hang. He could see the whole world from there, a world that made him sad to see because, for the first time, he saw his place in it. Suddenly he didn't care so much about Karen's tits. When he let go, he realized his mom would cry, but she could do it all at once now. And he liked the sense of falling.

Kaddish

My first published short story, From PLOTS WITH GUNS.

It was to laugh.

What a stupid fucking expression, but my old man said it all the time. It rolled off his tongue like careless spit. So I say it. My old man, so low on the totem pole he was halfway to Australia. So much an afterthought, he gave forgotten a bad reputation. When they drilled Manny Feingold's boys in the Chink's up on Empire Boulevard, Starker Mench's gang pissed their pants at the sight of my old man crawling out of the crapper, toilet paper trailing out the back of his trousers. He wasn't even worth the price of a bullet. One of Mench's boys threw a broom and a dust pan at my Pops.

"Start cleanin' up or say Kaddish. It's your choice."

My old man did both. He would have done a tap dance. All they had to do was ask.

It was to laugh.

Even when I don't say it, I think it. It's like one of them songs that gets stuck in your head sometimes. There are days I almost forget his stupid expressions, the sound of his voice and the weight of my Pops' subterranean legacy stops tugging at me, but then somewheres between my skull and scalp it settles back down into my brain.

I'm thinking it now, the blood pumping outta my *kishkas* in a sweet rhythm like the words outta that Olivier guy's yap. I don't understand half the shit that limey prick says, but I bet he could scream "fuck you" and make it land on your ears like a kiss. He's probably half a fag. Even still, I could die happy with that voice in my head. Instead, I got my old man's for company. I never heard my mother's voice, not so's I remember, anyways. She lit out on us before I could crawl. Smart move. What I don't get is what she saw in the loser in the first place. I bet she don't hear the old man clanging around her head no more. It would serve her right if she heard it on her deathbed. I'd like to be there for that.

"Remember me?" I'd whisper in her ear. "It's to laugh, no?"

Now I won't get that chance, but I'll save her a seat in hell like the old man's saving for me.

"I'm fuckin' bleedin'."

"Me, too. Didn't you hear, that's what happens when you get stabbed or shot? You wanna compare entrance wounds?"

"You stabbed me! What the fuck did you stab me for?"

"I didn't wanna waste bullets."

"I don't even know you. Do I know you?"

"My old man. You knew my old man."

"Call a fuckin' doctor. I'm dyin' here."

"That's the general idea."

"Who's your old man?"

"One of Manny Feingold boys."

"What happened at the Chink's, that was business. Your old man knew the price of admission when he got into ... Ah fuck, this hurts."

"And what, you think this hole you put in my belly feels like a dip in the pool after a *schwitz*?"

"Listen, I'm sorry about your old man, whoever the fuck he was. Now call an ambulance, for chrissakes!"

"Bite your tongue or the rabbi's gonna box your ears."

"You're a sick bastard, you know that?"

"Very sick. Sicker by the minute."

"Call a fuckin' ambulance!"

"No."

"Fuck you and your old man. I hope my boys took their time with him."

"Easy, that's blood dripping down your chin. You can't afford to let your heart pump any faster. You like Olivier?"

"What?"

"Olivier, the actor. You like him? I seen him in some of those Shakespeare movies. When he talks, it's like the rhythm of your heart."

"Anything! I'll do anything, just call somebody. I'm sorry I had your old man killed. It wasn't personal. Just call somebody, please!"

"Your boys didn't kill my old man. They should have, but they didn't."

"You stabbed me cause my boys didn't kill your old man? Is that what you're sayin'?"

"Something like that, yeah."

"You're Hymie's kid."

"Yeah."

"Holy fuck! It's to laugh."

"What'd'you say?"

"Hymie's wife was the best piece a skirt I ever had."

"What? What are you laughing at? Stop it!"

"Hey kid, forget the call. Just save me a seat."

It was to laugh.

Look at Me/Don't Look at Me

From CRIME PLUS MUSIC.

Five minutes to stage, Mr. Lake.

Terry James Lake remembered a time when his nerves were reserved for the confessional. And for the entire decade of the '60s, with a year of grace and spillage into the '70s, Terry had had much to confess. A darkly handsome man in possession of a bushel full of Southern charm and an Aw Shucks country smile, Terry had a way with the ladies and, upon occasion, when the drugs and the spirit moved him, with the men folk, too. The thing was that Terry James Lake—Terry Jim to his fans—was about as country as the D train and his Southern charm was strictly South Brooklyn.

"*Oy gevalt,* we've got to do something about that fucking accent of yours. You sound like an extra from *Guys and Dolls,* for chrissakes!" was the first thing the General had said to Terry over a

71

beer after Terry's set at Folk City. He gave Terry a soft, avuncular slap on the cheek. "Such a *punim*. With a face like that, the chicks, you'll have to beat them off with a stick once we ditch this folk music crap, clean you up, and get you a fancy electric guitar."

Terry was already a bit of a chameleon, so he had no problem with the notion of rearranging himself into any shape if it meant steady money and steady pussy. He'd already done a transformation of sorts from Geraldo Colangelo—Italian father, Puerto Rican mother—to Jerry Cole, the folkie with soul. It wasn't like he really loved folk music, anyway. He found a lot of it to be hokey crap that had as much to do with his life as a pizza pie with a wagon wheel.

He had even less patience for the purveyors and consumers of it. He had no love for the cafe owners who liked to think of themselves as Bohemian impresarios but were more like backstreet pimps. They loved you like a son, a younger brother, as a talent supreme. They loved you backstage and on stage. They loved you right up until payday. Then they grew alligator arms and stiff fingers that never quite reached deeply enough into their pockets. Every night for them was a rough night. Every week a rough week. Every month rougher than the last. Yet somehow they managed to stay in business.

Then there were the silly goofballs who sat out there in the dark "feeling it" and finding the deeper meaning in the traditional songs.

"Jimmy Crack Corn, my balls," he'd once shouted out in drunken disgust at a pal's rent party in the East Village. "And is Michael's boat ever getting to shore or what?" He just couldn't bear all the hushed and phony reverence. It was one thing when Lead Belly sang "Pick A Bale of Cotton", but it was something else when

three milk-skinned Princeton grads with matching plaid short-sleeve shirts, chinos, penny loafers, and five-dollar haircuts sang it.

He laughed now, remembering that night in February of '62. Talk about silence. All the people in the cold water flat in Alphabet City turned to stare at him after his outburst, a mixture of shock and contempt in their eyes. But not quite in everybody's eyes. One Beat chick with long straight brown hair that came to the waistline between her black turtleneck and black tights, smiled at him with her eyes. For the benefit of the other partygoers, she'd kept her mouth neutral. But there was nothing neutral about her mouth twenty minutes later in the stairwell.

He reserved his greatest contempt for his fellow performers, those Princeton grads with their standup basses, banjos, and Martin guitars. Them and the girl singer escapees from the Seven Sisters who de-sexed themselves in some bizarre, over-earnest gesture of martyrdom to Woody Guthrie, the Rosenbergs, and the working man. He called bullshit on them.

When his discharge from the service in '60 was greeted with substantially less fanfare than a certain other handsome, dark-haired singer's, Geraldo Colangelo didn't have many prospects lined up. His father got him a job unloading produce trucks at the Brooklyn Terminal Market. On a night off, he went into the Village with this girl from the old neighborhood and they stumbled into an open mic set at Café Wha? Some guy was strumming on a Sears' acoustic and croaking out songs Terry used to sing in Thursday morning assemblies at PS 58. It didn't escape Geraldo's notice that the singer, a scruffy, pimply-faced stick figure, was receiving enthusiastic applause, female adulation, and money in a hat being passed through the crowd. That was the moment Geraldo Colangelo shed his name, his skin, and his sore back for a new name and a used acoustic.

Folk music was a means to an end, a way to get into a holding pattern to see what was what and to figure an angle. The folk scene was strong, though Jerry sensed it wouldn't last. There were limits to its appeal to the wider teen audience, who, as far as Jerry could tell, didn't give a shit about the Bomb or segregation or tradition. But Jerry also knew he wasn't cut out to be a pretty white boy crooner like Paul Anka, Bobby Vee, or Bobby Vinton. He had the looks, but not quite the voice to carry off that type of thing. Besides, those guys struck him as Sinatra wannabes who were more suited to singing at weddings and bar mitzvahs than at a hop. The one thing folk afforded him was the chance to write his own songs. That much, he liked about folk. Not much else.

So when the General, Izzy Gettleman, offered to buy Jerry a beer after his set at Folk City, he couldn't get to Vinny's Tavern on Sullivan Street fast enough. Izzy was a famous manager, the Kike Colonel Parker, as he was called behind his back. Izzy was renowned for picking up talent wherever he could. The thing was that once the General took you on and you put your name on the dotted line, you belonged to him, lock, stock, and amplifier. You sang the songs he told you to sing, dressed the way he told you to dress, dated the people he told you to date. It was a deal with the devil, if a benevolent one.

We need you on stage now, Mr. Lake

Terry stared into the mirror in the makeshift dressing room, fussed with his now unnaturally black, shag-cut hair, finger combed his dyed mustache, and shook his head at the desiccated, made up face of the man looking back at him. He didn't like what he saw. Didn't like the ridiculous white, polyester suit with the high-waisted, flared pants and the red acetate shirt in which he had been outfitted. Especially didn't like the sparkly plastic stars pasted onto

the broad lapels of his silly jacket. He didn't much like the chunky platform shoes either, though they were the least embarrassing piece of his costume.

"And they said 60s fashion was a joke," he muttered to himself, derisively flicking his left lapel in disgust. "Yeah, right. Fucking clown suit for a clown."

He grabbed his signature guitar, the one Izzy had picked out for him at Manny's all those years ago, a '63 surf green Fender Telecaster that had taken on a robin's egg blue patina over time. He hated that he wasn't actually going to play it. That he wasn't even going to plug in when lip synching that hideous fucking song yet again. A song that had come to define him, overshadowing everything else he'd done before or since.

Izzy had done to Jerry exactly what he'd said he would do during that first meeting. They ditched the folk music scene, bought him the aforementioned Fender, recast him as a Southern boy, but not too Southern.

"From the south, sure, but not too country. Anybody asks, you say you don't like talking about your childhood. Just say you grew up poor and hungry. I think we both know from this, so it's not so much a lie." He patted Terry's face as was his wont. "Put some twang in your voice, but not too much twang. You're a white boy who loves Chuck Berry tunes and R&B. You're gonna write maybe some tunes of your own with that kinda feel. We're gonna get you some gigs up here in the north until you perfect that down home boy accent because up here they don't know from down there."

And it had worked. It had worked better than either the General or Jerry cum Terry Jim would have believed. It didn't hurt that the Beatles and the rest of the British Invasion legionnaires also loved Chuck Berry and R&B. And Terry Jim proved to be a pretty

respectable songwriter. By '66 he was a top forties fixture, even making his way into the top ten on three occasions: twice with cover tunes and once with his own hit, "Look at Me/Don't Look at Me". It was still the biggest hit he'd ever penned and the single thing he was most proud of. But no one wanted to hear a slow ballad about a facially disfigured war vet writing a goodbye letter to his girl, especially not these days. Vietnam was a recent bad memory everyone wanted to bury and forget. These days it was all disco all the time or that punk rock shit.

No, the only thing people ever wanted to hear from him whenever they bothered to want to hear from him was the stupid theme song from the TV show *Thriller Man*. *Thriller Man* was one of those peculiarly '60s' success stories of a French television show *called L'Agent Dangereux*. The hour-long show shot on location all over the world about a hunky American espionage agent named Gabriel and his stunning French sidekick, Gigi, was bought by CBS and shown on Saturday night at nine. But because the French title didn't work, neither did the original French theme song. Enter Terry James Lake, his guitar, and a song written by Deptford and Clark. The show lasted one season on American TV, but the theme song had become a radio staple. When he did the occasional '60s' rock revival show, the one song they demanded he play was "Thriller Man." No Chuck Berry covers. No hits of his own. Not "Look at Me/Don't Look at Me". Just that one fucking song.

There was a knock at the trailer door. He stepped out onto the metal landing. The stage handler, a pretty girl who looked about sixteen but was probably twenty-five, stared up at him impatiently. She wagged a finger at him, urging him to hurry up. She looked at him with disdain, like someone else's worn out shoe, which, he guessed, he was ... kind of. The kids assembled outside on the

sidewalk and inside had no idea who he was other than some old guy their parents listened to.

"Come on, Mr. Lake, we're only a minute or so from the opening credits and your intro," she said, pulling him along.

He stopped for a second outside the place to take it in. So this was 2001 Odyssey, the disco moon to Studio 54's sun, located only a mile or two from his old Carroll Gardens neighborhood. What a freakin' joke! It even had a stupid hand-painted sign. It was probably supposed to have the word space in its name, he thought, staring up at the floodlit placard on the top corner of the white/gray concrete block building, but the yo-yo who painted it either ran out of room or couldn't spell space. Whatever!

Taking this gig was a mistake, though Terry Jim didn't have much choice about taking paying gigs these days. He was good with a lot of things, with women and music. Jimi Hendrix had even sent him a fan letter about his guitar playing and offered to buy his Telecaster from him for an outrageous sum of money. He had had the letter framed and put up on the wall in his Park Avenue apartment. Problem was he no longer had the apartment or the letter because one of the things Terry wasn't good with was money. As long as he had been with the General, things were okay. He had never wanted for anything. The General put him on a generous allowance and invested his money for him.

Sometimes he missed the General. Izzy was more of a father to him than his own father had ever been, but it wasn't like Izzy hadn't fucked him. As Chuck Berry himself had once told Terry, "It ain't a matter of if they'll fuck you. It's a matter of how hard, how often, and where at."

One of the clauses in their contract gave control of Terry's publishing rights to the General's company. Izzy didn't exactly rob Terry blind, but he kept more of the money than he should have.

Terry resented that part of their deal. Still, he figured it was a price he was willing to pay for stardom. Not a bad attitude to have if tastes never changed and stardom lasted forever.

"Okay, Mr. Lake," the girl said to him when they got inside the club, "all you have to do when Dante calls your name, is to run onto the dance floor and wave your guitar above your head. Stay in the spotlight." She looked at her clipboard. "Just like in the run through at the studio, the announcer is going to introduce the show, then Dante. In turn, Dante will intro the guests. First the Tramps, then Vicki Sue Robinson, then you. When you come off the dance floor, I'll be waiting right here to take you back to your dressing room. You'll have fifty minutes until I come get you for your segment. You're on last. Dante, the other acts, and the dancers will join you on the dance floor in the last minute of Thriller Man. We'll lower your playback, so that Dante can thank the guests, thank the audience, and do a promo for next week's show of Dance Mania. You just keep pretending to play as the credits role. Got it?"

He nodded, gritting his teeth. Music came up. Heavy on drums and bass, with a scratchy guitar playing what passed for a melody

"Okay, here we go."

Live from 2001 Odyssey in Bay Ridge, Brooklyn, the birthplace of disco dancing and the setting for last year's smash movie Saturday Night Fever, starring John Travolta, it's Dante Ferrara's Dance Mania.

"Hello Brooklyn!" Dante yelled, running out to the middle of the dance floor. He was dressed in a bizarre, one-piece outfit of red lame and sequins. After the applause died down, after the cheers for Brooklyn calmed, he said, "Welcome to a very special episode of

Dance Mania, live from the mecca of disco, 2001 Odyssey. Tonight's show will feature our two round elimination dance contest and a bevy of special musical guests. The Tramps ... Vickie Sue Robinson ... and an oldie but a goodie, Terry James Lake here to sing his hit 'Thriller Man.'"

There had been no need for the applause to die down after Terry Jim circled the dance floor, a dazzling array of colored lights flashing beneath the soles of his clunky shoes. His name was met with lots of blank expressions and confused whispers, but at least there hadn't been any boos.

When he got back to his dressing room, she was waiting for him. Carla Saroyan, his poison. Carla was, for lack of a better term, his girlfriend-manager-agent. In terms of all three, Terry had run through many of each since the General died of a stroke on August 27, 1967. Not many people noticed the General's passing because it happened on the same day Brian Epstein, the Beatles' manager, died. Izzy's son, Bobby, had taken over for his dad, but he didn't have a stomach for the sharp-elbows, rough and tumble managerial aspects of the business. He did, however, have a taste for publishing royalties, a gluttonous, insatiable taste.

Fed up with Bobby Gettleman neglecting his bookings and squeezing every nickel out of his song royalties, Terry Jim left Bobby and accepted a ridiculously small settlement for his remaining percentage of the publishing rights. But the way Terry figured it, between the investments the General had made for him, his gigs, and the settlement, he'd be good. What he hadn't figured on was two very brief and very expensive marriages. He also hadn't figured on Led Zeppelin, and Emerson, Lake, and Palmer.

The early '70s had been unkind to Terry Jim. Squeezed out on the one side by Moogs and metal chords and on the other side by the Carpenters and Gilbert O'Sullivan, Terry couldn't get arrested.

From '71 to '74, he'd run through a series of managers and agents, many of whom made promises no one could have kept. Still, even the sleaziest of the bunch, which was really saying something, could claim it wasn't for a lack of trying. None of them, not the legitimate ones who'd taken Terry on out of respect for the General or Terry's talent nor the ones who had latched onto him to suck him dry of whatever juice he might have left, could create a demand out of thin air. By '75, he was tapped out, living back in the basement of his folks' house in Carroll Gardens and making whatever few bookings he could for himself.

Then he got a call from Lefty Farmer, a bass player with whom he'd done several recording sessions. Lefty, who'd heard Terry was down on his luck, said that he needed a singer and guitarist for a backup band he'd been hired to put together. Some girl singer from Toronto billed as the Canadian Linda Ronstadt, was doing gigs in the New York area. Terry Jim didn't think twice about it. The gigs and the girl singer were mostly forgettable, but not her manager.

Carla Saroyan had once been gorgeous, a cover girl model with impossibly black hair, perfect dark olive skin, brown eyes so dark they were nearly as black as her hair. Her body had been an amazing blend of curves and sinew, but it was her mouth that men and women alike could never see past. In the business, the modeling agencies used to refer to Carla as "The Mouth". She had made the bulk of her modeling money doing lipstick, lip gloss, and toothpaste ads.

By the time Terry met her, Carla's looks had faded some with age and stress. Modeling, it seemed, had an even shorter shelf life than rock stardom, which is why she decided to go into talent management. Carla and Terry were perfectly mismatched as they shared the same weaknesses: drugs, sex, and spending. Worse for

Terry, though, was Carla's appetite for gambling. She had the bug bad. She would as soon bet on cockroach races as the Belmont Stakes.

But for whatever reason, she delivered bookings for Terry where all the others had failed. She had gotten him this Dance Mania spot, though it had taken her a lot of convincing to get him to do it.

"It's a relaunch moment, baby. We're going to remind the older fans of your glory and introduce you to a new generation."

In his darker moments, which were in no short supply these days, he suspected Carla of trading herself for his gigs. He never asked. It wasn't that he didn't care. It was that desperation helped make him conveniently blind.

"Hi, lover," she cooed, tossing her cigarette onto the floor of the trailer and snuffing it out beneath her shoe. "You okay? You look nervous."

"You know the way I feel about this gig, how ridiculous I feel."

Then, before he could say another word, she kissed him hard on the lips, sliding her tongue into his mouth, slipping her hands beneath his suit jacket and pressing her long nails into his back.

"Let me make it all better like I always do," she whispered in his ear, dropping to her knees.

She rubbed her cheeks up against his crotch, reaching for his zipper. When she found the metal tab, she tugged it slowly down, fished out his semi-hard cock, and put it in her mouth. He got that jolt as he always did when Carla put him in her mouth, but he clamped his hands around her shoulders, pushed her away and pulled her up onto her feet.

"Stop it! Just stop it!"

"But lover—"

"No." He zipped up. "We've got to talk."

She lit another cigarette.

"Don't do that. I have to go on. You know what smoke does to my voice."

She cackled at him. "Yeah, and it really kills your voice on an eleven-year-old playback tape of 'Thriller Man.' Next thing you're gonna tell me is that it fucks up your lip synching."

"Don't be cruel."

"Stealing Elvis songs now, Geraldo."

"Don't call me that."

"Geraldo. Geraldo. Geraldo. What are you gonna do about it?"

He turned to look at himself in the mirror again. He felt even more ridiculous than he had before the stage assistant had come to retrieve him. And as he stared at himself it hit him that he just couldn't go through with it. That he'd sooner go back to singing "Michael Row Your Boat Ashore" or unloading lettuce crates off trucks at three in the morning than to sing—lip synch—"Thriller Man" again. That Carla's line about a relaunch moment was a load of crap that he forced himself to swallow one spoonful at a time. That he still had an ounce of pride left somewhere.

She poked him with a fingernail. "I said, what are you gonna do about it, Geraldo?"

Now it was his turn to laugh. "It's what I'm not going to do about it," he said, pouring on his phony down home accent like a ladle of red-eye gravy.

"What the fuck is that supposed to—"

"You know what it means, Carla. I'm not singing that fucking song again. Never. Not ever. Not tonight. Not—"

Her eyes got wide with panic. "But, Terry—"

"What happened to Geraldo?"

She snuffed out her cigarette and threw her arms around him. "I'm sorry, Terry. I'm sorry."

"Me, too, darlin'" There was his accent again. "But I'm outta here." He reached for his Telecaster.

"You have to do it, Terry. You have to."

"No I don't, Carla. It took this stupid disco dance show to make me see that. Took me having to get so low that I would go out and embarrass myself on national TV. Live TV!" He laughed again. "Live TV, what a joke. I was going to go out there and lip synch a fucking song I recorded a million years ago on live TV. They're not even going to let me plug in, for fuck's sake. I'm ashamed I ever let it get this far."

"No, Terry, it's you who doesn't understand," Carla said, her voice frosty and clear, her eyes narrowing. "People expect you to do this."

"People? Fuck people."

"Wrong answer, Terry. These are the kind of people who fuck you, not the kind that you fuck. How else do you think a washed-up fake with a half-limp dick like you got a gig on a national TV?"

"I suppose if I thought about it, I would say your oral talents and willingness to bed down anyone with a pulse had something to do with it."

She cackled again, only this time it was very shrill and brittle. "No one's that good, Terry. Not even me. You got this gig because I sold your contract to some people."

"Sold?"

"I owed these people, Terry. I owed them a lot and they were willing to let me off the hook if I gave them my rights to manage you and if you would make this appearance. They have power. They can get you a lot more gigs. So you see how it is, right?"

"Explain it to me, honey," he said, his accent all South Brooklyn. "Explain it so that even a dumb mope from Carroll Gardens can understand it."

She shrugged. "Okay, then. If you walk out of here, they're going to hurt me, Terry. They say it won't be too bad. That they'll just break my legs. They won't touch my face. Not this time."

"That's too bad, Carla. But once your legs heal, you'll still be able to spread 'em again" He wiped the neck of his guitar, then laid it in its case. Stood up. "And to think I really used to love you."

She ignored that. "It's a little late in the game for indignation and jealousy, don't you think? I'll be able to spread my legs, Terry, but you won't have any legs anymore. You don't go out there and do what you're supposed to do, you're dead. And it won't go easy for you. The guys I sold your contract to, they don't fuck around."

"What do they even want my contract for, anyway? I'm barely making enough for you to lose."

"Who knows? You were all I had left to barter. Maybe they think they can launder money with you as a front or maybe one of the old guys liked the way you used to sing. Maybe they want you to be the regular act at the Gemini Lounge on Flatbush Avenue. You ever hear of Roy DeMeo?"

"Why? He the guy who bought me?"

Carla shook her head. "He works for the guys who bought you and he's crazy. He likes killing people. He shoots you in the head, chops your body up, and throws it in the Fountain Avenue dump. And that's if he likes you. If he doesn't like you, he skips the shooting in the head part and goes right to the hacking you up part." She relaxed and came over by Terry again. "So stop being stupid about this and let me make it better the way I always do," Carla said, bending to her knees yet again. "They said I can still travel with you if that's what you want. Let me make you want that, Terry. Let me."

He let her.

It's time, Mr. Lake.

As they walked once again from the trailer, through the crowd assembled outside, and into the club, the stage girl explained once again how it was going to work, but it all sounded like blah, blah blah, blah blah, blah ... Terry was too busy time traveling to listen. He was back at the air base in Germany. Back offloading trucks. Back on stage at Café Wha? and Folk City. Back with the General having deli at Katz's on Houston Street, planning their next moves. Back in his apartment on Park Avenue, showing his Jimi Hendrix letter to everyone who came by. Back making appearances on *American Bandstand, Where the Action Is, Hootenanny,* and *The Ed Sullivan Show.*

"Okay, Mr. Lake," she said, "get ready. Remember go to the center of the dance floor, watch for the director's cue, and begin playing and lip synching. Try not to actually sing because we don't want the live mics to pick it up. Go!" She clutched him by the biceps and pushed him toward the dance floor, which again, was lit from below with an array of flashing colored lights.

The director gave him the cue, but there was a delay in the playback. So he began fingering the chords and plucking his silent strings ahead of the recording. Then came that twangy intro a few seconds behind where he was in the song. His lip synching was out of synch, so he was mouthing the lyrics—Gabe and Gigi lived the lives of nomads—before the vocal playback began. And somehow in the midst of that technical snafu it all came together for him. He realized he didn't give a fuck about Carla's legs or even his own. He didn't care about Roy DeMeo or his bosses or anyone else. He wasn't going to do it. He wasn't going to play this fucking song again, not ever.

He stopped fingering the chords. Stopped lip synching altogether. Then he started fingering and strumming again. Started singing, loudly. Loudly enough so that the open mics clearly picked up his voice. But he wasn't singing "Thriller Man."

Dante Ferrara turned to the director. "Go to commercial. Go to commercial. What the fuck is he singing?"

Carla, who'd followed Terry in, said, "You don't know this? It was a big hit, "Look at Me/Don't Look at Me.""

"Nah, that ain't it," said the pudgy faced man with the dead eyes and the slick black hair, standing over Ferrara's left shoulder. "It's a whatumacallit ... a swan song. Yeah, like that."

Carla opened her mouth to disagree, but when she looked into the man's bottomless eyes, she closed her mouth. She didn't bother trying to run, either. Why piss off the debt collector? She had heard a broken femur was terribly painful. She couldn't imagine how painful two would be. She figured she wouldn't have to imagine for very long. Terry had just seen to that. But like Terry had said, she'd be able to spread her legs again. She laughed to herself. She had never believed him when he said he hated that stupid "Thriller Man song." She believed him now. You couldn't have asked for more proof.

Mastermind

From LONG ISLAND NOIR.

Jeff Ziegfeld was always the exception to the rule: the dumb Jew, the blue-collar Jew, the tough Jew. No matter the Zen of the ethnic group the wheel of fortune got you born into, dumb and poor was the universal formula for tough. And he had to be tough because it's hard to be hard when your name's Jeffrey Ziegfeld. Didn't exactly make the kids on the block shit their pants when someone said, "Watch out or Ziggy'll kick your ass." He was extra tough because his dad liked to smack him around for the fun of it, all the time saying, "Remember, dickhead, no matter how strong you get, I'll always be able to kick your ass. I grew up the last white kid in Brownsville. And where'd you grow up? Lake Grove, a town with no lake and no grove. What a fucking joke. Kinda like you, huh, kid?"

J-Zig, as one of the other inmates at the jail in Riverhead had taken to calling him, could trace what had gone wrong with his life back to before he was born. Neither one of his parents had ever gotten out of high school or over moving out of Brooklyn. Long Island was a rootless, soulless place where everyone except the Shinnecock, the East End farmers, and the fishermen came from Northern Boulevard or the Grand Concourse or Pitkin Avenue. And even the natives were trading in their roots and souls for money. All the goddamned Indians wanted to do was to run slot machine and bingo parlors. The working farms had been converted into condos, McMansions, and golf courses that no one like J-Zig could afford to play. Not that J-Zig knew a rescue club from a lob wedge. The fishermen? Well, they'd become the cause célèbre of Billy Joel, Long Island's king of schlock 'n' roll. Billy Joel, born and bred in Hicksville. Hicksville, indeed.

J-Zig's head was somewhere else as he sat on the ratty Salvation Army couch in his dank basement apartment in Nesconset. Nesconset, a stone's throw from his mom's house in Lake Grove. It might just as well have been a million miles away for all he saw his mom since she'd remarried. He had plenty of reasons to hate his real father, but he hated O'Keefe, his mom's new husband, even more and that was really saying something. His stepfather, a retired city fireman with a belly like a beach ball and the manners of hyena, was a drunk and more than a little anti-Semitic. J-Zig didn't let that get to him. O'Keefe—if the moron had a first name, J-Zig didn't know it—hated everybody, himself most of all. Jews were probably only fourth or fifth on his list.

J-Zig had a terminal case of yearning exacerbated by persistent bouts of resentment. The thing about that was he was a lazy son of a bitch and about as ambitious as a dining room chair. There'd be no pulling himself up by his bootstraps—whatever the

fuck bootstraps were, anyhow—not for this likely lad. One way or the other he was a man destined to be a ward of the taxpaying public. He'd already tried on three of the state's myriad options: jail, welfare, and the old reliable, unemployment insurance. Truth was he found none of them very much to his liking. The food and company at the jail sucked. Welfare was okay as far as it went, but since he and the wife and her bastard son by another man's drunken indiscretion had split, he no longer qualified. He liked unemployment okay, but the bitch of it was you had to work for a while to qualify and J-Zig wasn't keen on that aspect of the equation. So he sold fake Ecstasy outside clubs and stolen car parts to pay the bills.

When he wasn't making do with the drugs or the hot car parts, he worked as muscle, doing collections for a loan shark and fence named Avi Ben-Levi. Ben-Levi was a crazy Israeli from Great Neck who put cash on the street and charged major vig to his desperate and pathetic clients. J-Zig hated his job except when it came to gamblers. He had no respect for gamblers. They'd borrow the money and blow it that day and then, when J-Zig would come to collect, they'd squeal and beg like little pussies. He liked to hear them scream when he snapped their bones like breadsticks. It was the business types he felt sorry for. All sorts of people borrowed money from Avi, but as broke as he could be at times, J-Zig knew better than to dip into a loan shark's well. Once they had you, they had you by the balls and then they squeezed and squeezed and squeezed until they milked you dry. Thing was, Ben-Levi didn't do the milking himself. It was always left to the muscle like J-Zig. It had been a few months since he'd worked for Ben-Levi because the Israeli had wounded J-Zig's pride. He'd come to the loan shark with a pretty good idea about how to streamline Ben-Levi's business.

"What, are you a mastermind all of a sudden? Listen, Ziegfeld, as a businessman, you are good muscle. Just do your job, get paid, and shut up." He waved his hand in front of J-Zig's face. "This ring and watch are worth more money than you will ever see in your life, so, please, either go to Wharton or keep your genius ideas to yourself."

Mastermind. The word had been stuck in J-Zig's head ever since that day. He burned to prove that Israeli cocksucker wrong, to repay Avi for mocking him. He wanted to shove Avi's sarcasm so far up his ass that they'd be able to see it in Tel Aviv. Trouble was, J-Zig couldn't figure out how to do it. He hadn't hit upon the right idea just yet, but he knew the right idea was out there waiting for him to find it. He could feel it sometimes like an itch on the bottom of his foot that he couldn't quite get to. If he could just reach it, J-Zig was sure he could finally escape the weight of the gravity that had held him down his entire miserable life.

Then it happened in a flash: the idea hit him like a kick in the balls. When he retraced his steps that day, he even understood the genesis of it. This in itself was a near miracle. Deductive reasoning and introspection weren't usually dishes on J-Zig's menu. The day started out like most others. Maybe a little better than recent days because he'd fallen into some stolen airbags at dirt cheap prices. God love tweakers. Meth heads didn't haggle, they just wanted enough cash to keep them buzzing for the next few weeks. Sometimes they got a little violent, but violence was something J-Zig could handle. He was better at it than most anyone stupid enough to take him on. He was empathetic to the tweakers' plight. Shit, who wouldn't get edgy when his world was spinning that much faster than everyone else's? Who wouldn't get wound up tight after not sleeping for days on end?

J-Zig had found a body shop in Selden willing to buy the boosted airbags at a fair price. Getting goods cheap didn't mean dick if you couldn't find someone to take them off your hands. The exchange of the airbags for cash went smoothly and the *gelt* in his pocket meant his expenses were covered for the next two months with a little something left over. Mick, his connection at the body shop, told J-Zig that they could handle as much merchandise he could bring in. In a tough economy everyone was looking to cut corners. This new connection and the cash were cool, but it wasn't his way to prove himself. What it was was a big weight off his shoulders and that helped clear his head.

For the first time in a long time, he had a little mad money and room to breathe. He decided to head a few miles west, straight down Middle Country Road, for the Smith Haven Mall. In Saudi Arabia, they have Mecca and Medina. On Long Island they have Roosevelt Field and the Smith Haven malls. I mean, who needs God when you've got the Gap? Everybody on the island, even lowlife mutts like Jeff Ziegfeld, prayed at the temple of conspicuous consumption. Say hallelujah. Say amen.

The second piece of the grand scheme planted its seed in J-Zig's brain as he turned left out of the body shop's driveway and toward the mall. A commercial came on the radio for Island World Gold and Jewelry Exchange. Long Island's biggest and most generous gold and jewelry exchange, so the announcer claimed, with branches in Floral Park, Bethpage, Massapequa, Mastic, Selden, Yaphank, and Riverhead. Selden! And there it was right in front of him, directly across Middle Country Road from the body shop— Island World Gold and Jewelry Exchange. Funny how he never noticed it before. A sign in the window read: MORE CASH ON HAND THAN ANY THREE OF OUR COMPETITORS COMBINED. Still, it didn't quite register in his thoughts. The only thing he was

thinking about was checking out the high school girls parading around the mall in skin-tight pants cut so low you could see the waistbands of their thongs peeking out the back. J-Zig was pretty successful with high school girls who had a thing for bad boys with good bodies. But when he got close to the mall, thoughts of teenage girls and their silky thongs went right out of his head.

There were two white and blue Suffolk County Police cruisers blocking the Middle Country Road entrances to the mall. The cops were out of their units, motioning for approaching cars to turn around and leave. J-Zig noticed the vast parking lots were empty and that there were Suffolk County PD cars all over the place, their cherry tops lit up like Times Square on New Year's Eve. There were fire engines and ambulances too.

"Excuse me, officer, what's going on?" he asked one of the cops, slowing his car to a crawl. J-Zig's tone was utterly respectful. He'd learned the hard way how to talk to cops. If you kissed their asses and licked their boots a little, they might tell you what you wanted to know.

"Prank," the cop said. "Some stupid kid called in a bomb threat. Okay, now let's keep it moving."

That's when it all clicked. Eu—fucking-reka!

It was week seven of his master plan and so far everything was going smoothly. If everything continued going that way—and he had no reason to think it wouldn't—he would hit Island World Gold and Jewelry Exchange in Selden that coming Thursday at 2 PM. J-Zig got stiff just thinking about what he'd been able to manage completely on his own. He was proudest of exhibiting three qualities he wasn't exactly known for: diligence, patience, and calm. He had written out the entire plan, step by step. He'd made a list of the equipment he needed and the research he had to do before even

thinking about pulling the job. He went over the lists again and again and again.

First thing he did was to get hold of the meth head who'd gotten him the airbags, because J-Zig needed a steady flow of funds to help finance the job. He promised the tweaker better prices for his merchandise if he could keep the supply of car parts coming. Mick at the body shop was good to his word and said he would pay top dollar for anything J-Zig could deliver. Greed and drugs were great motivators and within twenty-four hours, the tweaker was knocking on J-Zig's door and J-Zig was in turn knocking on the body shop's door. Everybody was happy.

Over the following weeks, whenever he went to the body shop for a transaction, he scoped out the external security setup at Island World. By his third trip, he was totally confident he hadn't missed anything. It was pretty basic stuff: a camera on the front door, one on the back door, one on the parking lot, one on the side street. He spent days in the abandoned Taco Bell parking lot with a pair of binoculars fixed on Island World. It got so he recognized the employees, their cars, the times they went to lunch. Most importantly, he took note that the armored car pick-up came at 2:15 PM every day of the week.

Next thing he did was to turn some of his car part profits into used gold jewelry at a flea market in Sayville. He knew that the stuff was gaudy crap, but that wasn't the point. He needed something to use as an excuse to scope out Island World from the inside. Unlike with the outside security, J-Zig would only get one shot, two at most, to survey the internal security. There would be cameras inside, some he knew he wouldn't be able to see, but that would sure as shit see him. He couldn't risk making too many scouting trips. One, his being there a lot would raise suspicions that he was in fact scouting out the place for a job. Two, he was a convicted felon. Admittedly, a

low-class felon, but a felon nonetheless. If Island World's security company was thorough, they might identify him and suspect he was using them to dispose of hot jewelry. He meant to set off some alarm bells, but not that way and not just yet.

He'd convinced a local commercial real estate broker that he was interested in a stand-alone building not unlike the one that housed Island World Gold and Jewelry Exchange. "For coins and other collectibles," he told the broker, who was then only too happy to give J-Zig the keys for a look-see.

When the rep from the same firm that did Island World's security met him at the vacant building, J-Zig realized he shouldn't have wasted time worrying about them being thorough. The rep was so eager to land the account, he volunteered more information than J-Zig could have hoped for.

"We do security for a client right down the road from here in Selden that does sort of what you have in mind for this place. It's roughly the same size and we can do the same setup."

The schmuck practically tripped over his own penis giving out details. And in an attempt to sell an even more elaborate system, the sales rep listed the pitfalls of the Island World setup and explained how a very clever criminal might defeat the system entirely. Some of it was beyond J-Zig's capabilities, but he didn't need to defeat the whole system, just part of it. He thanked the salesman, took his card, and told him he'd be in touch.

The other part of the plan was trickier and more dangerous. It was riskier because it directly involved the police. At random times and on different prepaid Wal-Mart cell phones, he called in various emergencies at the Smith Haven Mall. One Monday it was a car fire. One Wednesday it was a robbery. One Thursday it was a heart attack. One Friday it was a bomb threat. Bomb threat won in a landslide. The police response was incredible. Every cruiser in the

4th Precinct and half the fire departments on the North Shore of Suffolk County showed up at the mall. That would take care of the cops to his west. J-Zig was smart enough not to repeat the phone threat routine in the 6th Precinct, the precinct responsible for Selden, but he was willing to bet they would respond to a bomb threat at the local high school with the same sort of vigor the 4th Precinct cops responded to a bomb threat at the mall. When J-Zig pulled the job, the cops would be so preoccupied they wouldn't know what hit them.

What made this especially cool was how, for the first time in his whole fucked-up life, all the parts had fallen into place. The stars had finally aligned for him. All of it, from the bad economy to the kid's bomb prank, from the tweaker to Mick, from the radio commercial to Island World being right across the street from the body shop, had made it pretty easy. But now Thursday was here and the easy stuff was done. It was time to go to work.

He'd made all the calls as he pulled into the body shop's parking lot. As he stepped into the shop to greet Mick, the firehouse claxons erupted, calling for the volunteer firemen to get their asses to the firehouse. Then, as he walked to the back room of the body shop to use the bathroom and establish his alibi, J-Zig heard the police sirens wailing. By the time he slipped out the back door, all hell had broken loose. Emergency vehicles were flying down Middle Country Road in both directions: fire engines and ambulances and police cars, lots and lots of police cars. With all of the activity no one noticed him dash across the street. Certainly no one saw him slip into the latex gloves and Obama mask in the shadows along the back edge of Island World's parking lot. He had no doubt that Island World's two female employees were too busy to notice him. Every day at this time, they assembled their cash take and jewelry for the armored car pickup at 2:15. It was only when J-Zig threw the brick,

lit road flares, and smoke grenade—much easier to get than he thought it would be—through the side window of Island World Gold and Jewelry Exchange that the employees would sense something was terribly wrong. By then it would be too late.

It was magic. When the two women ran screaming and coughing out the back door, he ran in and scooped up the two bags. Before leaving, he checked out the back door and he couldn't believe his eyes. The two women were still running and hadn't bothered looking back. He was out of there and at the edge of the lot, out of sight of the cameras. He slipped the deposit bags, gloves, and his mask into the gym bag he had hidden there the night before with the brick, road flares, and grenade. If anything, the activity on Middle Country Road had intensified. Now there were news and police helicopters in the air. Getting back across the street was no easy thing, but he made it. He tossed the gym bag in the trunk of his car, walked through the body shop's back door—which he had made sure to keep slightly ajar with a small stone—ran to the bathroom, and flushed. He looked at his watch. 2:06 PM. The stars were still aligned, but that wasn't the beauty part of the deal, not by a long shot.

The sweetness was that J-Zig was going to get the chance to shove Avi Ben-Levi's own words up his ass after all. He had arranged for Ben-Levi, a man with all the right connections in the wrong world, to fence the jewelry. That's why J-Zig had taken the gold and diamonds and not just the cash, so he could get the chance to face Ben-Levi and gloat. He had fantasized about how the meeting would go for nearly seven weeks. After shaking hands with Mick to reestablish his alibi, he was going to go straight from the body shop to meet with Ben-Levi at his office in Great Neck. And as a kind of subtle and final fuck you to his former employer, J-Zig had

purchased a ticket on EL Al for a flight to Israel. Seemed as good a place to enjoy the spoils of victory as anywhere else.

J-Zig slammed the toilet door loud enough to be heard over the sirens and then stepped through the door into the shop itself. Mick was there waiting for him.

"We were gonna send a search party in there after you, for fuck's sake. What the fuck were you doing?" Mick asked.

"Stomach's been bothering me." J-Zig winked. "I wouldn't go in there for a while unless you get battle pay."

"I consider myself warned."

"What the fuck's going on out here anyway?" he asked, as innocent as a spring lamb, as a few more police cruisers flew by. "I heard all the commotion when I was in the can."

"Fuck if I know. Come on in the office, there's some friends I want you to meet."

J-Zig looked at his watch again. "Maybe another time, I've got—"

"Look, man, for what I've been paying you, you owe me this small favor."

It was tough to argue Mick's point, so he didn't bother. "Lead the way."

He was in the office, the door shut at his back, before he could quite make sense of what was going on. Even after seeing the shields hanging on chains around the necks of Mick's three friends and the 9mms strapped to their belts, it almost didn't register. Then he heard Mick, who was still behind him, say:

"Jeffrey Ziegfeld, you're under arrest." J-Zig felt Mick tug his wrists and slap on the cuffs. "You have the right to remain silent. Anything you say can and will be used against you in a court of law. You have the right to an attorney. If you cannot afford an attorney, one will be provided to you. Do you understand these rights?"

J-Zig didn't answer the question, but asked one of his own. "What are the charges?"

"What are the charges, he asks," said the fierce-looking detective standing directly in front of J-Zig. "Are you fucking kidding me or what? Hey, this guy missed his calling. He shoulda done standup."

J-Zig repeated the question. "What are the charges?"

"This guy can't be this dumb, can he?" the detective asked the cops behind him. Then he spoke directly to J-Zig. "Are you really that stupid?"

J-Zig repeated the question again. "What are the charges?"

"Okay, rocket scientist, let me give you a clue. My name is Detective Robert Ferraro and we're from the Suffolk County PD Auto Crime Task Force. You think maybe now you can figure it out or do I have to draw you a picture with crayons?"

J-Zig heard someone laughing. It took a second or two until he realized it was him.

"Mick, can you believe this guy? He's facing like a ten spot in prison and he's laughing his head off. Hey, shithead, what's so funny?" asked Ferraro.

"I am," said J-Zig.

"You wanna let us in on the joke?" Ferraro asked.

"The punch line won't be as funny to you if I just tell you, but you'll find out soon enough."

"Whatever. Mick, get this moron outta here."

Later that afternoon, when J-Zig's impounded car had been towed to the 6th Precinct, Mick and Ferraro searched it for more stolen parts. Nobody at the precinct paid the two auto crime task force detectives much mind. Who gave a fuck about some dumbass skell who was selling car parts to a police sting operation? They were too busy looking for the guy who jerked around half the first

responders in Suffolk County, ripped off Island World Gold and Jewelry Exchange, and then disappeared into thin air. After about ten minutes, Ferraro found the gym bag with the money, the jewelry, the gloves, and the Obama mask.

"Holy fuck, Mick!"

"What is it?"

"The punch line."

When J-Zig was arraigned the next morning at the courthouse in Central Islip, he seemed utterly calm. He turned and smiled at the crush of media squeezed into the courtroom. After the long list of charges were read, the judge asked for J-Zig's plea.

"Tell Avi Ben-Levi to go fuck himself!" is what he answered.

J-Zig knew it really didn't matter what he said. He was going to spend the rest of his now somewhat less miserable life in prison.

Portrait of The Killer as a Young Man

From DUBLIN NOIR.

Jaysus Christ, I hate fooking Americans! The donkeys worst among 'em. And them arse-licking cops worst of all. Them with their fifty-two paychecks and pensions, their red noses and "Danny Boy" tears. They think glen to glen is a conversation of like-named punters. Cunts all, every last one. Them that sees romance in the famine and the troubles. Yah, romance in a bloody holocaust and the smell of cordite in the streets of Derry. And they ease their guilt and fancy themselves Provo men because they open their wallets and sing Pogues songs and drown themselves in pubs with a gold harp above the threshold. What a load a shite.

Oh, and how they imagine us Irish in the worst possible sense; a race of toothless spud farmers in white cable knit sweaters and black rubber boots, spouting Joyce or Yeats, herding lambs with a switch in one hand and a pint of Guinness in the other. And what of our race of red-haired colleens? Why, they're out in lush pastures in their white blouses and green plaid skirts gathering clover and hunting for pots of gold. Bollix!

I hadn't meant to kill the first one. I had dreamed of it, for sure. Taking one of the cheery bastards who hopped into me cab and opening him up like an Easter lamb, tossing his innards out my windows as I drove the M-road back from Shannon. But like with sex, it never quite happens the way you dream it. I s'pose if I had planned it, it would never have come off at all. I had sat patiently for a year at the wheel and listened to my American cousins affect cartoon brogues, recite bad jokes, and spew inanities at the back of me head.

"Would you like a seven course Irish meal? A six pack and a patata."

"Top a the mernin' to ya, boyo."

"Where do you keep the leprechauns, in the trunk?"

"Hey, where's me Lucky Charms?"

"I speak Irish– Erin go bragh. Good, huh?"

"Is it true about the Irish Curse?"

"You don't have red hair!"

"Irish Spring. Sure it smells good on him, but I like it too."

I took all of it and more; let it build up like steam in the kettle, fester like a cut from the lid of a rusty tin. It got so that the loathing felt warm as a cup a tea armor-plated with Jameson's. I learned to bathe in it so that the thought of killing one of me American fares made me hard as a hurley soaked through with water and left to cure in a baking hot oven. Hate had always been a

comfort to me. What's more natural than hate save rage? I hate Pakis, tinkers even more. But nothing I had known before compared to how I hated Americans. It was my coming of age.

Then, out of the blue, I was triggered. A blowsy Yank, all muzzy and hog-eyed, got in me cab just outside Davy Byrne's Pub in Duke Street and asked to go to the Gresham Hotel in O'Connell St. Upper. He went quiet on me after first announcing he was ex of the NYPD. As if I gave a shite. Did he expect me to kiss his fooking ring? So many sheets to the wind was he that he'd seemed to lose his voice as well as his senses. Then catching his breath, he began to rant about the weather, but that isn't what set me off.

No– it was when he complained bitterly that us Irish drive as the Brits do, on the wrong side of the road. In America, he assured me, they would never put up with that shit. It was at that point I decided to no longer put up with this. Well, it wasn't so much a decision as a reflex. Why of all things *that* should have lit my candle, I cannot say, but light it, it did.

I detoured to a section of town where, at that hour, there would likely be no foot traffic at all. Feigning illness, I pulled into an alley near dark as my heart. I got out of the cab, having already slid me sawed-off baseball bat up me trouser leg. When he came to look after me as I knelt on the cobbles pretending to retch up me lungs, I slammed the bat into his shins with such fury to snap at least one. I nearly orgasmed at the crackle of his shattering bone. He tumbled mightily, his head smacking a brick wall as he toppled. Thud does not describe the sound of his skull against the stone. He was not dead, only damaged. I made sure to damage him well beyond dead. His face, what there was left of it, now red from blood and not from drink. I removed his watch, his jewelry, credit cards, the money from his wallet. I learned that from American TV.

"Was that a home run, fella?" I asked, tossing his pilfered wallet onto his body.

He was strangely silent.

There have been five more like him spread out over the last two years. I've made certain to alter the way in which I approach my victims, never again picking one up in me cab. They're such suckers for the glad hand and blarney that there's no challenge in it. They're kittens to cream. Nor have I repeated the method I've used to murder them. I've stabbed one, poisoned another, beaten one to death with me fists, strangled one, and used a shotgun on the last. When the Garda seemed to be putting two and two together, not usually a skill they possess, I was forced to kill at random. Not a drop of red, white or blue involved.

She was an Irish girl, pretty enough to interest the press. She was at Trinity studying some wanker named Kant. Had to swallow the laughter on hearing that. Dropped two roofies in her drink, fooked her every way to Sunday and stabbed her with the same knife I used to do in the American. I cut her in just the same way as I did the Yank. I think of him as the ugly American. Looked better when I was done with him than when I began.

I feel bad about her sometimes, like when I'm getting meself off. She's the only one I rue. Might have been a future for me with her and Kant, but I had to confuse the Garda. Worked like a charm. They need a new calculator. I figure I'll have to do the odd one every now and again to fook with their arses. No more pretty girls, though. No philosophy students. Kants, the bunch of them. I'll have to use that line. You think?

Shite, a fare out in front of Kavanagh's Pub and I was having a tickle with you lot. Do me the favor of keeping your gobs shut until I rid meself of the fare. Then we can get back to our business.

"Where to, sir?"

"Just drive. I'll tell ya when to stop."

"American?"

"Yeah."

Jaysus, I finally got a quiet one. No jokes nor brogues. And look at the face on him, Irish as a Galway swan and dour as a priest out of sacramental wine. I almost feel sorry for this one.

"Here on business or pleasure, you don't mind my asking?"

"Business."

"What kinda business you in?"

"Cop. I'm a cop."

I'll be fooked. An American cop, but nothing like the others. He didn't even tell me where. Usually takes no more than a few seconds in me backseat before they show me their friggin' shield sand tell me how long till they're vested in their bloody pensions. Then it's to the war stories. As if I gave a toss.

"Collins," I said, reaching me right mitt across my body and over the seat.

"Jack," he said, giving my hand a quick, uncomfortable shake.

Again, nothing like the others. All the others near crushed my hand, refusing to give it back until I pled for its release. Now as I see him in me rearview, I'd say he's had a fair amount of drink, but he's far from scuppered. He's in turmoil for sure, by the look on his face. Christ above, damned if I'm not concerned for the bastard.

"Is everything right by you, Jack?"

"Far from it, Collins."

"Is there anything I can do to ease your troubles, sir?"

"Yeah, can you pull over here? I'm feeling sick."

"It's a rough part of the old town, Jack. Are you sure you can't hold– "

"Pull over!"

Shite! Now he's out of me cab and down an blind fooking alley. It's been five minutes. Ah, let me go see how the poor bastard's doing.

Thwack!

"Sorry, Collins."

Thwack.

"It's nothing personal, but some shanty prick beat my father to death with a baseball bat down an alley not too far from here."

Thwack.

"I figured we owed you cocksuckers one."

Thwack.

"Shit, Collins, if I didn't know better, I'd swear you were smiling at me. Fuck you, asshole!"

Thwack.

Like I says, I hate fooking Americans, arse-licking cops worst of all.

The Frog

Introduced Gulliver Dowd. First published on the Plots with Guns website.

Gulliver Dowd was sure he had the Frog. Alternating his gaze between the snoring man laid across the metal grate and the picture he held his near-frozen hand, Dowd could understand why

Alain DeGail had escaped detection for so long. Bloated, bearded and tattered, the snoring man at his feet barely resembled the dapper little Frenchman in the picture. Monsieur DeGail had plummeted quite a ways down from his perch atop Boulevard Haussmann. The Armagnac lunches and Hermès silk ties and summers en Provence were all part of his past. Maybe they would be part of his future. They certainly were not part of his present. We

walk. We fall. We walk. We fall. It's only the heights from which we fall that distinguish us.

Napoleon in rags, Dowd thought as he crept quietly out of earshot to make the call. But he wasn't calling Bob Dylan to ask if he had had a man like Alain DeGail in mind when he'd written that lyric a million years ago. Rumor was that line was about Andy Warhol. Whatever.

"I got him," Gulliver whispered, giving his location.

"Ten minutes. Keep him there," were the terse instructions followed by a click.

Dowd yanked the phone away from his ear as if it had singed the side of his face. "No problem, asshole," he grunted at the phone. "I'll offer him some brie while we discuss Camus."

As was often the case, Gulliver Dowd had no clue as to the actual identity of his client. Who, for instance, should be so interested in the whereabouts of the former director of a French insurance company: His family? The cops? Jacques Chirac? Not only didn't he know who the client was, he didn't care. He couldn't afford the luxury. For reasons most obvious to himself, Dowd never met directly with prospective customers. What mattered was the job, the work. And in eight minutes or so, according to his watch, this job would be over. He had been told to find a man and he had found him. He had been given a number to call and he called it. Gulliver pocketed the phone and brushed his palms together.

But when he returned to his quarry, Dowd was dismayed at finding Monsieur DeGail awake, kneeling upright on his steel and cardboard bed, gathering his few ratty possessions together. DeGail had yet to notice him. Good. Several scenarios played out in Dowd's head. He could act the fellow tramp, a benign, even more miserable lost soul. He was, after all, born to the part. He could feign injury, beg for DeGail's help, distracting the French man until whoever was

going to show up showed up. He could play it the other way, pull his knife on the Frog. He could cut DeGail's Achilles tendon.

DeGail stood. Time for scenarios was at an end.

"*Comment ça-va* Monsieur DeGail?" Gulliver asked with an accent that was more Brooklyn than Bordeaux.

This approach had the desired effect of confusing DeGail. He stopped gathering his things and tilted his head at Gulliver like a one-eared dog listening to a cat fight on the other side of the kitchen door. Dowd's false confidence crumbled. Had he gotten the question right: How goes it? That's what he thought he asked. Who knows? His high school French had grown rusty in twenty years. Maybe he had asked about the weather. Either way, it had worked.

The Frog's confusion was fleeting. Even in the relative darkness, Gulliver could see DeGail trying to make sense of his situation. That's what he thought he saw in the Frenchman's distant, alcoholic eyes. His bloated, unshaven face was remaking itself—a kid's balloon animal untwisted and reshaped into a new creature. Dowd moved his hand slowly until he felt the hilt of his knife. He had worked too hard to find the Frog. He wasn't about to let his paycheck walk away, not even if it meant cutting DeGail's Achilles tendon.

Gulliver needn't have worried. There was no need for remedial surgery. For the thing he had seen forming on DeGail's face was a smile. But it didn't stop with a smile. DeGail added a soundtrack to the smile and made it a titter. The titter became a laugh. Eventually the tattered man was laughing so ferociously that it became a coughing fit. When the coughing waned, the Frenchman clapped his hands together, looked up to the sky, shaking his head in disbelief.

"My God!" he exclaimed. "My God. You are ridiculous. This is ridiculous, no?"

Yes. "No!" Dowd barked. But he was ridiculous and he knew it.

Everything but his physical appearance, and maybe even some of that, was Gulliver Dowd's own invention. The joke of it was no one would choose to invent Gulliver Dowd. Gulliver least of all. Well, maybe some sadistic fuck. God, maybe.

Dowd heard rapid footsteps behind him, growing louder as they grew nearer. DeGail stopped smiling. The Frenchman had sprung a leak, the humor of the situation draining right out of him. Now it was Gulliver who was smiling. This was not lost on DeGail. He bowed his head to the man who had finally found him.

"*Pardonnez moi, monsieur. Je suis désolé,*" he apologized, his voice drenched in pity enough for the both of them. "My rudeness was uncalled for."

Pity was the emotion Gulliver's presence seemed to elicit more than any other, hence he despised it. He had only one answer for pity other than his own. "Stick it up your ass, Frog. Pity is for the weak."

DeGail didn't debate the point. He was weak. "My wife, is it my wife who comes for me?" he implored.

"Don't know. Don't care."

The approaching footsteps slowed. Stopped. Two pair, Dowd thought. He did not turn immediately to look. Instead he watched DeGail's panicked face, his wide eyes.

"You Dowd?" someone, a man, asked. The question came from behind him.

Now he about-faced. There were two of them, big men; one black, the other white.

"Me? What have you boys been smokin'? I look like Dowd to you?" he mocked.

110

The white guy, hard, with a face like the side of a cliff, shook his head. "Nah, I guess not."

His buddy, an escapee from the NFL, smiled. But the ex-linebacker was curious about something other than when to blitz. "Where'd Dowd get to?"

"I didn't ask. He just threw me two twenties to baby sit your boy here until you showed."

"You, baby sit him! Dat's some funny shit, nigga."

"Whatever," cliff-face said impatiently. "Come on, Frenchie, your wife's waiting for you."

Dowd turned back to his quarry just in time to witness a wave of dread ripple across DeGail's bedraggled face. Gulliver laughed to himself. Marriage had the strangest effect on people. He didn't suppose he'd ever find out for himself.

Science Fiction / Crime

Accidentally Like a Martyr

Title borrowed from Warren Zevon. Originally appeared in The Darker Mask.

Jesus wept. Scarlet teardrops on my shoulder, standing beneath the crucifix at Our Lady of the Martyrs on Broxburn Street. Priest's head spilling itself onto the granite floor. Zevon playing in mine. Should have done, should have done, we all sigh ... Suppose that was the start of it ... or the finish. All depends on how you looked at it. Was no kiss that sealed my fate, but the first toke on the pipe. White smoke tugging at me like marionette strings. Crack called the tune and I danced. Danced faster and faster and faster still until my soul spun out of my body and stood beside me laughing. Look at you, asshole! Dance, motherfucker. Dance! I did.

Priest or pariah, it mattered not a wick. Just someone standing between me and the collection box. Knew it in my

molecules. Knowledge like hunger. Knowledge like thirst. Needed money. Needed rock. Needed my strings of smoke. Needed to dance.

"Get the fuck outta my way, old man!"

Put up a struggle. Fierce. Sour breath poured into my nostrils as we tangled. Bizarre. Could make out individual flecks of dandruff on his black cassock, the shoulders worn shiny with age.

Finally, he fell back. Head against the corner of the front pew, then bouncing off the granite. Stubborn old fuck, grabbed my leg. Pounded the stubbornness out of him. Then came the savior tears. Hole in the roof. Had to be. Outside, no rain. Smoked myself into oblivion.

Angels do come.

Came to me in a shroud of fire. Spoke not a word. Touched me where the tears had fallen; wooden Jesus tears in scarlet red. Lightning. Cold, electrifying lightning. Every muscle twitching. Torque of my own spasms near shredded me. Hunger vanquished. Smoke strings cut. Oblivion no more. Angel stirred the atmosphere. Taste of salvation and damnation in the air. Freedom and slavery; two sides of the same coin. The air stinks of sour breath, dead man's breath, sand man's breath.

Sleep— bottomless, empty,
lightless.

Woke up the next morning on a cot at the Martyrs' Mission off Skid Row. Don't ask how. Don't know. Magic comes in lightless sleep. Didn't recognize the man from the mirror; tanned, fit, well-muscled. A new scar above my heart. Jagged letter A, like pink candle wax. Adulterer? Unlikely. No scarlet letter for the ex-crackhead. Entire scarlet alphabet maybe. Felt healthy for the first time since the

busted kneecap in high school. Went from full ride running back to piece of shit in the blink of an eye. Knee healed. All of me healed, but for the jagged A. Healed, but unforgiven. Proof of it to come.

An hour later, breakfast. Eggs. Bacon. Coffee like brown piss. Not so sweet. Not enough sugar in the world. Plastic tray and Styrofoam cups. No way for a man to measure out his life. Life! Had my life back. Joke's on me. Mind clear for the first time in two years. Then came the touch.

A brother, beard of gray knots. His flesh bleached sickly brown, hollow, pockmarked. Skin, bone and methadone. Breath of the sewer. Man of the world. Man of the street. Man after my own heart. My old heart. Face wound tight with fury. Sat beside me, mumbling, nose running. Sneezed into my face. Filthy gloves on filthy hands. Glove fingers cut off. He wiped my face. The fatal touch. Judas kiss in ebony.

Lightning again. No angels this time. I disappeared. No, not so much disappeared as imprisoned inside my own skull. Strapped into a movie seat, etherized, forced to watch the show. Rest of the universe filled with rage. His rage. Black rage. Rainbow rage. Name was DeShawn Pembroke. Middle name? Rage. DeShawn meant to murder Horse, stick a shiv in his throat. Horse, another man of the street. Fat man. Big man. King of Needletown. DeShawn's grudge playing out.

Last night. DeShawn paying fix tribute to the King. But King Horse was King Pig. Takes the whole load for his own self. No scraps for DeShawn. Happy Horse. Happy Pig. Happy King. Good to be the Pig. Good to be the King. DeShawn running on fumes, hurting, needing to get well. Sucks to be DeShawn.

Ticker tape inside my skull — Times Square news flash:

*Ragerevengeragerevengeragerevengeragerevengeragerevengeragerevengera
gerevengeragerevengeragerevengeragerevengerevengerevengerevengereven
gerevengerevengerevengerevenge …*

Free! Straps cut. Movie over. Back inside my own head. Look at
DeShawn. On his knees, my right hand in both of his. Kissing my
hand. Tears streaming down his face. His face! The coil of fury gone.
DeShawn Pembroke, serene, a human being again.

"Thank you, brother! Praise the Lord! I'm healed. Christ
Almighty, I'm me again. Ain't felt like me since I was a kid. The
hunger … it's … it's—"

"—gone."

"How?"

Whispered, "Don't know, DeShawn." Sour priest breath in
my mouth. "Just don't know."

Looked up into my face. Shock in his wet eyes. "How you
know my name, man?"

"Don't know."

"Man, there's a lot you don't know, but you saved my soul.
My sins been washed away. I been absolved and redeemed. What
can I do for you, brother?"

"Let me finish my breakfast."

DeShawn gone. Appetite gone with him. Food sat in front of
me. Hungry eyes staring across the table. Push my tray across. Sloe-
eyed piranha devour the remains. Couldn't get my head around it.
Bellies full, men of the street yawn. Nothing in their world shocks
them. Angels and miracles come to them in pint bottles, pills,
packages. A hard crowd to impress. They drift. One stays, staring.
Torn map of Ireland on his ragged face. Gin blossoms in bloom.
Orange hair. Glare at him. Laughs, blue eyes twinkling. Familiar
eyes.

"Something funny?"

"Never pictured the Second Coming quite this way, did you, lad?" A Lucky Charms brogue. "Yeats spinning in his grave for sure. Turning and turning in a widening gyre, me arse."

"That s'posed to mean something to me?"

"Hosanna, hallelujah, and praise the lord!" Waved his gnarled hands above his head, face to the ceiling. "Touch me. Heal me!"

"You don't get the fuck outta here, I'll heal you, all right."

Gone.

Me too.

Streets on fire, feel like they're about to crumble beneath my feet. Gravity and weightlessness play tug of war. Wander all day. Aimlessly, blindly meandering. Can't remember a single thought. Didn't have any. Didn't notice a thing, just movement. A mindless shark on two legs; vacant as an abandoned hotel. Night falls on my shoulders.

Bang!

Trip over a tree root, land on the bad knee.

No pain.

Hands feel something in the dirt. Dig it up. End of a toothbrush sharpened to a fine point. Prison shiv. Finds its way into my back pocket. Man gotta watch out for himself. Dark here as my night's sleep. Dangerous kinda dark. Light ahead. Go to the light! Recognition. Homeless heaven. Needletown. No commemorative plaque, just metal, plastic, human detritus. Shapes move in the yellow sulfur light; worms under a blanket. Swan dive into the sea of worms.

Off to the left, on higher ground, surrounded by oaks, a tent of towels, tarp, plywood, rope. Xanadu of shanty town. Rosebud. Legs moving on their own to the castle. Smoke strings have been cut,

but replaced by DeShawn strings. Free will gone. I move. I move. I move. Feet landing one after the other, dance steps painted in the dirt with my name on them. My name, DeShawn.

The king is home in Xanadu. Fat man. Horse. Black skin shining in junkie sweat. Shiv in my hand. His eyes wide with panic. Shiv pressed to his neck.

"You shouldn't oughta piss on a brother like that," DeShawn's voice out of my mouth. "Man got his pride, even a man low on the pole as me, motherfucka."

Horse's eyes wider still with equal parts recognition, confusion. Moves his cracked lips. Nothing sound.

Plunge the shiv into his jugular. Slides right in, easy. Easy as love in the spring. An inch left above his skin. Scarlet fountain pumping to the beat of the fat man's heart. Thick wet fingers yank wildly at smooth, wet plastic. Blood as good as Teflon to a blind Horse. Fountain losing momentum. Bottom of my boot pushes the shiv all the way in beneath the skin. Fountain cum puddle. Horse is dead. My boot to his teeth. Beating a dead Horse. DeShawn's laughing in my head. Slip silently away from Xanadu.

The king is dead. Long live the king.

Never did get that.

They shoot horses, don't they? Not tonight. Tonight, Shivs "R" Us.

DeShawn gone forever.

Back in the woods, running. No heavy breaths, barely sweating. Stop to rest, anyway. Another light ahead. No sulfur streetlamps. A burning bush? Yeah right! A campfire. Shabby man, face to the fire, back to me.

"Warm your bones, Christ Junior." That comic brogue again. Gin blossom clown from the mission.

I sit.

"Angels do come," he says, laughs a yipping laugh like a jackal. "But from where?"

"Am I s'posed to understand that?"

"But you do, crackhead. You've killed two men in two nights; a priest and a king." Crossed himself. "Jesus and his Holy Mother, may God forgive."

"How—"

Ignored me. "Don't fret 'bout the priest. When his dick still worked, he planted more altar boys than Johnny Appleseed did trees. And Horse, a glutton. Worse, a bully. The Lord loves bullies least of all. Still ..."

"On intimate terms with the Lord, are you?"

"Like this." Twisted his misshapen fore- and middle fingers together.

"Fuck you!"

His blue eyes went red. Lightning from his fingertip. Pain in me beyond description. Felt my DNA unfurl.

"Watch yer mouth, lad. Just lay there still and listen. Shake yer head if you hear me?" Comic brogue gone. No one's after his Lucky Charms.

Can't shake my head fast enough. "Good. Now hear my word."

Shake it again.

"The die is cast. The clock is wound. Those who are marked for death cannot escape it. The priest was meant to perish as he did, but at whose hand? Agents of death present themselves as you presented yourself to me."

"But—"

"Silence! Hear my word!"

Pain blots out the universe.

"You will roam this earth, travel through time, cursed with immortality. You will save the souls of the worthy. You will own their sins as I own your soul. They will move on to the kingdom of heaven. Seconds, minutes, days, years, decades, even centuries may pass before you take on another mortal sin. If you should forget or grow complacent, touch your fingers to your heart and feel the brand I have left upon you. You are my Absolver."

Jagged A glowed through my shirt. Jagged A burnt through my shirt. Stink of burning hair, flesh, flannel.

"Just one more piece of advice, me boy," he said, the brogue returned. "Mind who you touch or let touch you. A kiss, a tear, the brush of a finger ... You'll just never know, will you? And old son, if I were you, there are certain centuries I would try mightily to avoid. Ta!"

And he was gone.

Was that yesterday or a million sins ago? No sense of time passage for me. No sense of place. Sleep again—

bottomless,

empty,

lightless.

Walking, always walking in some faceless town. Pain-free, perpetual— worse than the walking dead. Dead don't know what they're missing. Give my right arm for my bad old knee. Just need to feel something. Arm's not mine to give. None of me is. Been let out, rented, loaned, leased, mortgaged, co-oped, gentrified, electrified and deified. Only me in me lives in the basement, between the oil burner and infinity.

Daydreaming, my one last pleasure. Daydream of smoking rock, of pain, of dancing, of hustling old queers in the alleyways on Catona Boulevard. Sing B.B. The thrill is gone. Sure as fuck is, baby.

Sure as fuck is. Prove it to myself sometimes. Find a bar. Money on the bar.

"How much till I pass out? Put your money up."

Never lose. Done as much as two liters of Bacardi 151. Might as well have been drinking spring water. More likely to drown than get drunk. Buy some rock on the odd day. Smoke it. Snort it. Chew it. Shoot it. Rock candy gets me higher. Huff gas fumes, Carbona, you name it. Got so low as a '60s punk, sniffing model glue in a brown paper bag. Nothing. Got a jones to get my jones back.

Ain't tried suicide. Not directly, not yet. That will come.

Eyes open.

Legs stop moving.

Feel something.

For fuck's sake, I feel something!

Love.

First love.

Maggie Flynn.

Maggie Flynn loading groceries into a minivan.

Maggie Flynn—my first and me hers.

I look up. Corner of Sedgewick and Vine. Home. East Pollado, Illinois. Used to call it East Potato. Farms and more farms surround the dull town. Main crops, onions and potatoes, wheat and corn too. Sad town for a beautiful girl with ambition.

Maggie Flynn, still beautiful, older. Not old. Older than me. Time stopped for me. Ambition gone from Maggie Flynn. East Potato beat down. See it in thin gray threads twisting themselves through her hair like cancer. Choking cancer. Cancer of boredom. Slow death comes to Maggie Flynn. Her smile gone. Robotic Maggie. Heart still pounds for her, robot or not, ambition or not, smile or not.

Drops her bag. Tears. Looks up. Sees me.

Legs won't move. All my legs do is move. Not now.

Confusion in violet eyes. More tears.

"Is that you?" Her voice like prayer.

"Who else?" So lame.

"But you look ... You look, I don't know, so ..."

"I keep in shape. A lot of walking." No lie. "Eat healthy." Healthy! Yeah, right! I'll have another bottle of vodka, a side of glue and crack for dessert, please.

"Well, whatever it is you're doing, it's working. What are you doing here?"

1. God, in his infinite wisdom, sent me here.

2. I have no fucking idea.

3. Longing for you.

"Been a long time," I say. "Wondered what'd become of everyone." "No one comes back to East Potato."

"I did."

Answer hangs there in midair.

"Where are you staying?"

Felt the plastic diamond in my back pocket. Pulled it out. A key. Held it, dangling between us. Golden Silos Motor Inn, #8. Only the best for messengers of the Almighty.

"How about you?" I ask.

"Nothing about me. I still live in East Potato, don't I?"

"Family?"

Tears again.

"What is it?"

"Have dinner with me tonight," she says.

"What will your husband—"

"Larry's out of town tonight. He's always out of town. Please, I could use the company and we could talk."

Like Maggie Flynn needed to convince me.

"Sure."

"Thirty-one Shaumburg Way. Say, seven."

"Seven."

Leans over to kiss my cheek.

Back away. Avoid touching. Occupational hazard.

"What's wrong?"

You wouldn't believe me if I told you. "Oh nothing. Sorry."

Force myself to lean back in.

Lips land softly on my cheek. A jolt. Hint of darkness. Ignored it.

Maggie Flynn, tears in violet eyes.

Flowers.

Wine.

New clothes.

31 Shaumburg Way.

Victorian.

Wraparound front porch.

Wheelchair ramp.

Incongruous scar.

Hint of darkness.

Maggie Flynn on the other side of the door. Violet eyes. No tears.

She takes the flowers, the wine. A kiss again, softly on the lips. Force myself not to flinch. Smiles cover darker hints.

"I want you to meet someone," she says.

Heart sinks. Larry, back from out of town, no doubt.

Wrong.

Maggie Flynn brings me into a near dark room. Only light, green. Green light from monitors. Silent save the whoosh and whir

of machines. Nose-stinging medicinal tang. Small boy lies motionless in bed.

"I want you to meet my son Jeff."

Retreat into my silence.

"It's okay," she says. "Talk to him."

"Hey Jeff, nice to meet you."

"It's okay," she says, "to touch him."

Not okay. Wrong. Wrong. Wrong. How to explain? Maggie Flynn, let me explain about mortal sin? Touch the boy's forearm. Nothingness. Blessed nothingness.

Bow my head. "Thank God," comes out of my mouth, but Maggie Flynn mishears.

"He's beyond prayers."

"How?"

"I was supposed to drive Jeff to his soccer game, but I was mad at Larry and made him do it. Larry was upset with me for making him miss his stupid fishing show. He always drives too fast when he's angry. The road was wet and he plowed into a tree. Jeff was ejected from the car and ..." Tears.

Touch her to comfort her.

Hints of darkness hidden in shrouds of fog.

Wine.

Dinner.

Laughing.

Remembering.

More wine.

More remembering.

More wine.

To bed.

Our pain mixes. Sex, sweet and hungry, volatile, sadly exuberant.

Again.

Climax.

Fog lifts.

Dark hints no more.

Blackness of soul in full bloom.

Strapped into the chair again, a stranger in my own head. Maggie Flynn, her guilt all consuming. Depression so deep the stone drops forever. Rage at Larry. Her plan clear to me. Maggie rolls off me, asleep. Her blackness mine.

Straps released. Run. Run. All I think is to run. The front door. Knob in hand, turning. Pull back.

"And where do you think yer off to, old son? You've done yer work not," the lilting brogue pins me. Blue eyes twinkling.

"I can't."

"There's no can't for you, Absolver." Puts a twisted hand on my bare chest atop the scar. "You live yer days from sin to sin, lad."

"Other people's sins."

"Don't be a wanker. Would you rather stand up for yer own sins, murder chief amongst 'em?" Cups a hand to his ear. Waits. Silence. "No, I didn't think so. Now get yerself back in there and release the poor woman from her torments. You felt them. You know. What you suffer is nothing in comparison to her pain. Go!"

Close the door.

Turn back.

Bathroom.

Pills.

Five minutes spent grinding the pills into powder. Sense memories of razor blades, credit cards, and mirrors. Endless lines of coke sucked up coiled dollar bills. Burning nostrils, chemical drip in the back of the throat. Happy, numb, chatter. Nights spent doing

more, getting less. Cocaine paradox. No paradox tonight. A pinky brushes the powder into Pinot Noir. Stir and stir.

Maggie Flynn, groggy, smiling, propped up on an elbow. Her scent filling up the bedroom universe.

"Here." Hand her a glass.

Clink glasses. We sip. She tastes it. She knows. Panic. No need. Finishes the last drop.

"I had a dream," she says. "I thought I heard you talking to someone."

"Really? Who was I talking to?"

"Jeff. I know it's crazy, but ..."

"It's not crazy." I put down my glass, kiss her. "Go on."

"You two were talking and he got up out of his bed and walked in here and laid down in the crook of my arm. See, I told you it was crazy."

"Did it make you sad?"

"No. It was the most amazing thing."

Maggie Flynn's violet eyes flutter. Close. Take the glass from her hand. Her breathing slow and peaceful. Fluff pillows, slide them beneath her head. Pull the sheets across her, lifting her arms above them. Eyes still closed, but her hand lifts. Fingers slide across raised tissue on my chest. Her hand falls.

"Goodnight, Maggie Flynn."

A kiss.

Hits me. Different this time, somehow. Not like DeShawn Pembroke or the ten others between then and now. Still myself. Not a prisoner.

Jeff's room. Shut the door. Spoke too soon. Maggie Flynn's torment moves me. Unplug the monitors, the respirator. No whoosh and whir. No lighted screens. Sounds of a little boy struggling to breathe. Short struggle. Silence.

Cradle him. Lift him up. Maggie Flynn's bedroom. Lay Jeff at his mother's side, place Maggie's right arm around her boy. Brush his hair with my hand. Maggie Flynn's breathing slower, shallower. A whisper.

A last kiss.

"Goodbye, Maggie Flynn."

Job not done. One last sin for Maggie Flynn. Find the key to the gun cabinet and wait. Dawn will come. Hope Larry's angry. He drives fast when he's angry. Stink of sour breath in the air.

Walking, always walking in some faceless place. A river bank this time, sun warm on my face. Slight chill in morning air. Spring. But where? When? Doesn't matter so much anymore. Not after Maggie Flynn. Nothing worse than the trail of blood left behind in East Potato.

Ahead, a black-haired little boy skimming stones without much luck. Stomps his foot in disappointment with each throw.

"Where is this place?" I ask.

"Linz."

"What is the year?"

"Eighteen ninety-five," he says, still throwing the stones.

"And the day?"

"April twentieth, my birthday." He slips as he throws. "Help me up."

I begin to reach for him.

Gobble

From the Busted Flush edition of SOUL PATCH.

1998

Much to the dismay of Petersboro's children, Halloween that year had been graced with very un-gothic weather. The winds of central New York State were so still that the mounds of fallen leaves piled high in every front yard remained as inert as bronze sculptures. The closest thunderstorms were hundreds of miles away in the Ohio Valley and the temperature, though not quite summery, made life beneath the ghoulish greasepaints and cheap plastic masks nearly unbearable. Even the sun seemed unwilling to cooperate, fighting desperately not to be pushed down beneath the rim of the earth.

At the edge of the woods behind his house, Vijay Patel stopped to look back at the big Queen Anne Victorian from which he had just stealthily escaped. He hesitated, making certain his movements had gone undetected and that he wasn't being followed. His parents' room was still dark. In his little brother's room the dim glow of the nightlight—Raj was still afraid of the dark—leaked through the sides of the window shades. "Good!" Vijay said aloud, as if to convince himself before venturing into the woods. Somewhere, not too deep below the surface, he wished he had been caught trying to sneak out.

He clicked on his flashlight and made for the rendezvous with the other boys. Vijay had always been a loyal, obedient son and had never dared anything so bold as he was attempting tonight, but he was finished pretending belonging wasn't important. He ached to fit in, finally. Through two previous moves—first from Cupertino to Boston and then Boston to Dallas—he had suffered the loneliness and indignities that came with being the new kid in school. Vijay further suffered the added burden of his Indian heritage. Pride is a fragile thing in the heart of a twelve-year-old boy and he did not think he could bear being called sand nigger or 7-Eleven boy yet again. No, not again, not for any price. His dad had signed a multi-year contract with IotaSoft and had actually purchased the old Victorian, which Vijay could no longer make out through the thicket behind.

Twenty minutes later he emerged from the woods and, as the others had promised, he could see their bonfire burning a few hundred yards ahead, up the hill in the parking lot of the dilapidated strip mall. He held his flashlight to his watch. 11:45, right on schedule. He hesitated once again, turning slightly back toward home. Then remembering the thousand little cuts from his time in Boston and Dallas, he started up the hill.

The fire was brighter now. On the asphalt leading into the deserted shopping center, Vijay noticed the words GOBBLE HILL spray painted in big block letters on the road. The white paint was wet, fresh. The edges of the letters, however, were shadowy and indistinct, as if someone had painted these same letters over and over again, year after year on the same spot, but had failed to perfectly trace the outline.

Gobble Hill. Yes, Vijay had heard the place mentioned since his late August arrival in Petersboro. Adults whispered its name with their hands over their mouths like old ladies talking about cancer. The kids in school whispered it too, but with awe and reverence. As Halloween approached, he heard it more frequently. He had made some tentative inquiries about the place, to no good end. Tonight he would have his answers, but at what cost, he wondered?

"Well, fuck me, it's Patel. He showed up," said Matt Poole, a fat townie kid. "I didn't think you had the balls. Here, let me look at you." Poole shined a flashlight in Vijay's face. "White makeup, huh? I guess that'll work."

Vijay had been instructed to completely cover his face in either all white or all black grease paint. He wasn't afforded an explanation and he hadn't wanted to risk pushing for an answer. Poole was in all whiteface too.

"Here he is, guys." Matt shoved Vijay into the light of the bonfire.

Three other boys surrounded him, giving him an enthusiastic round of applause and exchanging high-fives. For the moment Vijay's trepidations were forgotten as he basked for the first time in the warm glow of acceptance, however fleeting.

Ricky Smith and Dylan Cohen, both in blackface, were there as well. Smith was another townie kid. Dylan, like Vijay, was a

transplant to Petersboro, and it was Dylan who had nominated Vijay for induction into this exclusive little club. The Cohens lived down the street from the Patels and both of Dylan's folks worked up at the glass cesspool—what the locals called IotaSoft's squat, round building at the edge of town. Vijay recognized the fourth kid from school, but didn't know his name. Unlike the others, this kid's face was half-white, half-black.

When things quieted down, the accepting smiles vanished. Vijay was prodded along to the last building in the strip mall. Like the other buildings, its glass windows and doors had been boarded over by several generations of plywood, but this last building was taller and at least twice as wide as the other units in the shopping center. And the plywood on this place was painted black. Vijay could see places where crosses had been nailed onto the plywood and then painted over. Suddenly, he was consumed by second thoughts.

"We know you got questions," said Dylan, seeing the obvious fear in his friend's eyes. "We'll answer them as soon as you get this over with. I swear."

The nameless boy just nodded his head yes.

"You bring what you was told to bring?" asked Rick Smith.

Vijay held up his flashlight, the adjustable-jaw pliers, and cheap plastic crucifix he had purchased the previous weekend at a garage sale.

"Good job," said Poole, spreading out a piece of paper on the sidewalk. They all closed ranks. "This place was called Jungle Jerry's Playplex and this here is a floor plan we made up for you. There's a hole in the concrete around back big enough for you to crawl through. It's hidden by weeds and shit."

"Are you sure I can get through?" Vijay asked, immediately regretting it. He sounded scared. "I mean—"

"If Fat Matt could do it," joked Rick, "then you sure as shit can."

"Shut up, you asswipe," screamed Poole.

Dylan tried to calm him down. "Don't worry about it. We've all done it. You'll be in and outta there like that." He snapped his fingers.

"Enough yappin'. It's almost time," Poole said, looking at his watch. "This is the deal. You gotta go inside and, see here," he said, pointing at the diagram, "this is where the maze, big slide, and ball pit used to be."

As Matt was speaking it occurred to Vijay that Petersboro was the least kid-friendly place he'd ever been to. There were barely any parks and no video arcades or amusement venues. None of the fast food places had play areas and you had to go to a neighboring town to see a movie.

"Hey, Patel!" Rick shouted. "Pay attention to Matt."

"Sorry, yes, I see."

"Okay, then," Matt continued. "You go to where the maze used to be and you take any piece of hardware you find lying around on the floor. Use your pliers if you have to. Put the crucifix down right on the spot you take the hardware from, get on your knees, and say a Hail, Mary. Then—"

"But ... but ... I am not ... Christian."

"Don't worry about it. Cohen's a Heeb and he did it." Poole handed Vijay a slip of paper with the words to the prayer.

"Hail, Mary, full of grace ... " Vijay mumbled.

"It's time," Rick said. "Everybody around back."

Vijay's feet were lead. He wanted to run and not stop until he was back in his bed, but he remembered the applause and the high-fives and the warmth of belonging. He walked to the back of

the building, but before he caught up with the others, the nameless boy stopped him and handed him an envelope.

"Put this under the crucifix," the nameless boy said.

"What is it?"

"A letter for my brother."

"Okay," Vijay agreed and shoved it in his pocket.

At the rear of the building, the boys moved the weeds out of the way and formed a semi-circle around Vijay as he crawled through the hole in the back wall. Emerging into the dank, lightless space that was once Jungle Jerry's Playplex, Vijay could hear the boys still chanting: "Gobble. Gobble. Gobble. Gobble ... "

1989

Corina Davis closed the book when she came to the realization that she had reread the same passage seven times. The author was blameless. Corina always found it impossible to concentrate on anything but the noise at Playplex. Even now, at dinnertime for most families, the decibel level was earsplitting, but the clanging bells and shrill whistles had a paradoxical calming effect on Tanya. Diagnosed at three with ADD, Tanya found peace in the unceasing din of Jungle Jerry's. So three times a week, Corina Davis loaded her daughter into her minivan and forced herself to reread passages.

Yet in spite of the good it did Tanya, Corina was unsure how much longer she could bear it. For beyond the obvious assault on her senses, Jungle Jerry's Playplex had come to symbolize everything she despised about Petersboro. It had not been an easy adjustment. The utter grayness of the place—broken only by rain or snow—was enough to drive her to distraction. Thirteen months ago, when Malcolm had phoned to tell her he'd landed the job as a special projects manager for a big high-tech firm in New York, she'd

had visions of Saturday nights on Broadway, lazy Sunday picnics in Central Park, and the occasional Knicks' game. What she got was unending potato bogs and biweekly trips to Tanya's occupational therapist in Syracuse. But Malcolm had worked too hard to wait for another opportunity. In business, African-American men didn't get second chances.

Ultimately, it wasn't the weather, the boredom, or Malcolm's impossible hours that got to Corina. It was the people, the townies— Peterites, officially. Puds to the IotaSoft transplants. They were as gray as the weather and incredibly resentful of the company that had saved the local economy from ruin. That people could hate her for her skin being the color of black coffee, Corina could almost reconcile, but to be hated because your minivan had an IotaSoft parking permit on the bumper defied understanding. And here at Playplex, at this hour, the place was rotten with Puds. Sitting across from Corina was the perfect Pud pinup girl: dressed in polyester, smoking a cigarette, smacking her kid for dropping his juice bottle, and yapping incessantly at the woman next to her. After Corina checked her watch, she felt like her sentence had been commuted. She walked to the ball pit to get Tanya.

Pat Holland looked after Marge Ritter's two boys during the week. Once a week, Marge would meet Pat and the boys at Playplex and treat them all to Pizza Hut afterwards.

"Did you see that?" Marge asked Pat, blowing smoke through her twisted lips.

"See what?"

"That one," Marge said, jutting her chin at the black woman calling for her kid in the ball pit. "Did you see the look she gave me? Lord, those people turn my stomach."

"Nig—"

"Them too, yeah, but I mean them IotaSoft snobs. They all think their shit don't stink."

"I know what you mean."

Marge lit up fresh cigarettes for Pat and herself. "How long has Tim Jr. been in there?"

"Thanks for the smoke. He's been in there a good hour."

"Get your brother," Marge ordered Mark.

. . .

"Christ, lady, calm down," the teenager snapped at Corina, unzippering the entrance to the ball pit. "Your kid's fine. Nobody drowns in a ball pit. What's her name again?"

"Tanya! Tanya! How many times do I have to—"

"Lady, you scream at me again and—"

That was it. Corina shoved the teenager aside and crawled into the ball pit herself. "Tanya, come on. Tanya, come to me. This isn't funny anymore."

"Get outta there!" the overwhelmed employee shouted after Corina.

"Tanya, honey, you come to Mama this instant," Corina shouted sternly, as if trying to make her daughter appear by an act of sheer will.

By now everyone in Jungle Jerry's had formed a crowd around the ball pit. Two uniformed security guards pushed their way through, one gently nudging Marge Ritter aside.

"What you suppose happened?" Pat asked.

"You know them people. They can't keep track of their kids and their fathers without a scorecard."

Pat didn't bother pointing out that Marge's two sons were fathered by different men, neither of whom had married Marge and both of whom had vanished into the ether. Just then, Mark appeared at his mother's side, tugging at her sleeve.

"Stop it!" she yanked her arm away. "I thought I told you to get your brother."

"But—"

"Go on."

Mark was crying. He turned to Pat Holland for help. She picked him up and asked the boy what was wrong.

"I can't find Timmy."

1998

Like a warehouse for darkness, Vijay thought, sweeping the beam of his flashlight from side to side. No cobwebs or ghouls or big hairy spiders, just an empty building with a dirty floor. The attic in his house was creepier. There, at least, the wood creaked beneath your feet and the asymmetry of the rafters threw ominous shadows. This place was as scary as a cardboard box. His fears were calmed not only by the musty sterility of the room, but by the nameless kid's silly ploy with the envelope. A letter for his brother! Yeah, right. They had him going pretty good until then, when his fears were amorphous and his initiation ritual unclear.

No one jumped out of the shadows, but as he approached the designated area, his newfound cockiness receded. For as the conical beam illuminated the linoleum floor, he could make out the silhouettes of several dust-covered crucifixes, a frayed and yellowed envelope beneath each cross. They were pretty spooky. Vijay swallowed hard, quickly aiming his flash away from the crucifixes. He moved to the opposite corner, farther into the demolished play area than the other boys had apparently been willing to wander. He figured the extra distance was worth it as long as the crucifixes were out of sight.

Within a few seconds, Vijay found some metal washers strewn about like spare change. He knelt down, scooped them up, put them in a back pocket, and got out the prayer cheat sheet. As instructed, he placed the nameless boy's envelope beneath the crucifix and recited the prayer: "Hail, Mary, full of grace. The Lord is with thee. Blessed art thou among women. Blessed is the fruit of thy womb, Jesus. Holy Mary, Mother of God, Pray for—"

He stopped, his eyes catching an unexpected reflection. There was something smooth and round lying about twenty feet to his left. It was hard to be sure of what the object was in the fading beam of his flashlight. He put the prayer paper under the crucifix, closed his eyes, and tried recalling the crude floor plan. He could see it in his mind's eye. "Yes!" He pumped his fist. "The ball pit!"

How cool was this? He would have more than just a few stinky old washers to show for his work. Vijay would have a ball too. Based upon where the crucifixes were, he was willing to bet none of the other boys, not even Dylan, had ventured this far or been this lucky. His flash grew dimmer still and Vijay chided himself for not having thought to replace the batteries before coming. To save what power the old batteries had left to give, he lined himself up with where he thought the ball would be and shut off the flashlight.

Vijay took slow, measured steps, crushing bits of dirt and flakes of concrete as he went. He was breathing hard and fast, his heart pounding inside his small chest. When he guessed he was pretty close to where he wanted to be, something cracked loudly under the weight of his Nikes. A stick, he thought, or a small piece of PVC piping. Not wanting to use up the batteries unnecessarily, he knelt down and felt for the ball in the darkness. Almost immediately, his fingers landed on their target. But something was wrong. The thing in his hand was rounded but irregular. It was way too hard to be a plastic ball. There were ridges and ... eyeholes!

Panicked, Vijay dropped the flashlight and the skull and ran into the darkness, swallowing his screams as he went. No matter what, he could not let the others hear him scream. Bang! There was head-splitting pain and his ears rang so loudly he could no longer even hear himself breathe. He felt himself spinning off into space even as the floor pulled him down, down, down. Then there was nothingness.

1989

Detective Jim Feherty had watched the grainy black-and-white security tape so many times it was beginning to dissolve into a gray blur. According to the time stamp, at 5:47:21 p.m., a white male child positively identified as ten-year-old Timothy Joseph Ritter Jr. enters the play area of Jungle Jerry's Playplex. Eleven minutes and thirteen seconds later, a black female child positively identified as five-year-old Tanya Davis is escorted to the ball pit by her mother. Several other children are seen to come and go, but neither the Ritter nor Davis child are seen to exit.

People told Feherty he had been mad to swap his NYPD gold shield for one in some cockamamie upstate town. Sometimes he thought he was crazy too, but felt he needed the quiet. And Petersboro was only a stone's throw from the best fishing in the state. That's the way he figured to ease into retirement: in waders or a rowboat with a rod and reel in hand. Jim Feherty just wanted to work cases that made some sense and he thought that's what this move offered. He had seen enough body parts in garbage bags and whenever he found himself second-guessing his decision to take this job, he thought about Billy Pesco.

On a beautiful spring day in 1987, Jim and his partner caught a homicide at a deli on Hillside Avenue in the Jamaica section of

Queens. There they found the owner, Billy Pesco, murdered behind the counter. His eyes were open, his body still warm, and his blood leaking out of three holes in his torso onto the wooden slats above the tile floor. Both Jim and his partner had the same thought.

"Robbery," they said simultaneously.

"Think again," said the uniform who had been first on the scene. "The register's full and that's a real Rolex there on Billy's wrist. And look under the counter. See that bank deposit bag? It's looks pretty full to me. And just between, you, me, and the Holy Ghost, Billy keeps a loaded Glock under there too."

Just then another uniform stuck her head into the store and asked the two detectives to please step outside. There, hands cuffed behind him, legs spread, face pressed to the hood of a patrol car, was a young Hispanic man. Next to him on the hood of the car was a hero sandwich half-wrapped in foil. Only one bite had been taken out of the sandwich. The female uniform waved an evidence bag at the detectives. Inside the bag was a .45 Browning automatic that had recently been fired.

"We found him two blocks away sitting on a stoop. He had the hero in one hand and the .45 in the other. His name's Alfredo Ordonez. I read him his rights already."

"You do this, Alfredo?" Jim Feherty asked.

"Yeah, I did that fuckeeng guy."

"Why?"

"Look at that hero, man. That's why."

Feherty picked the hero sandwich up in his gloved hand and took a careful look. "Corned beef. So what?"

Ordonez stared disbelievingly at the detective. "Look! Look at the hero. See the mayonnaise? He put fuckeeng mayonnaise on my corned beef."

"You put three bullets into a man at point blank range because he put mayonnaise on your hero?"

"I hate mayonnaise. I like mustard."

The next day, Feherty put in his papers.

As Jim Feherty pressed the rewind button yet again, there was a knock on the door. Before he could give his permission, an over-eager deputy sheriff stuck his head into the room. There had been a break in the case. A known pedophile, Thomas Horvath aka Dirty Tommy, had been identified by several Playplex employees as a man they had seen lurking about that day.

"We got him on tape from a second camera," the deputy said. "We got units rolling to his last known address right now."

"Any tape of him with the missing kids?" Feherty asked, never taking his eyes off the tape counter in the corner of the monitor.

"Nope."

"Let me know when he gets here."

Confused by Detective Feherty's apparent lack of enthusiasm, the deputy wondered about the detective's state of mind. Regardless of what Dirty Tommy did or did not do, Feherty thought, it wouldn't explain why the tape said those kids were still in there. And while taking note of the sour expression on Corina Davis' face as she walked Tanya to the ball pit, Jim Feherty swore he could smell corned beef.

1998

Dylan Cohen checked his watch and spoke up, "Something's fucked up. Vijay's been in there way too long. It's after twelve-thirty."

"Give him a few more minutes. He's just trying to scare us now," said Matt Poole, with little conviction.

143

Ricky Smith agreed.

"But what if he's hurt or something?" Dylan asked.

"Okay, hero, you go in after him," Poole said.

Dylan had nothing to say to that, but it was clear the boys were all nervous.

"Forget this, I'm going for help," Dylan said. "You guys want to split, go ahead. I got him into this and it's my problem. It'll take me five minutes to get to a phone, so that's how much time you've got."

Matt and Rick said they were sorry, but were certain their parents would kill them if they knew they had even come up here. When Dylan got around to asking the nameless kid, he'd already gone.

1989

The judge was accustomed to midnight arraignments and trials in nearly empty courtrooms. Nothing during his long tenure on the bench had prepared him for the circus that greeted him as he stepped to the bench.

"Be seated!" shouted the bailiff.

Although these proceedings were merely perfunctory and his comments already prepared, the salty old jurist made a show of seriously reading through the papers stacked high before him. In the end though, all he had to say was, "Thomas Horvath, you have been found in violation of the terms of your parole. I am therefore remanding you to the state correctional facility at Batavia to serve out the remainder of your original sentence. Have you anything to say to this court?"

A frightened looking man of fifty-eight rose to his feet, as did his court-appointed attorney. "Ya-Ya-Your Honor," he stammered.

"It's true I done some bad things in my time and if they didn't find that special room in my house, I woulda done some more. I don't wanna do them things, but I can't help it, I swear. So I guess it's a good thing that I'm going back inside. What I really wanna say is that, as God is my witness, I never done nothing to them two kids at that Playplex place. I know everybody thinks I did, but I didn't. I couldn't kill no kids. It's like they was gobbled up."

The judge had nothing to say to that and waved for the court officers to remove the prisoner from his courtroom. It was all over in five minutes.

Outside the courthouse, reporters shoved microphones and handheld cassette recorders in Detective Feherty's face. Cameras click-click-clicked. Television lights made the detective shield his eyes with his hand. Was he satisfied? Would they ever find the bodies? Was he proud to have put Dirty Tommy back where he belonged? Did he think Dirty Tommy used the secret room to torture and murder the missing kids?

"No comment," is what he said.

What he wanted to say, no one wanted to hear. Because although he had worked diligently to put Thomas Horvath back behind bars and had been the one to find the entrance to the secret room in Horvath's basement, Jim Feherty believed every word of Dirty Tommy's statement to the court.

Malcolm had wanted to stay home with her, but Corina refused and sent him off to work. Alone, she watched the live reports from outside the courthouse. She felt sorry for Detective Feherty. He seemed so ill at ease in the spotlight. He had always been so gentle and patient with her, never defending himself against her grief-driven rages. He had done his best. Everybody had, even the Puds, but no one could tell her what had happened to her precious child.

She turned off the TV and swallowed the last handful of pills. Corina went into Tanya's room, folded herself into her daughter's long unused bed, and went to sleep forever.

1998

Jim Feherty didn't bother with clocks. They only frustrated him these days. He knew it was late, very late and that he should have been asleep for hours. But sleep came harder and harder to him, so that it barely seemed worth the effort. Even so, he was annoyed to have someone knocking at his cabin door at this time of night.

"I'm coming, for chrissakes! Hold your horses," he screamed, throwing on a flannel shirt and pulling his .38 off the top of the refrigerator. Before opening the door, Feherty popped on the porch light and took a peep at his late-night visitor through the side window. The guy looked harmless enough in his corduroy blazer, sweater, and running shoes, but you never know.

"Jeff Kinnock, Finger Lakes Tribune," the pale man on the porch said, holding up his press credentials.

"I'm already a subscriber."

"Sir, I'm not—"

Jim Feherty was laughing too hard for the reporter to finish his sentence. Although he'd lived on the outskirts of Petersboro for eleven years, the retired detective had never gotten used to how tone-deaf upstaters were to sarcasm. He tucked the .38 in his waistband.

"Let me guess," Feherty said. "It's Halloween, so you got a brilliant idea to write a follow-up piece on those missing kids, right? I hate to bust your cherry, kid, but I've averaged one hotshot media type a year for the past nine years who had the same brilliant idea. But you are the first one who thought to show up this late."

Kinnock said, "Nice speech, but I break stories. I just came here to get a reaction to a tip I got from a source that another kid's gone missing at the Playplex building."

"You headed over there?"

"Of course."

"Come on," Feherty said, grabbing his hunting jacket. "We'll talk on the way."

They exchanged few words until they were getting pretty close to the abandoned shopping center. Feherty finally asked the reporter to repeat what his source had said as closely as he could remember it. Kinnock complied. There wasn't much there, no details, really, only that a young boy had gone missing. Feherty was disappointed and was embarrassed by his disappointment. He found his heart was divided into warring camps. On one hand, he hoped it all just turned out to be a Halloween prank. On the other...

Kinnock seemed to read Feherty's mind. "You hope it's real, don't you? That it's not a prank?"

"You're smart for a reporter. When I was a young detective in the city I was on a rape task force for a few months. We had this one guy who was a real monster, but a smart one. After averaging a rape a week for two months, he just stopped, and his trail went cold. We figured he got killed, arrested for something else, or moved to another city, but I remember hearing the lead detectives talking about the next victim. It was like they were praying for him to strike again so they could have fresh evidence. Now I'm just like them."

"It's natural," Kinnock said. "Nothing to feel guilty about."

"You think? Then why don't I sleep nights? I've spent part of each day for the last nine years hoping for some other kid to vanish so I could satisfy my curiosity. You try living with that."

At the bottom of the hill leading up to the old shopping center, a sheriff's deputy waved the reporter's car to a halt. Kinnock

rolled down his window and raised his hand to show his credentials, but Feherty grabbed his wrist. When the deputy recognized the retired detective, he waved the car through without hesitation.

When the overwhelming nausea welled up in him, Vijay Patel no longer regretted having been too nervous to eat dinner. Yet when he rolled over and tried to stand, his body exacted a heavy toll. With each futile heave, the pain in his head grew worse. He was blind with pain, but not deaf from it. He somehow sensed he was no longer alone and even in the midst of his body's revolt, Vijay took comfort in that. The comfort was short-lived, for the pain drove him back into the refuge of unconsciousness.

This time when he felt himself coming to, Vijay did not rush to stand or even to open his eyes. He took deep, hungry breaths, rubbing his hands along his sore abdomen. The retching had ceased for the moment and the fire in his head, though not extinguished, was at least under control. He counted to three and slowly opened his eyes. There was no light to hurt them, but they hurt just the same. He got to his knees in pieces, carefully monitoring himself for signs of coming nausea. Again, he was aware of another presence. Breathing! He heard breathing.

"Who's there?" he called out, his voice cracking.

No answer.

"Don't try anything. I've got a knife," he said.

Again, no answer.

On hands and knees he groped for the lost flashlight, but it was useless. He remembered the feel of the skull in his hand and realized that it had been a bone cracking under his foot, not plastic piping. Still, he decided he needed to get out of there at all costs. He crawled slowly on hands and knees, making sure to rest every few

feet. After his third rest, he put his hand down and it didn't hit floor. He recognized the feel of denim under his fingers. As he recoiled, something snatched his wrist.

As Kinnock snaked his car through the maze of emergency vehicles, he turned to Feherty. "You don't think Horvath did it, do you?"

"I wish I did. Then maybe I could sleep nights. But we didn't have a case then and we've got less now. Look, pedophiles have certain profiles and tastes. They don't usually include a range that would stretch from a black, hyperactive five-year-old girl to a white ten-year-old boy. And how is this guy stupid enough to get caught on one video camera just lurking about, but genius enough to somehow vanish with two kids simultaneously without getting caught on another camera? I mean, this is Dirty Tommy Horvath, not Professor fucking Moriarty. No, he didn't do it."

"Then what happened?"

"Christ knows, but I don't. Maybe there are some things that aren't knowable and this is one of them. What I know is this: those kids went in there and never came out."

"So you're saying—"

"Look, Kinnock, we investigated this as thoroughly as any case I ever worked on. And just for the record, I don't buy into what the psychics and the psychos say. Those kids weren't abducted by aliens. Jungle Jerry's isn't haunted. The shopping center isn't built on an Indian burial ground. There's no ancient temple under there, no sacrificial altar. If Atlantis is lost, we didn't find it. If you want witches, take the thruway east to Massachusetts. All I know is that those kids are gone."

When they got out of Kinnock's car, the reporter and Feherty walked into the middle of a wild shoving match. A sour-faced, middle-aged woman had latched herself around the arm of a slight,

confused-looking man in his early forties. He was handsome, dark-skinned, his black hair worn slick to his head. Pulling at the man's other arm with equal ferocity was another woman—the wife, Feherty thought—also darkly complexioned and confused. The second woman held a sleeping boy tightly to her chest with her other arm.

The first woman was screaming something about accepting the Lord Jesus Christ as the one and true savior while trying to pull the man to his knees. To his credit, he would not be pulled down, but his wife's grip interfered with his efforts to pull free of the other woman. The wife shouted something at him in a foreign tongue. He growled back and finally pulled free. The first woman went down to her hands and knees and Feherty helped her up.

"Marge Ritter!" He couldn't believe his eyes. "What the hell are you doing here?"

She smiled serenely. "The Lord's called again."

"What are you talking about?"

"He's called Mark to join him at his brother's side. Praise be to God!"

"Mark's gone?"

"Along with their boy," she said, pointing at the Patels.

Having helped Marge to her feet, Feherty let go of her. His worst fears and hopes realized, he walked away, stunned and guilty. Kinnock caught up.

"When things got bad, did you ever think about turning to religion to answer the unknowable questions?" the reporter asked.

"No, not for a minute. I thought about doing what Corina Davis did. She swallowed two fists full of pills the day Horvath was sent back to prison. Anyway, me and God don't see eye to eye on things."

"Most cops I know are pretty religious."

"I'm not most cops. Let me tell you a story, okay?" Feherty wasn't really asking.

"Sure."

"One day I was going to dinner at my first partner's house and I stopped by a liquor store to get some wine. On the counter there's one of these jars for spare change to raise money. On the jar, there's a picture of a little girl and a story about how the family needs money for a bone marrow transplant. So when the cashier gives me back my change, I go to throw a few bucks in the jar, but she tells me not to bother because the kid died the day before. 'Thanks for reminding me,' she says. And I watch her pull it off the counter."

"And I should extrapolate from this what exactly?"

"Nothing. I'm not done and don't use words like extrapolate. They give me hives. So I get to my partner's house and he's like sky high. He tells me that after two years of trying, he and his wife have finally sold their house. While we're toasting their good fortune, his wife tells me that it was God's will, selling the house. Seems she buried a St. Joseph's medal upside down in the front yard and the Almighty took care of the rest. It wasn't much of a dinner after that."

"Why?"

"I don't guess they appreciated my criticizing God for being too preoccupied with selling their ranch house in Massapequa to save a little girl's life."

Before Kinnock could say a word, all hell broke loose. One of the plywood panels at the front of Jungle Jerry's came crashing down and a volunteer fireman was helped through the vacant window. He held a boy crooked in his arms. In some heretofore unacknowledged part of himself, Feherty struggled with the impossible dream that the boy was Tim Ritter Jr. But before Feherty could even move, a second fireman came through. He too was

carrying a body in his arms. Feherty's heart jumped into his throat, but Marge Ritter's shrill screams dashed the retired detective's hopes.

"Marky. That's my son, Mark," Marge screamed, tears streaming down her face. "Oh my goodness."

Feherty saw that the boy's face was covered in half-white, half-black makeup and understood Marge's shock. The other boy's face was covered in ghostly white.

"You Detective Feherty?" a state trooper whispered in Jim's ear.

"Yup."

"Please come with me, sir," he said, putting a finger across his lips. "There's something inside the detectives want you to see."

When Kinnock moved to follow, the trooper stopped him. "Not you, sir. I'm sorry."

Feherty shrugged his shoulders and followed the trooper around to the rear of the building. Just as the boys had held the weeds back for Vijay, the trooper held the weeds back for Feherty. Once inside, Feherty got weak-kneed. It had been a long time, but it all came rushing back to him, all of it. There was enough ambient light because the fireman had knocked down the plywood, but he knew the place so well he could have navigated all its twists and turns in utter blackness. Up ahead of him, Feherty heard confused whispers and saw flashlights cutting swaths in the semi-darkness. As he walked on, he took note of the dusty crucifixes and yellowed envelopes. He reached a line of police tape behind which people scurried about. A pretty, red-haired detective dipped under the yellow tape and greeted Feherty.

"You won't remember me," the detective said, holding out her right hand. "I'm Kaitlin Darby. I worked the original case when I

was in uniform. I saw you outside and thought you deserved to see this. And I guess maybe I need your help explaining it."

All business, Feherty said, "What've we got?"

She lifted the yellow tape for him. "See for yourself."

As Feherty stepped under the tape, all the buzz and activity came to a halt and everyone shined their flashlights at something on the floor. Feherty gasped as he recognized the clothing in which the skeletons were dressed. "Give me a pair of gloves," he said. "Come on. Now!"

Detective Darby handed him a pair of latex gloves. As she did, she said, "This is fucked up, isn't it? I've heard of elaborate hoaxes, but this takes the cake. Someone went through a lot of trouble for a stupid hoax. I mean, to get the skeletons just right and to match the clothing perfectly. There are some twisted puppies out there."

Feherty didn't say a word but got down on his hands and knees and carefully looked over the nearly perfect skeletons.

"The smaller skull's over there," Darby said. "One of the kids must've picked it up. One of them also cracked that femur there. I don't think these kids were the perps who pulled this off. Way too complicated and exact."

Feherty grumbled something that meant he agreed with her. He touched the fabric of the blouse around the smaller skeleton right arm. Maybe Darby was right and this was all an elaborate hoax, but when he lifted up the right sleeve of the bright green blouse, Feherty couldn't believe his eyes. Along the underarm seam was a sloppy repair done in brown thread. He heard the distant echo of Corina Davis' voice as she explained how Tanya had ripped the sleeve during her mother-in-law's last visit.

"Malcolm's mom is half blind and has arthritis. She sewed the seam up. I meant to redo it, but I never got around to it."

153

Jim Feherty had never shared that fact with anyone. He scrambled over to the larger skeleton dressed in a Guns N' Roses sweatshirt, jeans, white socks, and Converse sneakers. Without asking permission, he broke just about every rule he knew about maintaining the integrity of a crime scene. He grabbed the left-hand bones and pushed back the sleeve of the sweatshirt. And when he saw what he was looking for, Feherty got lightheaded.

"What are you doing?" Darby screamed at him.

He held up the ulna bone. "See this spot here, that thick ring of bone growth around an old fracture?"

"Yeah."

"He fell out of tree when he was six."

"Who did?"

"Timothy Joseph Ritter Jr. did. This is him and that's Tanya Davis."

"Get the fuck outta here!" Detective Darby was more than skeptical. "The clothes don't look any older than they did when the kids went missing."

"Hey, X-rays and dental records are easy enough to get and I bet Malcolm Davis will identify these clothes. And there's no arguing with DNA. But that'll be a waste of time. These are them, I'd bet my life on it."

"So," Darby said, "I guess you were wrong about Horvath. I know you thought he was innocent of this, but look. He must have kept the bones hidden and the clothes in cold storage. Then when he got out, he came back here and did this. The sick fuck must've gotten a real charge out of it."

Jim Feherty shook his head no. "Dirty Tommy never got out, not while he was breathing, anyway. One of his buddies up in Batavia stuck the sharpened end of a spoon through his heart about two years after he went back inside and in those two years he didn't

have any visitors or phone calls. The only mail he got was hate mail."

Word of the skeletons hadn't yet spread outside and Jim Feherty meant to be gone by the time it did. First, like a benevolent spirit, he watched from the shadows as the two boys were loaded into the waiting ambulance. When it pulled away, Jim turned and began walking down the hill to catch a cab in town. Kinnock caught up to him before he got very far. Feherty decided to tell the reporter what the cops had found inside Jungle Jerry's.

Kinnock was dumbfounded, but managed to ask, "Who? How?"

"I don't know," Feherty said, pointing at the words GOBBLE HILL at his feet. "See that? When the judge revoked Horvath's parole, Tommy said those kids must've been gobbled up. Well, maybe he was right. Maybe they were just gobbled up and now they've been spit out. Ever see an owl pellet? Who really knows why anything happens or how? Maybe God was too busy selling real estate that day and only got back around to these dead kids tonight. Who knows anything?"

Jim Feherty patted Kinnock on the shoulder and started back down the hill. The reporter called after him, but Feherty didn't answer. With the scent of corned beef and mayonnaise filling up the pre-dawn air, he just waved and disappeared into the dark. It was time to finally sleep.

Slider

So good it inspired a poem. From MURDER AND MAYHEM IN MUSKEGO.

1

Red flags on black poles planted in the sand every few hundred feet along the length of Brighton Beach. Black poles barely sway. Red fabric limp in the stillness and fog. Red flags mean no lifeguards on duty. Venture into the Atlantic, you do so at your own peril.

2

Thousands of windows look out onto the fog-heavy boardwalk, the beige sand, gray stone- jetties, the shoreline, the now invisible ocean beyond. Not one pair of eyes has taken notice of the body rocking in the cold, soulless arms of the surf at water's edge. It is sin enough for a body to molder in a shallow, leaf-covered grave in the middle of a

forgotten woods. There is something achingly perverse about it bobbing up and down in the shallows with only swirling gulls and hungry crabs paying it any mind. Especially this body—bloated and blue—once so perfect.

3

This is some wicked fog, Stallion thinks, peering through the landed cloud at the strike zone chalked onto the brick wall of PS 209. The pitching rubber is a crack in the schoolyard cement forty-five feet away from the beige brick wall. He winds up and releases the Pennsy Pinky with a sharp snap of his wrist and fingers. That's the trick of a good slider: the grip, the fingers, not just the wrist. Stallion imagines he can follow the trajectory of the tightly spinning ball as it cuts through the mist between the mound and the chalk box. He swears he can see a visible, transient memory in its wake: a smoke ring, a contrail, a stickball worm hole. Then gravity yanks at it. The rotation of the ball skews ever so slightly. The ball veers down and to the right.

4

Dina D'Agostino was the neighborhood wet dream. There wasn't a guy from Coney Island Avenue to Shell Road, from the boardwalk to Avenue X, except maybe Jerry "Fagberg" Feinberg, who didn't jerk off imagining what fifteen minutes with Dag might be like. Ask not what Dina D'Agostino can do for you. Ask what you can do for Dina D'Agostino. To this day, Pete McIlroy—Ish because he's half Pol-ish and half Ir-ish—got hand happy thinking about the time the two of them walked all the way to Plumb Beach. That was the night Anthony Peritorre broke up with her. His mom called her a freakin' hoo'wa (Brooklynese for whore). Although Dag was crying so hard her body shuddered, she laid down on the sand with him, let him

slip his hand under her halter, slip his tongue into her mouth, slip his fingers under her panties—her pubic hair was matted cashmere. Sometimes, even now, he imagined he could still smell the musk and feel her magic on his hand. Of all things that persisted from his childhood, his memory of Dag was strongest.

5

Through the fog a pair of Ukrainian eyes sees a bruise on the water—driftwood perhaps, perhaps the carcass of a lost dolphin. He imagines its story. It is what this ancient man does, he sees things and creates a past for them. Everything, he thinks, must has a past. Everything needs a past for it to have value. He has no need to embellish or create one for himself. The cruel forces of history have molded a past for him, one he cannot escape. The bodies, all the bodies he carries with him, give him no warmth, no peace, but they remind him.

He remembers.

First in the woods outside Kiev, the bodies-in-waiting kneeling at the edge of the trench. Some cried. Some begged. Most silent. None prayed that he could hear. Then the pop, pop, pop, pop of the Lugers and Walthers. With each bullet came the metal metamorphosis of human beings into cascading lumps of meat. Then—

the quicklime
the dirt
more bullets
more meat
more quicklime
more dirt
more
and

more

and

more ...

Layers and layers like a trifle.

But what of the dolphin?

The dolphin, he thinks, has used up its life. Old and sick, it has separated itself from its family. Lost in strange waters, too tired to go on, it has beached itself in this odd little world where creatures swim upright through a dry sea.

6

No matter how much he tries, Stallion can't focus. His heart races, but not from pitching, not from stickball. He watches the pitch, Ish recoiling to swing.

7

Ish swings, his eyes locked on the spot in the air where he calculates the spinning pink ball will begin to veer down, to the right, under his bat-handled fists, and kiss the inside corner of the chalk box. For thirty years, he has swung and missed or taken the pitch, watching the ball all the way to the wall, witnessing the puff of dust as the ball bites the chalk and flattens against the brick. For thirty years, since they were seven, Stallion's slider has for the most part eluded Ish's bat. It's not that Ish never hits it—he does, but late in the game, when:

 1) Stallion's arm is fucked.

 2) When some of the piss is out of the slider.

 3) When the spin loosens up.

 4) When it flattens out.

 5) When it comes in like a helicopter.

But even then, he hits it straight down off his shin. And this is the third inning and Stallion is just getting warm and his arm is still full of vinegar.

Time slows down.

Ish is a camera.

He sees the ball so clearly it hurts. He sees the bat connect with the ball a few inches out in front of him, the rubber bending around the wood of the skinny bat, the ball flying away, disappearing into the fog, landing over the fence to the basketball courts. Ish's joy is short-lived. He knows something is wrong.

The universe is disturbed.

8

Old and sick, removed from his family to die in a strange little world, he is the dolphin. Dolphins are intelligent creatures. They recognize themselves in mirrors, teach each other how to hunt, to play with rings of bubbles. Too intelligent, he thinks, to believe in God. In this way, he is also the dolphin. After the Kiev woods, he was arrested by the Soviets and forced to serve in one of Stalin's suicide units. No gulag during the Great Patriotic War. No, just bullet catchers to waste fascist ammunition. Coming close to the dolphin, he remembers his comrade commander's inspirational pep talk. "My dear comrades, if you retreat a single inch or do not press forward, we will shoot you in the back and make stew meat of your worthless carcasses."

He survives, but to what good end? To die in this place, alone? For his whole life he has been passed from one butcher to the next. He reaches water's edge, the gulls squawking at him. The crabs ignore him. Some claw and peck away, unwilling to relinquish their prize.

The old man is not a dolphin.

The dolphin is not a dolphin,
but a blue and bloated mermaid spit out by the sea.

9

Stickball is Brooklyn Zen, a meditation born of spare parts: a broom
handle, a rubber ball, chalk, a crack in the concrete, a wall,
imagination. Om. But Stallion and Ish are done now, out of the
trance, back to their lives.

10

Sick with worry, Anna-Marie D'Agostino dials the phone and listens
to it ring. A woman picks up,

"Hello."

"Is Peter there?"

Peter? No one calls her husband Peter. It's Ish. Everyone,
even his captain calls him Ish.

"Peter? Do you mean Ish?"

Anna-Marie is flustered. "Peter, the kid from Manhattan
Court."

The wife puts her hand over the phone, turns, and screams,
"Ish, it's for you."

11

The old man has told his story first to the policeman and now to the
detective over and over.

1) I'm an old man.

2) I walk on the beach.

3) I thought it was a dolphin.

4) No, I didn't touch her.

5) I didn't see anyone else.

6) How did I know she was dead? I have seen dead bodies before.

Really? (Detective lifts eyebrow.) How many?

1) Many more than you will ever see.

Where? (Dubious)

2) The Ukraine.

3) Poland.

4) Germany.

Okay, you can go. I have your name and number just in case.

So that is that, the old man thinks. He is dismissed. As he walks back to the boardwalk, he writes the mermaid's history.

12

"She asked for Peter," the wife says, handing him the phone. "She says she's Dag's mom. Who's Dag?"

Ish doesn't answer. His eyes get big. He swallows hard. Into the phone, "This is Peter."

"Peter, the kid from Manhattan Court? You're a cop now, right?"

"Yeah, Mrs. D'Agostino, a detective. You're Dina's mom. Is something wrong?"

"Dag's missing , that's why I'm calling. I haven't heard from her in days."

"Days, huh? Is that a long time for her not to be in touch?"

"Calls me every day. Comes over all the time, checking on me because I got the diabetes."

"Have you called around ... friends, other family, like that?"

"I called the cops."

"You called the police?"

"Yeah, but it was a waste of time. The cop said she was an adult and that she'd turn up."

"But she hasn't?"

"No."

"How did you get this number, Mrs. D'Agostino?"

"I'm calling to tell you my girl's missing and you're—"

"I'm gonna look into it. I promise, but you gotta tell me—"

"Dina keeps a book. Only one name I recognized from the old neighborhood. Yours."

Ish smiles in spite of himself, the feel of cashmere on his fingers.

13

The old man is done with history, with all but one last body, with life. He doesn't hesitate to kick the stool out from under his own feet. Swinging from side to side, he thinks, I should have done this sixty years ago.

So much less pain.

So much less pain.

So much less pain.

So much less pain.

So much less pain.

No pain at all.

Nothing.

14

The dolphin is Jane Doe for only a few hours, until the boy who once clumsily rubbed her nipples and pawed her breasts, the boy who only once lost his fingers in the soft down beneath her panties, looks at the sea water and crab-ravaged body on the stainless-steel table.

Turns to the ME, "That's her, Dina D'Agostino. I'll call the mother."

15

Ish looks at the photos of his wet dream's body, how she looked when she washed up on Brighton Beach.

Detective Conrad watches him. The case is his, the memories are Ish's.

"Old girlfriend?"

"Not exactly. Once when we were kids ... How'd ya know?"

"I'm a detective. I got a shield to prove it and everything."

"Funny man, Conrad, but seriously, how'd ya know?"

"That look on your face. What's the word ... wistful? Tough to be wistful looking at that mess unless you were seeing something else in your head."

"I guess I was remembering her as a kid. God!"

"See how she's dressed." Conrad said. "Hope you don't got a Madonna thing for her memory. Mary, Mother of God, didn't exactly dress like that. That one shoe she's wearing there got a heel high enough to make my nose bleed."

"I see how she's dressed. No, I don't suppose she was going to a quilting bee or for happy hour at Ruby Tuesday. You got her address book? When her mom called me, she mentioned an address book."

"Your name's in it, McIlroy, you know that, right?"

"So what?"

"Lotsa men's names are in it. My guess, clients."

"Well, I wasn't one of 'em. If that's what you're—"

"I had to ask. You'd've asked. Here." Conrad slid the phone book across the table.

Ish thumbed through the pages, stopped breathing for a second. Hoped Conrad hadn't noticed.

"Recognize any names in there?"

Ish lied, "No."

Conrad didn't believe him. Conrad didn't believe anyone. Conrad didn't believe himself.

16

The name painted on the back of the boat was Slider III and Ish didn't take any special care approaching her. Him, his wife and kids, had been on board Slider II and Slider III more times than he could count. The original Slider was something else. She wasn't much. Maybe that's why Ish loved her most of all. Those were good days, party days, fishing days, days when Stallion and him could just go out into Jamaica Bay and drink or get high, watching the jets fly their glide paths into JFK. Sometimes they brought girls onto the boat with them, but mostly it was just Stallion and him hanging out. Where had those days gone?

17

Stallion was bleaching the deck. He'd already taken care of the cabin. Had the sheets and the rest of the shit from the cabin bundled up into a black garbage bag. It was about time to take her out of the water anyway. He thinks, if he had done it a week ago, when he should have, maybe ...

If, If, if ...
Maybe
Maybe
Maybe ...
what a fuckin' waste of time.
Then he heard the footsteps on the dock coming his way.
He turns, mop in hand, "Hey, Ish."

18

"Hey, Stallion. Cleaning her up. Gonna take her out of the water soon?"

"Yeah, one last trip for the season and then I'll take her out of the water tomorrow. You wanna come?"

"Depends."

"On what?"

"On the truth."

"Funny, Ish, all the years I known you, you never talked in riddles before."

"Never felt like it before."

"So why tonight?"

"Grieving an old flame. You remember Dina D'Agostino?"

"Dag? Sure. Who wouldn't remember her? Didn't you fuck her once?"

"Nope. I guess I wished I had. I guess that one night I coulda. She woulda let me, I think, but she woulda let me do anything to her that night."

"Too bad for you."

"That's strange, Stallion."

"Yeah, what?"

"You didn't ask me how she died."

"How'd she die?"

"Strangled, but she was also tortured. She was a real mess. Washed up on Brighton Beach. The crabs and gulls had gotten to her."

"Too bad. How'd you hear about it?"

"Her mom. She found a book Dag kept in her apartment. Mine was the only name she recognized in the book, so she called. Heard I was a cop and figured I could help."

"A book, huh?"

"Yeah. Like I said, Stallion, her mom only recognized one name in the book, but I recognized another name in the book: Joseph Stallone. I haven't thought of you as Joey Stallone since we were kids."

"I don't think of you as Pete. So what?"

"You sound a little stressed there, Stallion. Something wrong?"

"You hit a homer off me today."

"I hit homers off you before."

"Never off my slider. Never, not once in thirty years."

"I don't suppose you ever murdered anybody before, Stallion. Sure, it's easy when you're raging, but when you calm down ... Why'd ya have to beat her like that? You musta made a fuckin' mess. I could smell the bleach from the end of the dock."

"I didn't—"

Ish showed Stallion his Glock. "I'm gonna kill you soon, Stallion. You can tell me why you did it and get it off your chest or you can take it with you. All the same to me."

Stallion laughed. It was a nervous little laugh, weak, unconvincing. "Get the fuck outta here. You ain't gonna kill—"

The shot ripped through Stallion's liver and he crashed to the deck, his right arm hanging over the side of the boat .

"Wanna bet?" Ish said. "You got a few more minutes to think it over, Stallion." Ish took out a .38 drop piece he'd kept in his garage for years, wrapped Stallion's fingers around it, and fired into the dock. "Last chance, Stallion."

"She ... she ... she ..." Stallion was dead.

19

When the cops broke into the old man's apartment after the complaints about the foul odor, they found the rotted carcass of dolphin.

The Prophet

From SCOUNDRELS.

Rubes, boobs, marks, suckers, saps, and stooges ... Rubes, boobs, marks, suckers, saps, and stooges ... Rubes, boobs, marks, suckers, saps, and stooges ...

The words went round and round in Barney Peters' head like one of those carnival rides he had spent his youth setting up and breaking down. His father was a carnie spieler, his mom a cooch dancer. Barney had about as much use for them as they for him: none. But the carnie circuit was his schooling and it was where he'd met his second father and mentor, Willis Mansard, or, as he was known in the world of geeks, grafters, and grifters, the Cruelty Man. Why the name? Because it was said of Willis Mansard that he lacked both heart and conscience. His reputation was that he would scam his own grandmother on her deathbed if it suited his purposes. In

his world, damnations of that nature were grace notes of admiration and respect. The Cruelty Man wore his moniker proudly until the day a profoundly annoyed congregation of Baptists spiked him to a cross of creosote-soaked railroad ties before putting him to the flame. How was Cruelty to have known, after all, that the majority of the male congregants in that part of southern Indiana were comprised of Klan members? Ah, the blessed Klan, whose notion of turning the other cheek gave newfound meaning to the concept of Christian forgiveness.

Rubes, boobs, marks, suckers, saps, and stooges ... Rubes, boobs, marks, suckers, saps, and stooges ... Rubes, boobs, marks, suckers, saps, and stooges ...

The words went round and round to the rhythm of the rails. Ka-ching ka-ching ... ka-ching ka-ching ... ka-ching ka-ching ... And so it went, Barney staring at the star-poisoned sky through a two-foot hole in the boxcar roof. He wasn't alone in the boxcar neither. A man was never alone with nothing more than his own thoughts nowadays, not with the world gone into the crapper. There were five hobos sharing the dirty straw bedding with him, the boxcar reeking of the cattle that had been herded out into the pens at Chicago to await their slaughter. While the steers themselves were gone, the earthy, gut-turning ammonia stink of their piss and manure clung to the straw like a baby monkey to its mama's titty. His companions were dead asleep as much from the need to escape the stench as from the cheap hooch they'd passed around. Barney hadn't slept in four days. He was determined never to sleep again, not after what he'd seen in Goshen. He didn't even want to close his eyes.

It wasn't as if he hadn't run the Godwallop Con or, as some favored, the Rapture Play before. The Cruelty Man had taught it to him in its myriad incarnations early on in their partnership. At first, Barney had played the kid. Then as he grew, he acted most often as

the shill. He'd made the play with Cruelty any number of times and after Cruelty's demise, Barney'd run versions of the swindle himself with a bunch of interchangeable partners and all sorts of kids. The kids were always the trickiest part of the grift. After Barney had grown too old to play the innocent, it would sometimes take Cruelty and him weeks to scout out a kid who could carry it off. But since the Crash in '29, there had been an explosion of fresh talent from which to choose. Poverty and desperation put a lot of boys out on the road to fend for themselves. Those same factors also made the god-fearing boobs even more susceptible to the con. The Godwallop always worked like a charm ... until Goshen.

Cruelty used to say, "Religion is the greatest con of all. I can't testify as to whether Jesus was the King of the Jews, but I am here to tell you he was the King of the Grifters and Lazarus was nothing but a shill. Believers are the biggest suckers of them all. They are as near as asking to be taken as a spinster aunt on a whiskey and opium bender. You ever been to tent revival, boy?" Cruelty never waited for Barney to answer. "It's nothing but second-rate flimflam dressed up in a lot of hokum and hallelujahs. I played the cripple in them shows more times than a man has fingers and toes to count on. Say enough amens and praise the Lords and you'll have them in your hip pocket."

He was right of course. There were a hundred gaffes you could run on the bible bangers that you wouldn't dare run on anyone else for fear of getting your liver cut out and fed to you while you were dying. There was the Splinter of the Cross play, where you claimed to have in your possession a piece of the cross upon which Jesus had been crucified. The papists fell for that one in a big way. Them and their fetish for sacred objects was a grifter's goldmine. There were ten variations of that con alone, but since the Cruelty Man had gotten his on a fiery cross, Barney hadn't had the

heart to run it. That was the thing that distinguished him from his mentor: Barney was cursed with a conscience of sorts, at least the remnants of one. Whereas Cruelty could step on a mark's throat until he choked out every penny from the rube's pockets, Barney would let a markup for air.

"That will be your undoing, boy," Cruelty warned. "Once you've taken them, they are not going to see leaving them some crumbs as an act of kindness. You might as well bleed them dry once you've opened up the vein. Their judgement will be equally harsh regardless of how much blood you leave behind."

Barney knew Cruelty was right. Cut off three of a man's limbs, he ain't going to thank you for not relieving him of the fourth. Cruelty had also advised his protégé that the further outside the city you went, the easier it was to prey on the believers.

"The more straw in their teeth and shit on their shoes, the easier the score," he used to say.

Cruelty was right about that too. The boonies, that's where Barney had made his living since Willis Mansard's death. And Goshen was as far away from a city as you could get while staying within the confines of the contiguous United States. It was a pretty well-to-do little farming community. Well-to-do meaning three notches above dirt poor at most times, but flush these days. Goshen was founded by a group of like-minded Christian zealots in the years after the War of Northern Aggression. They were the kind of good Christians who quoted liberally from Hebrews while despising Jews as usurious Christ-killers; the kind of good Christians who claimed to love all brother and sister Christians while hating Catholics more than the Jews; the kind of good Christians who considered the colored races less than subhuman yet used them to pick their crops and sometimes raise up their children. They treated women like slaves. Didn't drink, didn't smoke, didn't dance, didn't

sing anything but the psalms, didn't spare the rod. To say they were severe was to be unkind to severe. In other words, they were perfect stooges.

It was all perfect. That should have been the first sign to Barney that he should queer the Goshen play himself and take it to Missouri or Arkansas. Cruelty had warned him a hundred times about perfection.

"When it all goes right, it's all wrong, boy. You best throw in your cards and take the game out of state."

Barney couldn't bring himself to fold the play. For once he had the funds to do it right, to run the gaffe with style. This was not to say that Cruelty and him hadn't showed their high strutting stuff, but they were always having to compromise, to make do. All Barney'd ever hear from Willis Mansard was how he had run big stock scams in KC and St. Lou.

"That was the cream on the top of the cream at the top of the bottle. Big money in, bigger money out. That was living, boy. Fancy suits, fancier dames, champagne and fish eggs on crackers. We wore spats on our feet, not shitkickers. Problem with them plays, though, is once you run 'em in a town, you're burned. Word spreads in the city and from city to city faster than you could set up shop. No, son, your best shot is to stay out here with the hayseeds and haystacks."

Barney knew it was dumb to try and prove a point to a dead man, but he'd done dumber things. He was sure Cruelty would be so proud of him. Everything was aces. He'd found a pure red heifer at a dairy farm ten miles outside Goshen. The farmer either didn't care a lick for bible prophecy or cared more about the fifty dollars— half now, half later—Barney had paid him for the beast and to continue to shelter and feed it until show time. Pure red heifers weren't easy to come by when you needed them. Even now, even after Goshen, Barney laughed to himself about some of the stunts he

and Cruelty had pulled to get around that part of the prophecy. They'd once even used lady's hair dye mixed with shoe polish to cover a spotted brown cow. Takes a lot of hair dye and shoe polish to cover a cow head to hoof. Barney had been scared to death they would get found out.

"Now don't you worry none, boy," Willis told him. "These country folk got some strange notions about what the Good Book says and even stranger ideas of what it means. Most of them can't read and those that can usually just twist it up to suit their needs. You and me, we got nothing on these yokel preachers and prophets."

The good fortune Barney had stumbling across the red heifer was nothing compared to the luck he'd had with the kid. The rest of it was nothing if the kid couldn't pull off the play. And the kid Barney found was worth ten red heifers. He was born to the part. Near twelve years old, but looking small and young for his years. Had the kind of blond hair that was closer to white than yellow and when the wind wasn't blowing it this way or that, it fell in a long limp sheet to the nape of his neck. Had them cold blue eyes looked like they were made out of river ice. He was milk-white complected. With his full face and soft jawline, the boy might've been an angel, but his gnarled mouth put the kibosh on that angel stuff. There were cottontails had prettier upper lips than this kid. Even with his mouth clamped up tight, you could see the hint of his teeth. Your child prophet always needed an affliction or deformity. That's what sold the hustle. When Barney'd done his child prophesying for Cruelty, he'd done it with a stammer.

"... and the peo—peo—people of the p—p—pri—prince who is to c—c—come will de—de—de—destroy the city and the sanctuary. From Da—Da—Daniel, n—n—nine:twenty-sss-sss-six. "

Worked, but it sure did get on folks' nerves. Cruelty used to joke that they gave up their worldly goods just so's they wouldn't have to listen to the child prophet struggle so with his preaching. Cruelty told his protégé he was really happy when he'd grown out of the part.

"No wonder to me why Pharaoh let go his grip on the Hebrews. Forget the angel of death. Probably couldn't take Moses and all that stuttering and stammering and such. Boy, I don't suppose I could take much more of it neither. If I had to sit through it one more time, I might've started praying for the End Days my own self."

With the night sky passing overhead, Barney was thinking back to the Monday when the kid wandered into Goshen as if out of the wilderness. He remembered saying to himself that even if he was having second thoughts about the Second Coming, the time for him to crumb the play had since passed. For weeks he had greased the gears of the yahoo grapevine with whispers and innuendoes of a boy preacher carrying the true gospel. With the world in the outhouse and with believers looking to the Lord for answers, it hadn't taken much for the whispers to become shouts, for the shouts to echo across the valleys, for the echoes to become a fever. It had also seemed to Barney that the Almighty grifter himself had taken a hand in setting up the con. For soon after Barney's whisperings had taken root, Goshen and the surrounding area was beset by a plague of traveling preachers, tent revivals, and bible salesmen. Barnabas Bixby the Bible Man was the guise under which Barney had taken up temporary residence in town. It was against this backdrop of false prophets and profiteers that the barefoot, hare-lipped boy — carrying nothing but a beaten, leather bound bible — strode into town to feed the fevered souls of Goshen tales of the four horsemen.

Barney or, more accurately, Barnabas Bixby, had done such a good job of priming the apocalypse pump that the kid's arrival alone seemed itself a fulfillment of biblical prophecy. When he walked down Main Street, cars and tractors, horses pulling carts, swung to the curb. People on the dusty street stood staring, their maws hanging open with a mixture of fear, hope, and awe. An old woman fainted dead away. Another sobbed. One shrieked, "We are delivered." But it was only when an old man pointed and called out, "It's him! It's the Prophet! The Boy," that Barney knew this would be something special. When the men bought into the con even before you got it going, you had them. But the set up, as good as it was, as perfect the timing, they were nothing compared to what happened next.

The kid stopped in the middle of the street in front of the general store on one side and Bock's Boarding House across the way. Bowing his head and raising up his arms up so that his silhouette looked like the letter Y in the afternoon sun, he held himself perfectly still and waited ... and waited ... and waited. He waited for the murmur to die down, for all engine noise to stop, for pin-drop silence. It didn't take but a moment for him to get it neither. Barney, watching through his open window at the boarding house had never seen anything like it. Then, when the kid had the silence he had seemed to want, he lifted his head, lowered his arms, and turned to look at Josephus Waring, owner of the general store. He did not speak in words, but Waring understood. The bespeckled, apron-clad Waring picked up a wooden fruit crate, carried it to the center of the street, and laid it at the feet of the boy prophet. He turned it upside down.

"Thank you, sir," said the Boy in a hush that everyone on the street could hear. Even Barney, perched up on the second floor.

That was one of the things that made the kid so good. Hare-lipped as he was, he spoke as clear as polished glass and never seemed to have the need to shout. It was that uncanny calmness that had drawn Barney to him in the first place, that and his perfect affliction of course.

"A storm is coming," the Boy spoke in that hushed voice. "A storm that will sweep all of us away in one form or another. In spite of what you may have heard, that storm, brothers and sisters, is not years away but nearly upon us."

And Barney would be goddamned if an icy gust of wind didn't just then blow down Main Street, kicking up dust into the faces of the crowd gathering around the Boy. The Boy himself did not blink or turn away even as the yokels grabbed their collars, pulling them tight to their necks and shielding their eyes with their hands. They all moved closer and closer to the Boy. Soon it seemed everyone for miles around was at the Boy's feet. Barney didn't hear the blare of Gabriel's horn for the din of cash registers ringing in his head.

"You have been told there are signs and omens, trials and tribulations to come before the End Times. And so there are, and so there shall be, but as in all ways of the Lord, there is mystery too. The signs are there for us to read, but we are blind. We have been blinded by the devil himself. Over the next few days, the people of Goshen will see again, for the Lord has sent me to peel the blackness from your eyes. For the next six days I will be right here at this same hour, in this very spot, on this very crate, and I will deliver sight unto you. Come if you will or come not. Attending me won't win you the Lord's favor and save you nor will the opposite be true. Being raised up or left behind is your own doing; not mine, not the Lord's, your own. Come and behold or come not at all, but be

saved." The kid stepped off the fruit crate, turned, and walked out of town the way he walked in.

Barney lifted his eyes to the ceiling of his spare, little room and whispered, "Willis, are you seeing this? Are you hearing this?"

Barnabas Bixby the Bible Man didn't begin his part in the con until day four of the boy prophet's preaching on Main Street. No, for those first three days he was content to watch from his box seat on the second story of the boarding house. As Cruelty had taught him, you had to be patient, you had to let a thing build a momentum all its own.

"Listen up good, son. You cannot pick a crop before its time. Corn, for instance. You pick corn too green and all it's ever gonna be is green corn. The best scams are the ones you just set in motion and let roll down the mountain of their own accord. Let the thing breathe like wine. You'll know when to pour it."

So it was with the Godwallop. You had to let it breathe. And man oh man was this Rapture Play breathing. Each day, the crowd had doubled until Main Street was crawling with rubes, boobs, marks, saps, suckers, and stooges from near and far. On that Tuesday, the Boy eased into things with stuff the people of Goshen had no doubt already heard from every itinerant preacher who had passed through the area for the last decade and a half. He spoke on how many of the warning signs had already shown themselves, on how the Dust Bowl, the Great War were all a part of biblical prophecy. Except when the Boy said those things, it was different from when them other preachers said them. When they would have shouted, he whispered. When they would have pounded their fists into their palms with rage, he stood stone still, calm and serene.

"The apocalypse is not a time for fear or anger for those of us who have accepted the Lord Jesus Christ as our savior and master,"

he told the crowd in his signature hush. "It is a time for peace and reflection, for forgiveness of those who would not be taken up. We should not revile them, but pity them."

On Wednesday, the Boy explained how others had misinterpreted the Good Book. That, in fact, the Jews had already returned to Zion. That they had never really left.

"The Hebrews are God's chosen people and they are a shrewd and stubborn people. They have never fully abandoned the land the Lord gave to them as their birthright. For years they have worked secretly to rebuild the temple. The foundation is already in place. And soon, when they take back all of Israel and their language is restored, the first stone walls shall rise."

The lines—written by Cruelty over thirty years earlier—worked beautifully with the assembled crowd. It appealed to their bone deep anti-Semitism. No one in attendance had trouble believing that the Jews had plotted secretly and were clever enough to fool the A-rabs or them Brit sons of bitches. Barney and the Boy didn't need the Almighty's help with this part of the con. They had another, almost as powerful ally in this: Henry Ford. His railings against the Jews were as a good as gospel with the good people of Goshen. Yet here again, the boy took the words from Cruelty's script and made them his own. And good god damn if the kid didn't almost have the crowd crying for the poor Jews who would make the Second Coming possible, but who would not reap its benefits.

On Thursday, it was Barnabas Bixby's time to shine. Of course by then, none of the yahoos and yokels would remember that it was Barnabas Bixby who had whispered in their ears about the boy preacher. That was the thing. It didn't take much whispering to get this play rolling down the metaphorical mountain that Cruelty had talked about. And when he whispered in those ears, Barnabas

181

Bixby had made sure to couch his words in ambiguity so that if anyone did recall his identity, they could not say he was a liar.

The Boy had stepped up his game some. He wasn't screaming exactly. He never had to scream, but he was speaking more rapidly, more excitedly so that his deformity was very pronounced. It gave him a snarling, feral look that belied his usually calm demeanor. That day he was speaking of the mongrel hordes, of the secret pact between the Bolsheviks, the yellow-skinned Chinese, and the brown-skinned Indians. How their armies were already two hundred million strong and growing and how they would overrun the world like a tidal wave. And just when he got them thoroughly whipped up and near breathless at the thought of these mud people ruining the world, the Boy returned to his usually hushed tones.

"But none of this, my brothers and sisters, no army of any kind will do the damage to this world that the upheaval of the earth itself. We will see in this in the earthquakes that will—"

"False prophet!" someone cried out from the crowd— Barnabas Bixby, pointing a bible directly at the Boy. "You are a false prophet. Let me quote to all of you from Matthew, words most of you know by heart. 'For many will come in my name, saying I am Christ, and will mislead many. And many false prophets will arise and mislead many.' And don't give us any of your mumbo jumbo talk about how clever the Hebrews are and mysteries we don't understand."

"You know your Matthew, sir," the Boy bowed his head in respect. The bow wasn't in the script nor was what followed. "Let me quote some Matthew to you. 'And in various places there will be famines and earthquakes.'"

Barney wasn't concerned at the kid's playing it off the cuff. He had done masterfully so far and didn't see how a little variation from the script could hurt. Besides, Barney had run this so many

times that he felt he could get the play back on track if the kid strayed too far.

"Very good, prophet." Barnabas applauded by thumping the bible. "Well, when will these earthquakes—"

Just then, a chorus of barking and howling dogs rose up in the distance. The horses that some of the farmers used to haul their goods reared up, neighing wildly. Cows that had been brought into town for sale and that had stayed placid in their corals bolted, creating a small stampede. Pigs in their holding pens shrieked and squealed as if being slaughtered. There was a moment of utter stillness and then the ground rumbled and shook. People scattered, running to and fro. The stores swayed, some bricks falling from the boarding house façade. And then just as suddenly ... nothing. Stillness once again. In that moment, Barney realized he was no longer in control of the hustle, but that the hustle was in control of him. Yet, he'd been at this too long to turn and run.

"Do you still name me a false prophet, sir?" the Boy called to him, but with no anger or belligerence in his quiet voice.

"Trickster! Huckster!" Barney cried out. "Everyone gets lucky now and again."

"That is true," the Boy agreed. "So tomorrow let us see. Let the good people of Goshen bear witness tomorrow on this very street."

"To what, another one of your tricks?"

"Let us all see what tomorrow brings, sir. What do you good people of Goshen say," the Boy asked, his arms extended, palms up, to the crowd. "If tomorrow I can reveal more of the Lord's signs, will you follow the word of the Lord? Will you put your faith in me that I am his messenger?"

The crowd, now reassembled and packed even more tightly than before the eruption, gave out a low roar of approval. Some

shouted hallelujah. Some amen. And Barney, who had to acknowledge that even he had been temporarily stunned by the events of the last few moments, breathed again. Because no matter what forces were at work here, the play was back on track. After tomorrow's second helping of God would come the Wallop and after that Barney and the kid would be flush. He'd be hip deep in women, real scotch whiskey, and lighting dollar cigars with ten-dollar bills. So lost was he in his fantasy, Barnabas Bixby nearly missed his cue.

"We'll just see 'bout that, Boy. 'Cause come tomorrow, I'll name the sign you have to produce for these good people. No more of your tricks and tomfoolery tomorrow. I imagine you won't get too much peaceful sleep tonight, thinking about all the possibilities and how you plan to pull one over like you done today."

"Maybe so, sir. Maybe so. Let us see what tomorrow brings."

With that, the Boy stepped of his crate, moved through the crowd and disappeared at the edge of town as he always did.

The gathering crowd was enormous. There was still near five minutes to go before the appointed hour and everything was set. Barney had managed to sneak out of town in the dead of night and get to the farm where the red heifer was being kept. He was feeling so confident in how things would turn out that not only did he pay the dairy farmer the twenty-five bucks he owned him, he threw in an extra ten spot on top of it. Now all there was left for Barnabas Bixby to do was to wade into the crowd, dare the Boy to produce a pure red heifer, and watch the yahoos be awed and amazed as the cow ambled down Main Street. Once that happened, the Boy would have them. He would beseech them to give up all their worldly goods as proof of their belief in their savior. Of course, the Boy

would "suggest" they give their money and most valuable goods to that stubborn and foolish disbeliever, Barnabas Bixby.

Bixby was not without supporters among the townsfolk. That was perfect, because it was always the last minute converts who coughed up the most treasure to the disbeliever. His supporters clapped him on the back and applauded as Barnabas strode out of Bock's Boarding House in his best black suit, bible clutched in hand. They had even set up a fruit crate next to the Boy's for him to stand on. Just as he stepped up onto it, a small, blond figure strode barefoot down Main Street. The roar was deafening as the crowd parted for the Boy. He offered his right hand to Bixby, who, as planned, refused to shake it. God once again seemed to be taking a hand in it as the dark, roiling storm clouds moved in to blot out the sun. A vicious wind came up, blowing hats off heads. What great theater, Barney thought, no carnie had anything on this.

When he saw the crowd extended all the way to the end of Main Street and that it filled the wooden sidewalks so that they pressed p against the storefronts, Barnabas Bixby spoke the words everyone in Goshen had been waiting exactly twenty-four hours to hear.

"Speak to the sons of Israel that they bring you an unblemished red heifer in which is no defect and on which no yoke has ever been placed. Numbers 19:2-7," Barnabas bellowed as deeply and loudly as he could manage. There was a gasp from the crowd. Unlike yesterday's rumblings of the earth, which might very well have been a matter of lucky timing, they didn't see how the Boy could, out of thin air and with no preparation, produce a perfect red heifer. Although he kept his face stern, inside Barney was smiling. Then, he saw a man in the crowd, an unwelcome one, pushing his way toward him. It was the dairy farmer. He couldn't get to Barney,

so he stopped in his tracks and mouthed, "The cow is dead. The cow is dead."

Barnabas Bixby kept his stern expression, only inside the smile had vanished. Without the red heifer, it would all fall apart. Everything depended on that damned red cow. Cruelty's words rang loudly as a thousand steeple bells in his head, "When it all goes right, it's all wrong." But there was no turning back now and the kid was so good, Barney hoped he'd be able to improvise something when the red heifer failed to make its grand entrance. Apparently, the kid had been paying attention and noticed the dairy farmer too.

When the Boy lifted up his arms, a hush fell over the crowd. "Is there an animal doctor among you?"

A heavyset man with wire rim glasses raised his hand and called out, "I'm Franklin Dunbar, Doctor of Veterinary Medicine and I see to most of the livestock in these parts."

"Dr. Dunbar, " the Boy said, "will you please go into the cow pen. There you will find a spotted brown cow fat with calf and about as ready to drop that calf as can be. Will you fetch her and bring it here presently?"

Dunbar did not make answer, but turned on his heel and headed toward the holding pens. What, Barney wondered, was the kid up to? He knew the kid was good, better than good, but was he that good? No, nobody, not even Willis Mansard was that good. Besides, the kid didn't have any money with which to work a side scam or to arrange a fallback. That was their deal: the kid only got his share if the play hit gold. Barney was still doing the mental permutations when Dr. Dunbar returned, a big bellied, spotted brown cow trailing behind him. Again, the crowd parted like the Red Sea for Moses and the Hebrews.

The Boy stepped down from his crate. He walked over to the cow and ran his hands along her flanks. He then stepped back up

onto the crate. "Behold!" said the Boy and almost immediately, the cow laid on her side. Within seconds, hoofs and the nose of a calf showed out beneath the tail of the mother. It wasn't five minutes before she had dropped the calf to Main Street in the most effortless birth Dr. Franklin Dunbar had ever seen. And when the doctor was done cleaning off the newborn, the calf stood on wobbly legs as if to show the assembled masses her pure, unblemished red hide. The crowd was stunned silent.

Barnabas Bixby, his heart in his throat, carried on. "By what means of evil and sorcery have you done this, false prophet?"

"By the will of the Lord, sir. By his will a thousand such calves may be born, here or in the Holy Land. Even today, such a calf is born there as here," The Boy then turned to the crowd. "The end is at hand, brothers and sisters, but for those of you who truly believe, it is the beginning of heaven without end. Tomorrow, bring all your worldly goods, your cash money and jewelry, any such material thing you have ever loved before God and lay it down here in this street for soon the horn will sound and you will be risen." During the tumult that arose in the wake of his pronouncement, the Boy leaned over to his partner and whispered, "Meet me tonight on the other side of the animal pens just before sunrise." Then he stepped down off his crate and vanished as he always did.

Barney never met the Boy. He waited until Goshen was asleep and ran. He had been running ever since. He had left behind everything he owned, every stitch of clothing save those on his back. He'd left his bag of flim flam props and disguises, his fake money and false papers. Now the sun was leaking through the roof of the boxcar and there was a squealing of brakes.

"Come on, fella," one of the hobos said, pulling at Barney's arm. "Best get going while the getting's good or you'll catch a beating from one of the railroad bulls or the yardmen."

Barney jumped out when they yanked the door back and he tumbled down the side of a small hill. The 'bo who had urged him to jump told Barney he knew of a camp deep in the woods just a few miles from where they'd landed. Barney figured he was in no position to be choosy and he was so damned hungry he would have gone anywhere as long as there was the chance of a meal. Once into the woods, the hobo excused himself saying he needed to let a little water out. Barney took the opportunity to do the same. When he was done, he sat down, back against a tree and waited for his traveling companion to resurface. After a few minutes, when the hobo didn't reappear, Barney called out to him.

"Over here!" the 'bo answered back.

"Phewwww!" Barney said to himself.

Except when Barney followed the voice, he didn't find the man. Instead he stumbled over something. When he looked back to see what it was, he found he couldn't breathe. For there on the forest floor was the carcass of a perfect red calf, throat slit, eyes open and unseeing. Barney heard a twig snap behind him and spun his head around. The Boy!

"Behold," was what he said and laughed at Barney. Then he took his right index finger and rubbed it over his hare-lip. With that, the deformity vanished. "Come on, con man, we've got a world to save one town at a time."

Concentration Camp

Feeding the Crocodile

From JEWISH NOIR.

*T*he baker sang as he always sang while kneading the dough. It was a sad song, a song that once made his late wife spill her tears into the mother yeast, the yeast he still used to make his loaves rise. *Although his son thought he was a superstitious old fool, the baker swore that his Anya's soul lived in the yeast and no one could convince him otherwise. It was why his bread was so prized by all the people of this small Polish town.*

Everyone, Jew and gentile alike, Bolsheviks and National Socialists from the German side of the border, came to Baruch's tiny shop in the ghetto. And it was a fight over the last loaf in the shop that had led to the blood feud between the two families.

Exhausted and hungry, Isaac Becker closed his tattered notebook.

"More!" barked Kleinmann. "What happens to the old baker's daughter? Does she escape Poland with the documents? Does Pavel, the dirty Bolshevik scum, help her or turn her over to the Gestapo to save his own worthless hide? More!"

"Not tonight, I'm afraid, Herr Lieutenant Kleinmann. I am feeling weak. There was much much work on the ash heap today. Have you ever shoveled wet ashes?"

"You Jews! Always complaining. Always ungrateful. Remember, Becker, if not for me, you would be in the heap and not on it."

"I remember. Every day, I remember. I thank the God of Israel for your kindness."

"Good, then write well tonight, Becker. Pray to that God of yours to inspire you, for I will dream again of the old baker's daughter and what will become of her."

"But my rations ... what about—"

"You will have your crusts and soup," Kleinmann said, cutting Becker off mid-question as he always did.

It was as ritualized as the dance of bees, these nightly exchanges between Werner Kleinmann, the SS lieutenant, and Isaac Becker, the Jew. With the exception of Becker's tales, even the words they spoke had become formalized, as if they were the names of words instead of the words themselves. Any implied irony or threat that may have been a part of the ritual when the dance partners took their first awkward steps together had long since been forgotten.

"Thank you, Herr Lieutenant Kleinmann." Becker bowed as he always did, as was expected.

Becker waited for the words. You're welcome, Isaac. These words never came. The lieutenant dismissed the prisoner with a curt, backhanded slap of the air as a finger of flame might snap at an impudent moth. Lately it dawned on Becker that things omitted

from a ritual are part of the ritual too, but this revelation did not quench his thirst or fill his belly.

Closing the door behind him and plodding through the mud back to his barracks, Becker cursed Kleinmann in several tongues. In hell, one is educated in many things. He loved Hungarian curses best of all. He delighted at the sound and rhythm of the language, and the creativity of the curses was unparalleled. He had never been to Hungary and once had dreamed of some day visiting. But he had months ago stopped dreaming of walking the streets of Budapest and just listening to the people chatter about the magnificent and the mundane. His current hell was as close to Budapest as he would ever get.

So caught up was he in his cursing, Becker hadn't noticed the approach of Jacob Weisen. Weisen and Becker were from the same small village on the German side of the Polish border. They had met for the first time when they were five, their hate for one another immediate and mutual. The depth of their loathing was beyond social, beyond merely molecular. It was metaphysical. At home, they had managed, for the most part, to avoid contact. That proved impossible in the camp, their having been assigned to the same barracks. Worse for Becker was Weisen's position as head of the retribution squad.

A death camp is a special kind of prison, but a prison nonetheless. In all prisons, there are rules and there are lines and there are lines not to be crossed, ever. Given the cheapness of life and the ever-hungry machinery of death behind the barbed wire and electrical fences, no one seemed keen on appeals or second chances. This was especially true of the prisoner enforcers. Yes, at its basest level, life inside this place was all about survival: a few more minutes, an extra day, two weeks, perhaps a month. But at what price? How close to the line should one step?

"So, Isaac Becker, you have again been feeding the crocodile," prodded Weisen.

"The crocodile? What nonsense are you talking now, Weisen?"

"Have you never heard it said that the frightened man feeds the crocodile in the hope that he will be eaten last?"

"I am a teller of tales, not a chef. I work on the heap just like you and the rest of the men in our barracks."

"But you eat better than us, don't you?"

This stunned Becker. Lieutenant Kleinmann had assured Isaac that none of the other prisoners would ever learn of their special arrangement. The change in Becker's expression was not lost on Weisen.

"How typical of you to assume you are the only lost soul in hell to have made a deal with the devil. Fool! Do you ever wonder where your rewards come from? For every one of your extra rations, there is a little more smoke, the heap gets a little taller."

Becker felt as if Weisen had just whacked him across the ribs with a plank. He was short of breath, suddenly nauseous, and might've vomited right there in the mud had there been enough food in his system to bring back up. He had never wanted to consider from where his extra rations had come. He hadn't wanted to think about it because he knew. He had known from that first day the lieutenant pulled him off the pile.

"You are the storyteller," said the SS man. "In such a place as this, your talent is a commodity as precious as gold fillings and hidden diamonds, Becker." The SS man had pointed at the crematoria. "If a man's soul is gray when he is stationed here, the smoke will blacken it. If a man's soul is already black ..."

"And yours, Herr Lieutenant Kleinmann, what is its hue?"

"Never mind my soul, storyteller. Your job is to make sure that a little sun shines through the smoke."

And so the deal had been struck. Becker would provide the sun, Kleinmann the bread and soup.

"What's the matter? You've gone gray, Becker," Weisen asked, snapping the storyteller back into the moment. "You walk a very thin tightrope between us and the crocodile. His protection extends only so far. One day soon, you will be part of the pile and your rations will go to some other scum who has traded in your soul for one more day in paradise. Sooner or later, Becker, we are all eaten by one crocodile or another."

Becker opened up his mouth to explain, but the words would not come. He knew he could not risk telling another inmate of his plan. Weisen's threats had only reinforced Becker's belief that there were no secrets in Hades.

When he was certain that the baker's daughter was well into the tunnel beneath the shul, Pavel twisted the hand grenade fuse and pulled Herr Ernst, the Gestapo man, close by his black leather lapels. First, confusion washed across the crystalline azure sea of the Nazi's eyes, then fear like a raging storm roiled the waters. Herr Ernst pounded his fists against the Russian's chest, but to no avail. Pavel simply smiled.

In that brief second, he was as at peace as any man who had ever lived. He could see his mother's weathered face set against the swaying field of golden wheat, her red and blue babushka snapping in the wind. He smelled the sweet aroma of onions frying in chicken fat and the fragrant steam rising from the boiling buckwheat. When he was certain there was no turning back, Pavel released Ernst's lapels. He pressed his fingers softly to his mouth, remembering the feel of Esther's lips against his. Then nothing.

When the old baker heard the explosion from the street outside the shul, he smiled and pressed the stolen Luger to his temple, his tears pouring into the mother yeast. He would not survive to knead the next batch of dough. That would be for new hands, but he and his wife would live on, their souls bubbling up together as long as the new baker fed the yeast. Perhaps they would live forever.

Becker closed the tattered notebook.

It was time for the dance of bees to begin, but it did not. When Becker looked up, he noticed tears streaming down Kleinmann's cheeks. In that moment Becker felt a level of revulsion and hate for Kleinmann, for his own writing, for himself that he never imagined possible. How, in this place where the worst atrocities were perpetrated by one human against another on an hourly basis, could his story make Kleinmann weep? He had witnessed Kleinmann execute prisoners for the mildest perceived slight, even for slipping on the heap, sometimes simply for sport. Nor was Becker blind to the teenage girls Kleinmann had brought into his office. The crocodile was hungry for more than stories.

"Bravo, Becker. Bravo!" The lieutenant raved, wiping away tears between claps. "Thank you. Thank you."

At last, Kleinmann uttered the words Becker had longed to hear.

"There will be meat for you tonight, Isaac Becker. Triple rations."

In his head, Becker heard Weisen's voice. Triple rations. The smoke grows more dense. The heap grows taller still.

The SS man smiled. "Or maybe you would prefer some companionship instead? Man does not live by bread alone, eh, Becker?"

Now Becker wanted to rip his own eyes out of their sockets. "That is most kind, Herr Lieutenant Kleinmann, but the rations will be fine." On the verge of tears himself, Isaac Becker stood to go.

"I have not dismissed you, Becker. Here, bring me your book, that magic book of yours."

Becker's body clenched in fear. "The magic is in me, not the book."

"The book, Becker! Now!"

What choice did he have really? He slid the book across the desk to the SS man. The Nazi stroked the book, patted it, picked it up and caressed it. Then, when he opened the book, Becker had to prop himself against the desk for fear of fainting. The scowl on Kleinmann's face did nothing to improve Becker's equilibrium.

"What is this, Becker? What language is this?" he growled at the storyteller.

Becker sighed silently, thankful for the lieutenant's lack of language skills. He got some string back in his legs and said, "Hungarian, sir, Magyar."

"Hungarian! The Magyars were once Aryans but are now inbred pigs. Why don't you write in German or even Yiddish? Is this some kind of trick, Jew?"

"I don't dispute you about the Hungarians, Herr Lieutenant Kleinmann, but their language sings to me. Learning the language has occupied my mind here and it helps me with my writing. Even you, sir, have said that one's mind must be occupied in such a place as this."

The scowl evaporated. "Yes, I have said this. Whatever helps you with your magic. I suppose the language in which you write is irrelevant, so long as when you read to me ..." Kleinmann again became emotional. "You are dismissed. Go to the rear of Building

Five. Your rations will be waiting." Becker stood his ground. "What is it now? I said you can go."

"But my book, Herr— "

"You have no possessions here, Becker, only the illusion of possession. That illusion is solely dependent upon me. Savor your meat. Take the night off from your writing. Tomorrow, I will keep you off the ash heap and I will have a new notebook for you and pens, the best pens."

Becker dared not show his anger. He bowed, turned, hurried through the door, and, for the first time in his life, sought out the company of Jacob Weisen.

"do you know what they will do to you if you are caught, Becker? For this, it won't be anything as gentle as the gas and that's no treat," Weisen warned. "It would be better if they shot you."

"No. You must see it happens as we discussed it."

Weisen shook his head. "All this for a book of tales. If I had known you were such a fool, I wouldn't have despised you quite so much."

"Then it is a fool's errand and I will pay for the folly, not you."

"Very well."

Becker grabbed Weisen's forearm. "You will give the book to the Gypsy and he will get it out of the camp."

"You have my word."

Jacob Weisen had explained how it was possible to get back to Kleinmann's office without drawing unwanted attention. This part of the camp was dark and not well patrolled. No need, really. On those rare occasions when prisoners got loose, they did not run to the ash heap. They knew they would get there soon enough without

helping their murderers. Now Isaac Becker, the teller of tales, lay face down in the mud, waiting. For nearly an hour he had listened to Kleinmann forcing himself on one of the blank-faced girls. Bitch! the pig would call her, slapping her hard as he grunted. Then there was silence. A few minutes later, two guards showed up at his office door.

"She looks like she could use delousing," one of the guards joked.

"Yes, a shower would do her well," said the other.

"No, not this one, not tonight. I am in high spirits tonight. Clean her up and send her to the enlisted men's brothel," Kleinmann said, as if he were a genie granting the girl her first wish.

Shortly after the guards left, the lieutenant headed to his quarters.

He had unexpected company.

"Becker, what are you doing here? Are you mad? You know this isn't permitted. You could be shot and there isn't a thing I could do about it. Come, walk in the shadows with me." He looped his arm through Becker's and pulled him into the dark.

"My book, please, Herr Lieutenant Kleinmann."

"What did you say, Becker? Did you again call it your book? You Jews are a stubborn race. I—"

Pushing the SS man against the side of an empty hut, Isaac Becker covered Kleinmann's mouth with his muddied hand and plunged a sharpened wedge of glass—the other end padded with a stolen sock—into the SS man's liver. When he was certain it was in very deep, Becker snapped the glass off so there would be no hope of removing the makeshift blade. Just like in his story, there was confusion in the blue eyes of the victim, then fear. Death came soon enough and more mercifully than it would come for Isaac Becker.

The storyteller took back his precious book and retraced the path Weisen had laid out for him.

It took Becker three days to die on the cross. They had tortured him first and then let him heal enough to make the crucifixion worth their trouble. The cross had been centrally placed so the prisoners would be forced to pass by the dying man while going to and from their barracks. Those prisoners who lacked ringside seats had been marched over to watch the long spikes driven into the storyteller's body.

"You got the book out?" Weisen asked the Gypsy, both staring out at the cross.

"This morning in a bag under the ashes for the local farmers. They use it for fertilizer, you know, the ashes. One of the farmers is a Polish Resistance man."

"Where is the book going?"

"An address in Budapest somewhere, I think."

Weisen turned to the Gypsy. "Did you look in the book?"

"I can't read. Did you?"

"No. Becker gave it to your man before the guards came for him. I wonder what was in it."

"Nothing worth that, I can tell you," the Gypsy said, pointing to the crows pecking at the storyteller's body.

"It was to him."

The Gypsy laughed. "No it wasn't. The first time they jolted him with electricity or burnt him with lit cigarettes, I can tell you, he stopped thinking it was worth it."

"Then it was a good thing there was no turning back. Still, I wonder what was in that book."

"Enough! Wondering won't feed us or keep us alive in this place," the Gypsy said. "I'm hungry."

So both men turned their backs on Becker and went behind the barracks to divide up the extra rations Weisen had received for turning in his old nemesis.

Somewhere a crocodile closed his eyes and fell into a deep sleep.

Jibber Jabber

From ONCE UPON A CRIME.

His father was a collector of things, all sorts of things, but James McCabe collected nothing. He did not relate to things, not even the splayed fingers he sometimes fanned before his opaque blue eyes. If not for the laws of physics, he would not relate to the floor on which he knelt, intermittently rocking his days away with inexhaustible energy. He was disconnected, unattached, self-contained, an eight-year-old universe unto himself. The doctors, shrinks, therapists, and teachers at the developmental center could only speculate about the nature of that universe. His was a silent universe, disinterested in revelation and selfish of clues.

He had cried at birth. It was the only sound ever to have escaped from inside him. He had never cooed or grunted, coughed or called out. His next sound would be his second. His next word his

first. His mother fooled herself that she could divine the mysteries of her son's moods and desires by the rhythm of his rocking, by the shadows his fingers cast on the walls, even by which room James wandered into. She might as well have rolled animal bones.

James McCabe's father had long since cut ties with his son. He treated the boy with the utter disinterest which the boy himself displayed. If only the boy could have shown minimal contempt, that would have been enough for the father. He understood contempt, but he could not stomach disinterest. Love was never an issue. To his father, James was less than the least of his possessions. Objects are created without the potential for emotion. One's own love, pride, and vanity had to be enough for both you and the thing itself.

The day the two universes collided, each forever changing, James McCabe, temporarily inert, found himself in a dark corner of the room that held his father's most prized possessions. The glass and oak case was more shrine than display. People came from all over to stand and gawk at the things in the case. Two sets of eager footfalls thumped against the big cabin's floorboards. As was always the case, it was impossible to know if James was aware they were coming toward him.

"Here we are, Mr. Smith."

Peter McCabe made a rather too formal gesture with his arm, but he couldn't help himself. Although he had shown his collection to many strangers, he could contain neither his pride nor his avarice. To see Peter McCabe's shrine cost you. It was a C-note just to stand near the case and peer through the glass. Five times that if you wished to handle pieces from the collection.

McCabe handed Smith a fresh pair of white gloves and put on a pair himself.

Reading Smith's expression, McCabe said, "Yes, it's always hard to know where to begin. This is a personal favorite. Here." He

reached for a meticulously preserved hardcover, carefully covered in acid free plastic.

"Mein Kampf."

Smith was unimpressed.

McCabe did not overreact. "Yes, but not just any copy. Notice that the inscription is to Neville Chamberlain and that Hitler's signature is particularly bold and powerful."

Smith was still unmoved. McCabe replaced the book in the case and began nervously reciting a laundry list of other pieces from the collection.

"There's the sutures removed from Hitler's body after the attempt on his life, one of Eichmann's prototypes for the Death's Head hats, an ampule of blue dye Dr. Mengele used to inject into the eyes of children, a pair of the doctor's spectacles, Martin Bormann's Luger, a bar of human soap, a pelvic bone ashtray, a bottle of ashes from Crematorium Number Two at ..."

So distracted was McCabe by his own narcissistic recitation, that he was unconscious of Smith removing his top coat. And though the reflection of the yellow star sewn onto the chest of Smith's suit jacket was plain to see in the spotless glass of the case, that too escaped McCabe's notice. He missed it as his visitor slid the tire iron from beneath his right sleeve and into his white-gloved hand. He barely noticed as Smith screaming "Never Again" so loudly that his wife could hear it in the shed. Even as Smith raised the crooked metal rod—his bland, hollow face transformed into something barely recognizable as human—McCabe was oblivious. With the nauseating thud of the iron against his skull, it was already too late to rue his lack of attentiveness.

Peter McCabe's face smashed directly into the case, loose shards embedding themselves in his flesh. Jagged glass wedged in place peeled away parts of his neck and right ear as gravity pulled

him to the floor. So much blood appeared in an instant that the oak and glass itself seemed to bleed. But Smith was far from finished. He swung the iron again and again, smashing almost every breakable object in the shrine. He dropped the iron, pulled a flask of gasoline out of his inside jacket pocket, and doused the case. He patted his pocket, feeling for a pack of matches. He became frantic when he could not feel that familiar shape in any of his pockets.

He found the matches in the pocket of his bulky top coat he had dropped behind him. As he struck the match, something else caught his attention. He heard James before he saw him. Rather he heard the floorboards creaking as the boy began rocking in the corner. Smith was transfixed by James' unseeing eyes. Not recognizing an ounce of humanity in them, Smith realized what he had become. A mist of profound shame filled his lungs. He wanted to approach the boy, but could not move. His hesitation proved fatal.

"You son of a bitch!"

The spell was broken and Smith looked toward the open door. The shotgun blast nearly took off his head and the inertia nudged his lifeless body into the ruined display case. Smith's last moment of consciousness was consumed by his shame and the heat of the match on his fingertips. The gasoline ignited. The spread of the buckshot and the impact of Smith's body finished the work he had started. The few shrine items that had remained intact, either exploded or crashed to the floor. The room quickly filled with smoke.

The fire was well extinguished and Peter McCabe had been helicoptered to the area trauma center. Mr. Smith's burned body had long since been delivered to the medical examiner's office. Smith, really Avi Pearlmutter, was the grandson of concentration camp

survivors, a full-time cultist, and part-time schizophrenic. James and his mother had both been treated for smoke inhalation and released.

The miracle was patient in coming. It waited until the stillness of night had fully descended and James' mom was halfway to visit her comatose husband. It waited until James' Aunt Greta had stripped off and burned her eight-year-old nephew's smoke-corrupted clothing. It waited until she led James into the upstairs bathroom, the shower already running. Then all patience evaporated and the miracle fairly exploded. James McCabe, the eight-year old universe, came undone.

The instant his bare feet touched the cold tile floor, James spoke. Well, it wasn't speech, exactly. He wasn't saying words, not so's Greta could make them out, anyway, but they weren't just random sounds either. They were like make believe words. And there was another change in James, maybe even more profound than the nonsense words. His whole body posture, the manner of his movements changed. The awkward, ungainly jerkiness with which he had moved his entire life was gone.

"One minute he was one of them fidgety little birds and then he was a swan," she would later tell her sister. "First he started to jibber-jabber and then ... Lord Jesus, sis, he moved so graceful-like."

And the movements, like the sounds that came from his mouth, were not random. Although he was naked, James removed invisible clothes. He pressed them, patted out wrinkles, hung them on unseen hooks. He balled up see-through socks, placing them in phantom shoes.

"Then he looked me straight in the eye and started that jibber-jabbering all over again. It was spooky, sis, like your boy was asking me a question. I didn't know what to do, so I just showered him. When he got out, he dried himself all up and put back on them invisible clothes and started them spooky questions again. When I

told him his momma would be home tomorrow, he smiled. He smiled at me, sis. The boy don't never smile. He went right to bed."

There was dark-clouded joy on the outskirts of town for a month or two. Although he had been burned, hit by stray buckshot, and suffered a seriously fractured skull, Peter McCabe's prognosis for survival was improved. His prognosis for a full recovery was less rosy. The damage to the skin and musculature of his face and neck would require several reconstructive procedures. The trauma caused by the blow to the back of his head, the subsequent collision of his forehead with the case, and the blood loss had left him addled, aphasic, weak.

On the other hand, James McCabe's metamorphosis was international news. Yet for all the coverage, each story filed bore a marked similarity to the ones before and after it.

"... the eight-year-old son of a white supremacist diagnosed with a

severe form of Pervasive Developmental Disorder or autism, as it's

more commonly known, witnessed a brutal attack on his father by ...

In the hours immediately following the attack, James McCabe, who

had never uttered a word nor made a sound after his birth ..."

So it went, at least at first. Then the tabloids moved onto the next sensation, but before they all left, The World Planet Star made the McCabes one hundred and fifty thousand dollars richer. Next came the religious fanatics, cultists, and crazies. They were harder to bear, for they came with their own predetermined agendas, agendas having nothing to do with rating points and ad revenues. One group erected a likeness of James nailed to a wooden yellow star. Another

took to acting out James' newfound undressing rituals. In the wake of the crazies came the intelligentsia, the critics, and the academics. They came to piss on the whole spectacle, on the McCabes, and each other. The academics, without ever examining the boy, concluded that this was no miracle, that the original diagnosis of PDD was completely misguided. Ultimately, James McCabe was judged a freak, an oddity, a future roadside attraction like a two-headed snake.

McCabe's Miracle, as it had come to be known, had become his mother's nightmare. For as the months went on, James' speech and rituals grew exponentially. From one minute to the next his voice, his tone, his posture would change. The syllables that poured out of him seemed endless and endlessly senseless. There was no more understanding him now that he spoke than when his mother read his finger shadows. She found herself yearning for his past silence and hating herself for it.

And her husband's rehab had all but consumed the largess of The World Planet Star. His problem was quite the opposite of her son's. Although he had yet to speak again, Peter McCabe was less confused and had come part of the way back to his old self. Unfortunately, his face still looked like a train wreck.

The next change in the collision of the two universes happened in the personal hygiene aisle of the supermarket. It took the shape of a bent old man, his posture that of a twisted tree limb. Even before he approached her, James' mother noticed the crooked man. So out of place, she thought, so shabby; the band of his black hat stained with sweat, his white shirt gone yellow with age. As she pushed the cart ahead of her and he hobbled towards her, she saw the dandruff on the shoulders of his threadbare black coat and the age spots on his ashen, unshaven face. She reached for the soap.

"Soap!" the old man exclaimed. "You know they made soap from human beings, the people your husband so admires."

She knew about the soap, the lampshades, about all of it.

"Get outta my way or I'll call– "

"But if you call security, Mrs. McCabe, I wouldn't be able to help you with your son. And if I don't help him ... I don't think a woman like you could take much more of him, his talking and talking. Am I right? I can see in your eyes that I am right. Here's my card. I'm staying in the Best Western. If you want my help, I'll be there until Thursday."

She hesitated.

"Take it. Take it!" he said, shoving the card into her hand.

She did just to be rid of him. He touched the brim of his hat. She saw his hand was gnarled, scarred by fire.

"I'll await your call. Good day."

She did not turn to watch his retreat. Instead she stared at the card, as frayed and ragged as the man who had given it to her.

CHAIM FEINGOLD

That's what the card said, as if saying his name alone were enough. It would have to be, for it gave no address, no phone number, no fax, no email address, no website. She made to crumple the already withered card, but she did not. She would call. She knew she would as sure as Feingold, whoever he was, knew she would. She was desperate and desperation makes for strange allies.

Feingold came to the cabin that night after dark. Once again put his fingers to his hat in the way of greeting and deference. That was his only concession to manners. He brushed past her, moving his ancient bent frame with an unexpected grace and power.

"Show me where is the room!" he barked.

"The room?"

"Where the husband was clubbed. Where he kept his foul things and the boy was in the corner. Show me!"

She led the way. "But it's all been–"

"Mrs. McCabe, do you want my help? Yes! Then please do as I say."

When they got to the room which had once held the shrine, Feingold had Mrs. McCabe describe in detail about where everything was situated, where her husband had fallen, where her boy had been, where Pearlmutter's body had come to rest ...

"And your husband's horrible trinkets, they were all destroyed? The soap, the ashes, all of it?"

"All of it," she said. "The room filled up quick with smoke. I got my husband out first. He was bleeding so. Then I came and got my boy."

"So, the boy was in the room here for some time, no? A few minutes maybe, yes?"

"A minute or two at least."

Feingold rubbed his cheek, grinning a contemptuous grin. It was a grin that frightened James' mother, a woman who didn't frighten easily.

"Mr. Feingold, how did you find us?"

"On the TV. I saw him on the TV and I recognized ... Well, the way he moved and spoke. You wouldn't understand. Let's just say I became a student of your son and his miracle. Where is the boy?"

She hesitated.

"The boy!" he shouted. "Where is the boy?"

"In the bathroom. He seems his most comfortable in there."

"Comfortable, ha!" His laugh was as bent as his spine.

Both of them stood at the open door of the bathroom, Feingold staring in stunned disbelief as James ran through a never-

ending series of undressing rituals, each different from the next, and nonsense questions asked with wildly different intonation patterns. Silent tears streamed down the old man's cheeks. It had been one thing to see the boy on TV and something else again to stand in the room before him. Feingold's whole body shook. Although she was standing behind him and to one side, Mrs. McCabe could see the old man's reaction in the bathroom mirror.

The old man collected himself, walked up to the boy and placed a gnarled hand on James's shoulder.

"*Was ist dien nomen?*" he asked the boy.

A pause. Then he continued with his rituals.

"*Was ist Ihr Name?*"

Another pause. Back to the rituals.

"Wat is uw naam?"

James crooked his head slightly if he almost understood, but continued.

"*Barmilyen egyezes kiejtes nelkul?*"

James stopped dead in his tracks, looked over each shoulder as if making sure no one was watching or listening. When he was secure that only Feingold could hear he whispered a blue streak. Feingold gave the boy a long avuncular hug and, in the same foreign tongue in which the boy had whispered to him, told James to put his clothes back on, that his shower could wait. Dutifully, he did as the old man instructed, sitting himself down quietly on the cool tile floor. He told the boy not to worry, that he'd be right back, and closed the bathroom door behind him.

Mrs. McCabe was on her knees in the hallway, head upturned to the rafters, hands folded prayerfully. When she was done muttering, she turned to Feingold.

"How did you— What did you—"

"I asked his name, what it was in Yiddish, German, Dutch, and finally Hungarian."

"But he doesn't—"

"—speak Hungarian. He doesn't speak English, yes? He doesn't speak at all. He still does not, Mrs. McCabe."

"I don't understand."

"Why should you? How could such a person as you or your husband understand? The boy, your boy, is not speaking. At the moment, that is not your son, but a thirteen-year-old girl from Budapest named Magda Nagy whose father was teaching comparative literature at the University of Warsaw when the Nazis invaded. For her, it's nineteen forty-four. Less than an hour ago, her whole family got off the train at the gates of Auschwitz. Her father, mother, and older brother were taken away and she was sent for a delousing shower."

"That's crazy!"

"Crazy! You know what she asked, Magda? First, where her family had gone. Then, what hook number she should place her clothes on. That's what the bastards would tell the unfortunates before they herded them into the gas chambers and locked the steel doors behind them. 'Remember what hook number you placed your clothes on so you can retrieve them when you come out of the shower.' That's what they told them, these people you and your husband admire. She's not even a Jew, Magda."

Mrs. McCabe did not have the strength to argue. "But how did you know? Until you just now spoke to James—Madga , whoever, he, I mean, she didn't speak Hungarian. That was jibber-jabber coming out of my boy's mouth."

"Yes and no. It was Yiddish and German, Dutch and Hungarian, Polish and Russian, Romanian and ten other languages jumbled together, sometimes spoken backwards with no native

accent. It was the languages of all the people what bodies became ashes and lampshades, soap and ... It is the language of the smoke."

"But how did you know? How could you know?"

"That is my business alone. I am going in that bathroom now. And when I come out, maybe we will both have back something we lost: you only a few months ago, me a lifetime ago."

When Chaim Feingold stepped back into the bathroom and closed the door behind him, he stood up on the bathtub's edge. In the Yiddish of his youth, Feingold shouted as if above the din of a crowded room crammed with people, though only James McCabe was there to hear him.

"Is my sister, Shandel Feingold here? Shandel!" he called, hoping that the girl he had recognized on TV in the guise of James McCabe could be reached. "Shandel! Shandel!"

"Chaim! Chaim! Here, over here I am," she answered across time and space.

And for hours, the crooked old man held his dead sister in his arms.

It was three more months before Peter McCabe was deemed well enough to come home. And when he arrived, he found a very different cabin and a very different family than the ones he had left. James had returned to his silence, but the opacity of his blue eyes was gone. You cannot have the dead speak through you and be unchanged. He was no longer a universe unto himself and had learned to indicate through gestures his likes and dislikes. Peter swore the boy almost smiled at him.

Mrs. McCabe had found the God she had run away from twenty years before. She went to church every day, asking forgiveness for herself and her husband. She had taken what was left of the money and donated it to the Holocaust Museum in

Washington in the name of Magda Nagy. She sold most of their property to pay for her husband's rehab.

Still aphasic, McCabe asked his wife, "My 'hings, 'hat 'appened 'o my 'hings?"

"They're gone and we're never to speak of them again."

He grew very agitated, his arms flexing and shaking. Then she told him about Feingold and how he said James' jibber-jabber was the language of the smoke.

Peter McCabe began laughing wildly, crazily. His eyes got wide, his face red. Then he started choking, coughing. His wife was frantic not knowing what to do. Eventually, he settled back down, tears in the corners of his eyes.

"Lang'age a smoke." He shook his head. He didn't have the heart to tell his wife that he had made the soap himself and that the bottle of ashes had come from their own fireplace.

Moe Prager

Breakage

Nominated for 2018 Shamus Award. Originally published in Down & Out Magazine.

Brooklyn, 1984

Traffic was buzzing across the metal grate of the Brooklyn Bridge roadway. It was a raw and treacherous day with a wind that cut through you, leaving jagged little holes in its wake. A day so wet and cold that it even made newborn babies' bones ache. But Klaus and I were inside Bordeaux in Brooklyn, dried off and drinking piping hot coffee from the deli across Montague Street. Klaus's mood was diametrically opposed to the weather, his mix tape of Squeeze, Nick Lowe, Graham Parker, and Elvis Costello was playing full blast on the stereo. He was dressed in ripped blue jeans and beat-to-death black cowboy boots two sizes too large for

his feet. And for the irony of it, he wore a red satin Western shirt with the likenesses of Donny and Marie Osmond ironed on the back.

"You're in a good mood today," I said, taking a sip of my coffee.

He put his hand on his hip and raised an eyebrow. "What makes you say that, Boss?"

I pointed at the speaker above the cash register. "British Pub Rockers usually means you've met someone new. When it's Joy Division, The Cure, and Depeche Mode ..."

"You're awfully observant ... for a straight man."

"I'll take that as a compliment."

"You should. I don't think your brother Aaron has even picked up on the fact that I'm gay."

"My brother Aaron stopped noticing anything but good wines and his wife during Nixon's first term."

Klaus was an escapee from points west and from a family who viewed with equal disdain his love of Punk, New Wave, and men. He was my favorite employee and someone I secretly admired for his ability to throw off the chains his upbringing had forged for him. I'd done a little bit of that myself by becoming a member of the NYPD. Jewish parents don't brag about their sons getting their badges and guns. They shake their heads and whisper about it like how they discuss Aunt Sadie's cancer. And I'd married a *shiksa*, but she'd insisted on converting. Hey, Hitler, wait, don't forget about me! I thought she was crazy, but once Katy made up her mind there was no changing it.

No, in the end, I wasn't very unconventional. I had a wife and a daughter I loved beyond measure. I had a mortgage and lived only a few miles away from where I grew up, a few miles from where I had served in the Six-O Precinct. I had a bad knee, a pension, and was in business with my big brother, a business I hated

a bit more with each passing day. The one unconventional thing I
clung to was the PI work I did every now and again. But even that
conceit was slipping away. It had been months since anyone had
come knocking. So indeed, it was a great surprise when someone
finally came around seeking my help. It was an even bigger surprise
to see who that someone was.

Israel Roth and I weren't a natural fit as friends. He was forty
years my senior, a concentration camp survivor, and a man with
deep guilt over his faithlessness as a husband and his failure as a
father. We'd met a few years ago when I was up in the Catskill
Mountains investigating an old fire that had killed some girls with
whom I'd gone to high school. The friendship between Mr. Roth and
I persisted after I went back home to Brooklyn and he to Florida. It
grew into something else. Maybe he saw me as the son he could
have a second chance with. I know I saw him as the loving
grandfather I'd never had.

I threw my arms around him. "Mr. Roth."

"*Oy gevalt*, Mr. Moe, you're squeezing my *kishkas* out
already."

I relaxed my grip and held him by the biceps at arm's length.
"It's great to see you, but what are you doing up here? Is something
wrong?"

"You sound like my Hannah, may she rest in peace. Always
something had to be wrong."

He didn't fool me. I may not have been his real son, but I
knew him well enough by now to understand. He wouldn't be in
New York at this time of year if there wasn't trouble.

"Come on downstairs to my office and we'll talk. Would you
like Klaus to get you some coffee from across the street?"

He rubbed the gray stubble on his wizened face. "Coffee? I
wouldn't say no to black coffee. Maybe with a little something in it

to warm an old man's soul on a miserable day. You have an open bottle of whiskey in this place somewheres?"

"There's a bottle of Dewar's in my desk drawer."

Klaus was already out the door before I could ask. Although the store was empty of customers, I couldn't leave the register unattended, so I lowered the music and asked Mr. Roth once again about his being in New York.

"Mr. Moe," he said, the corners of his mouth turned down, "I need from you a favor."

"Anything for you, Izzy. You know that."

He made a face as if he caught a whiff of something foul in the air and tilted his head. "It's not for me, this favor, not exactly."

"Who then?"

He didn't answer. Instead he walked to the big plate glass window of the brownstone Aaron and I had converted into our second wine shop. He pointed outside at the snow that was just beginning to fall.

"You know why I live in Florida most of the year, Mr. Moe? Not because I love the weather there. I don't. Between the humidity and the heat and the bugs and the alligators ... oy! But this weather, this weather I hate even worse because this weather brings Auschwitz home to me." He was still facing away from me and he couldn't seem to be able to force himself to stop staring at the gloom and the snow beyond the glass. "Sure, I was there in summer, too, but this is the weather I remember and when I remember this I remember all of it: the stink and the smoke and snow and the tears and the brutality."

He buried his head in his hands and cried silently for a few seconds. I had never seen him this way. We had spoken of the camps before, but he didn't usually react with this much emotion.

"Are you okay, Izzy?" I asked after giving him a minute.

"I will be. Don't you worry, boychik."

Klaus came back in and handed me Mr. Roth's coffee.

"It'll be easier if Moe walks downstairs with it."

"Thank you, Klaus," Mr. Roth said. "You're a good boy."

"My parents would disagree."

Mr. Roth let out a sigh and patted Klaus's cheek. "With what parents don't know of their own children, you could fill a book."

I picked up my coffee and had Israel Roth follow me downstairs to my office. I did business in my office, but what I did there most of the time was hide. I only agreed to partner up with Aaron after I was put out to pasture by the NYPD. I was injured in the line of duty, but I was nobody's hero. I wasn't shot. I didn't fall off a roof while chasing a suspect. I wasn't in a car crash during a high-speed pursuit. Me, I was the victim of a conspiracy between a freshly waxed precinct floor and a piece of carbon paper. Cops who saw it happen say my knee bent in such a way that even Gumby would've winced. Good thing my head hit the floor and knocked me out. These days, I never know which aches worse, my knee or my heart. I miss the job something fierce.

When I got Mr. Roth situated in the leather chair across from my desk, I poured a little Dewar's in his coffee and mine. I poured more in his because he seemed to need it. As he got some of it into his system, I filled him in on Sarah and Katy and how well the wine business was doing. When I ran out of small talk, Mr. Roth filled the silence.

"Hershel Tannenbaum was from my town. He worked on the ash pile with me in the camp," he said, holding his cup out for another dose of Dewar's. He took a sip and went on. "We were the lucky ones, though. We were working on the ashes, not in the ashes like our families."

"The favor you're asking is for Mr. Tannenbaum."

223

"Wait. Wait, Mr. Moe. Patience. Hershel had a wife, Shana. You know what means Shana in Yiddish?"

"Beautiful."

My knowing that pleased Israel Roth. "Very good. Well, Shana was a perfect name for her. She was considered the most beautiful of all the women, Jewish or not, where we were from. Hershel was a little older than her and not a Clark Gable by any means, but he was a furrier, a wealthy man. Shana's parents were from dirt, so a *shidduch* was made."

"An arranged marriage."

"Just so, boychik. They had no children, thank God, when they rounded us up. But when we got to the camp ... you know about how we were separated out like cattle. The very old and the very young were gassed right away. Oven fodder. Others, like Hershel and me, were sent here or there to work themselves to death. For most of our time on the ashes, Hershel had convinced himself, and wisely so, I think, that Shana was already dead and with us in the ashes."

"But ..."

"Yes, Mr. Moe, but. As I told you once, we weren't one big happy family there in the camp. We all did things to survive that we would never have believed we were capable of. Let me tell you something about the worst aspects of human nature. They persist even when you are reduced to your lowest form. You are capable of callousness and pettiness when you have been turned into a lizard or a worm."

"This is all very fascinating, Izzy, but—"

"Oy, enough with the impatience. Shush already."

"Sorry."

"One man who worked with us on the ash heap, a Hungarian intellectual, a goy named Bela Nagy, he despised

Hershel. He thought Hershel never pulled his weight and moaned too much. Maybe Bela was right. Hershel was a complainer, but since I was glad to have a landsman with me, I forgave Hershel his foibles. Bela, he couldn't forgive. So one day on the pile he comes to stand between me and Hershel and I know this is trouble. 'I've got good news for you, Tannenbaum,' says Bela to Hershel. 'Your wife, the beautiful one, is alive.'

"Mr. Moe, to this day I have never seen such an expression as I saw on Hershel's face. He fell down to his knees, tears streaming from his eyes, and he raised up his hands in a gesture of thanks to God that was so genuine that it made chills on my spine that I feel now as I tell you. But I looked away from Hershel and on Bela's face I saw a different expression. It is the face of a jackal. He says nothing. Not even when Hershel rises up from his knees and embraces him. Then, as they pull away from each other, Bela says, 'Yes, your Shana is alive and while you work on the pile, she works on her knees. She is the Queen of the doll house. I bet she enjoys her work more than you do and complains less. What do you think, Tannenbaum?"

"Doll house?"

"You know what means Joy Division?"

By the look on my face, Izzy could see that I did. What my expression couldn't tell him was how I knew that a Joy Division was a brothel in a concentration camp populated by mostly Jewish women prisoners. I knew only because Klaus had explained to me how the English band by that name chose it. "So, yes, Moses, Shana, the beautiful wife of Tannenbaum the furrier had been turned into a *kurveh*, a whore for the men who were slaughtering us. It took everything I had to not have Hershel do something stupid. Anything he would have done, like hitting Bela over the head with his shovel or lashing out at one of the guards, would have gotten him killed. I

am ashamed to say I wasn't so much frightened for him as for myself. The guards weren't very discriminating when they started killing and there were thousands of men getting off trains day and night who could have easily replaced us."

"What happened?"

"Nothing. Well, not nothing. I saw to Bela in my own way."

I poured more Dewar's in my coffee and gulped. "You killed him?"

Mr. Roth leaned forward and rubbed his forehead. When he looked up, he said, "I couldn't risk him coming to Hershel every few days and instigating him. We would all be dead. So for two days I didn't eat and I planted my bread rations in Bela's bunk and ..."

"You ratted him out as an SS mole to the enforcers in your barracks and the extra rations was your proof he was collaborating."

"As I said, in the camps we did things ... terrible things. The next day the guards found Bela face down in the shit pit with his throat cut. Do you hate me, Mr. Moe? Already I have a son who hates me, but I—"

"I don't hate you, Izzy. I can't imagine what I might do in that place. How can I judge? But please get to the favor."

"After the camp was liberated, I came to America, but Hershel he went first to England, then to Israel, then here, last week he shows up at my door in Florida. We kept in touch. He never married again and never wanted to know what became of Shana. But last year Hershel was told he was dying and wanted to make his peace. It wasn't easy for him, finding anything about her. Those of us who lived through the camps ... we don't like to talk about things what happened in there. And for a woman in one of the brothels, you can only imagine their shame. Hershel and me, we were gravediggers of a kind. But Shana and those women, they gave pleasure to the Nazis."

"They were being raped, Izzy, night after night."

"I know, I know," Mr. Roth was practically shouting. "I understand, but do you understand the torment for them? As deep as the rest of us push those memories away, those women, they hide deeper what they did in the camps."

"If Hershel has found her, what do you need me for?"

"She's in New York somewhere, this is all he is sure of. But how sure can he be, really?" Mr. Roth shrugged. "It was so many years ago. There were hundreds of Shanas, likely many Shana Tannenbaums in the camps and there was such confusion after the war and in the resettlement camps ... Hershel's a sick old man, Moses." Izzy only ever called me that when he was very serious. He took a thick white envelope out of his inside jacket pocket and tossed it onto my desk. "All the information Hershel has gathered is in there. Please, for me, look for her."

"Of course."

"Hershel can pay you."

"We can talk about that later," I said. "Let me do some asking around. And if I find her—"

"Call me," he said. "Hershel is staying at a hotel in the city. You have the number."

When Mr. Roth left, I opened the envelope and read through the documents Hershel Tannenbaum had supplied. I had to give the old man credit. He had done a lot of research. I couldn't imagine the hoops he had to jump through or how long he had to wait to obtain some of these things. The paper trail was pretty convoluted and it included documents in several languages I didn't understand. After Auschwitz was liberated, the trail got very confusing. The Soviets and the resettlement organizations weren't quite as good at record keeping as the Nazis. They were probably too busy trying to keep

people alive long enough to get information from them. And the record of Shana Tannenbaum's journey was filled with years' long gaps and stays in many countries: East then West Germany, Spain, Italy, Argentina, and, most recently, the USA.

There were photocopies of passport stamps, visa applications, and visas. There were blurry, grainy, black and white photos, copies of medical reports. Yet, as I scanned the documents, all I could think about was the horror these women must have endured, knowing that their being raped and abused by the men who were killing their families and neighbors was their only means of survival. I imagined Katy and Sarah being put in that predicament and when I did, I drank more Dewar's, a lot more.

Among all of the documents and grainy pictures, was a photo of Shana Tannenbaum in her wedding dress. I stared at her face for what felt like hours. It was a beautiful face to be sure, a face like the young Lauren Bacall's, but more innocent, I think. Yet as gorgeous as she was, it was her eyes that held my attention. They seemed to reach through time and invite me into her soul. I had never been one to believe in such things. My time as a cop and as a PI had taught me the opposite. Eyes were a liar's greatest asset. There was hope in Shana's eyes, but there was something else, too. A sadness, a sense of what was to come.

I spent a lot of the day making copies and drinking more Dewar's.

I met Larry McDonald at the Hound's Tooth, a cop bar by the Fulton Fish Market. Larry was a captain, working at 1 PP. We had been part of a trio at the Six-O, the Three Stooges: Moe Prager, Larry Mac, and our Curly, Rico Tripoli. Unlike the real Curly, Rico had a head of thick, wavy black hair. I guess we should have been called Moe, Larry, and Wavy. For a few years we were inseparable. But

men, even cops, grow up and apart. Rico, once closer to me than my own brother, had sold himself for a gold shield and had lost me in the process. Larry had one vice, ambition, and was too busy climbing the ladder for friendship to matter. Still, I could count on Larry to do me an occasional solid. Ambitious people know there's no commodity like favors owed. He never knew when I could do him some good and help him get to where he was going. I was never clear on where that was, exactly. I only ever knew it wasn't where he was at that moment.

"For fuck's sake, Moe," he said, hugging me, "you smell like you got a head start."

"Yeah, I had a few Dewar's today."

He gave me a sideways glance. "Things okay between you and Katy?"

"It's not that," I said, waving to the barman.

"Then what?"

I slid copies of Hershel Tannenbaum's documents to Larry and as he had a few Johnnie Walker Reds, I told him the story Mr. Roth had told me.

"She is beautiful," Larry said, staring at the copy of Shana Tannenbaum's wedding photo.

"She's in her mid-seventies, Larry. Relax."

"It's a sad story. I hear lots of sad stories, but what do you want me to do about it? All those Nazis who fucked her are dead and she's probably deader inside than all of them put together. What does this Hershel guy think is going to happen, butterflies are going to lift them both up and they're gonna fly off and be happy together?"

"I don't know what he expects except that he doesn't have long to live. And I'm not doing it for him, anyway."

A smile broke across his handsome face. "You want me to find her. Okay, but ..."

"What can I do for you, Larry?" It was always quid pro quo with him, but at least he wasn't coy about it.

"A case of good champagne, not that cheap American shit."

"Technically, champagne can only come from France, but okay. You have anything in mind?"

"I trust you, Moe. You never screwed me before. I don't think you'll start now."

"One Police Plaza is just the other side of the bridge. You get the info, you hop on the bridge and come over to the Brooklyn store. I'll have a case of really good stuff waiting."

Larry sucked down his last drink and kissed me on the forehead. "I miss the old days, Moe. The three of us against the whole fucking world."

"I miss them, too, whether the world was against us or not."

"I'll get you what you need. No sweat."

And he was gone.

I got the call three days later that Larry Mac would be headed over that afternoon and to have his champagne waiting. I'd already prepared a case with some Dom Pérignon —as he would expect— and two other vintages he'd have no clue about: Veuve Cliquot Grande Dame and Krug Grande Cuvée. Aaron would have shot me for bartering these wines for information, but broken bottles were just the cost of doing business. And as far as my big brother would know, the bottles going into Larry's cellar would be shown in the quarterly inventory as breakage.

The case was up front by the register and when Larry Mac came to collect, Klaus directed him down to my office.

"What's with the guy upstairs?" Larry asked, sitting himself in the chair Mr. Roth had sat in a few days earlier.

"He's gay. What about it?"

Larry clapped his hands and laughed at me. "What the fuck do I care if he's queer? I was talking about his outfit, you schmuck. He looks like an escapee from CBGB."

"I don't think he's escaped yet," I said. "So, you got the info for me?"

The smile on Larry's face disappeared and it was replaced with a wary expression.

"What's with the face?"

He handed me the documents I had given him at the Hound's Tooth and a folded sheet of paper. "It's all there."

"The face, Larry. What's up?"

"The next day, after we met at the bar, I got caught up with a big case, so I couldn't get the info for you right away."

I shrugged. "So what?"

"Moe, it took me about five minutes to find this woman. Maybe less. I mean, she's not in the phone book, but it's not like I had to dig very hard."

"The point being ..."

Larry shook his head at me. "C'mon, Prager, I thought Jews were supposed to be smarter than the rest of us."

"Only smarter than you, Larry."

"Not this time, asshole. I read through all those documents you gave me. Doesn't it strike you odd that this Hershel guy traced his wife all over the fucking world to how many countries over the course of like forty plus years and then suddenly here he can't find her?"

I hated when Larry was right, but he was right. I had been so caught up in Mr. Roth's tale and so lost in Shana Tannenbaum's eyes

that I had ignored my own common sense. I admitted he had a point, shook his hand, and sent him back upstairs to collect his champagne.

When he got to the office door, he turned back around to me, "Watch your ass, Moe. Something's not kosher, boyo."

When I was sure Larry was gone, I went upstairs and told Klaus I was going to take a long lunch.

"How long, Boss?"

"As long as it takes."

I sat in my car at the corner of Diamond Street and Norman Avenue in Greenpoint and watched the comings and goings from the dive bar across the street. According to Larry Mac's information, Shana Tannenbaum lived in an apartment over the bar. I wasn't sure what I was looking for, exactly, or why I was there at all. But I had known Larry McDonald a long time and he was a hell of a cop, ambition notwithstanding. If he said something wasn't right, something wasn't right. I'd be damned if I knew what or why.

It was kind of strange that Shana Tannenbaum had chosen to live out her last years in Greenpoint, an almost exclusively Polish neighborhood across the East River from Manhattan. Even the signs on the stores were in Polish. And given that Auschwitz was in Poland, I would have thought Shana would have wanted to live in a more Jewish neighborhood, like Brighton Beach or Midwood. But when I thought about it some more, I guess there was an odd kind of logic in it. Here in Greenpoint, there was less of a chance for her to run into other survivors, especially other survivors who might remember her from the old country or remember how she had managed to survive. Here she would be just another old woman pulling her wire shopping cart to the laundromat or from the supermarket.

I'd been there for about forty minutes when I saw a door open across the street. Out of the door came a bent old woman with a cane. Was it Shana Tannenbaum? She seemed about the correct age and if the bend was taken out of her spine, she would have been the right size. The hair sticking out from beneath her babushka was steel gray, so that was no help. I was too far away to get a perfect view, but I was close enough to see she wore thick glasses and that the left side of her face sagged. A stroke victim. Was this the most beautiful woman in Mr. Roth's town? Was this the woman in the wedding gown, the woman with the haunting eyes? She turned left and limped down Norman Avenue toward McGuinness Boulevard. I got out of my car and followed.

Fifteen minutes later, the woman I thought might be Shana Tannenbaum went into a Polish restaurant on Manhattan Avenue. I watched through a side window as she sat alone at a red vinyl booth. She didn't look at the menu and ordered before the waitress could walk away. And within a few minutes, the waitress brought the woman a bowl of soup and crackers. I felt like an idiot standing out there in the cold and slush, staring at an old woman breaking crackers into her soup. I went into the restaurant. Even if the woman turned out not to be Shana, I felt like having soup myself.

I sat far enough away from her so that she wouldn't notice me and ordered a bowl of mushroom barley. I needn't have worried. Shana Tannenbaum was too preoccupied with her soup, because eating it was a labor for her. From where I sat, the droop in her face was very evident and some of every spoonful she put in her mouth leaked back out. Between the glasses, the babushka she hadn't removed, and the sag in her face, it was impossible for me to know if this was her. I ate slowly and waited until she was done with her soup before I approached.

"Excuse me," I said softly, walking up to her table. "Are you Shana Tannenbaum?"

She looked up from her nearly empty bowl, took off her glasses, and stared up at me. I knew immediately she was not Shana, at least not the Shana Tannenbaum I was looking for.

"Yeth," she answered in that lispy, nasally voice that stroke victims sometimes have.

I think she knew I knew she was lying. She gestured for me to sit. Then she pushed up the sleeve of her ratty green sweater and showed me the number tattooed on her forearm. She did it without much enthusiasm, as if she understood it would take more than that to convince me.

I nodded. "You were in the camps, but you're not her."

"How do you know?" she asked, speaking slowly that I might understand her.

"Your eyes."

I took the wedding gown photo of the young Shana out of my coat pocket and handed it to her.

Tears streamed down her wrinkled cheeks.

"She was the most beautiful woman I had ever met and she had such eyes. Mine are blue, but nothing like hers."

"Who are you?"

"Since the day the Russians came, I have been Shana. Before that I was Emilka Stanislawa of Krakow, a patriot who fought the Nazis. But when they captured me, they executed my family and sent me to the camp. That was where I met Shana."

"In the—"

She reached her frail hand across the table and put her fingers across my lips. She shook her head. "Please, no, don't say these words."

"Shana is dead?"

Now Emilka was crying much as Mr. Roth had cried in front of me the other day. I could feel the waitress watching us, but I didn't much care.

"After a few months, she cut her own throat in the bath. When the Russians set us free, I couldn't go back home. I had no family to go home to and if word ever got out what I did in the camp ..."

"So you became Shana Tannenbaum."

"It was easy for me to get the Russians to do what I asked. I was used to letting men do as they wished. Only with the Russians I could at least ask for something in return."

I ordered us some tea. As we sipped it—tea was an even bigger struggle for her than the soup—Emilka told me the rest of her story. Then, finally, she asked me what I was doing there. When I opened my mouth to answer, I saw her eyes get big. Panicked even. She was looking over my left shoulder. I turned to see an elderly man, a hunched skeleton with ashen skin barely disguising his skull. He wore a hugely oversized blue cashmere coat with a mink collar. Hershel Tannenbaum. He held a .38 in the shaking bones of his right hand. It was pointed at Emilka.

Then I saw in his eyes, what Emilka must have seen in mine earlier. Hershel Tannenbaum realized this woman was not his wife. I stood up and put myself directly in front of Emilka.

"Mr. Tannenbaum, Shana is—"

But before I could finish the sentence, he pressed the muzzle of the .38 under his chin and squeezed the trigger.

Mr. Roth, Emilka Stanislawa, the rent-a-rabbi, and I were the only people at the cemetery when they planted Hershel Tannenbaum in the earth. I couldn't get it out of my head that this man had tracked down the woman he thought was his wife just so he might kill her.

And for what? Because he thought the things he imagined she had done to survive were somehow less worthy than the things he had done?

"I don't understand it either, Mr. Moe," Izzy said to me after we had dropped Emilka back at her Greenpoint apartment, so she could go back to being Shana Tannenbaum. "He was so sick. That's why he needed you at the end. He had nothing left in him but anger."

"It was enough for him to follow me around."

"Who knows what went on in his head all these years?"

"He was going to kill her because he was ashamed. Madness."

"They broke us in that place, Moses. They broke us. They broke our families, our bodies, and our hearts. Some more than others."

The next day I drove him to the airport. I got back to Bordeaux in Brooklyn at about 2:00 that afternoon. Klaus was dressed all in black. His breakup color. Joy Division's "Love Will Tear Us apart" was playing on the store sound system.

"Klaus."

"What is it, Boss?"

"I don't ever want to hear this song again."

Requiem for Spider

First published in an online anthology years ago.

Her heart was lonelier than Sergeant Pepper's and the whole fucking band. I could see that from across the bar, not that across the bar was like seeing across space and time. It was more like twenty feet and, at that time of night, the view was relatively unobstructed. She had last call girl written all over her. Don't misunderstand, she wasn't a call girl. She wasn't even much of a girl anymore. Thirty, at least, she hadn't fit that description for quite some time. What I mean to say is that she was the kind of woman who probably had more than her share of men, but only because she understood that desperation was her ally. She was that pair of shoes on the discount rack you bought because you needed shoes and you only had so much money and the store was closing.

When the bartender screamed "Last call for alcohol," it was her mating song. She was a last call girl.

I watched her quarry approach, lean into her, buy her a drink; watched them leave, him on unsteady legs, her propping him up. I imagined the sting she would feel tomorrow morning when she saw that look in his eyes, when he was no longer too-full of drink and desperation, no longer in need of that last pair of shoes, when dashed hopes would again break her lonely heart. But as fascinating as she was, she wasn't why I was here.

I was here because I was bored. It was that simple. I couldn't stand another minute as a shopkeeper, selling wines to nouveau riche assholes who understood even less about quality than I understood about the role of subatomic particles in the structure of the universe. What they thought they understood was the implication of price, which meant they understood very little about substance or value. Well, fuck, when your president is an ex-actor— and not a very good one—and the world of high finance turns on junk bonds and hostile takeovers, value and substance don't count for much, do they? I was here because I'd taken the kind of gig I vowed never to take when I got my investigator's license. I was here to watch Spider's back and this particular spider lacked the evolutionary adaption of rear-facing eyes to do the job himself.

Having grown up around the corner from one another, Spider and I had been friends for as long as I could remember. Dick Thomas got the handle Spider because he was a gangly bastard as a kid, all arms and legs, each limb seemingly with a mind of its own. He wore thick glasses and dressed like an unmade bed, but he stuck out for all sorts of reasons in the old neighborhood. In a place where you were either Jewish or Italian, a place where Jews could recite the Hail Mary and the Catholic kids ate bagels and lox, being a Wasp marked you as a freak. We had no clue what Protestants did or what

they were about. Another thing about Spider was that he always had a book in his hand. Always. He once told me he had visited worlds the rest of us couldn't even imagine. I suppose he told me because he thought I was smart enough to understand or maybe it was because I was the one kid in the neighborhood who, even then, had his back.

If our senior class at Lincoln had voted on the least likely among us to become a gangster, Spider Thomas would've won in a landslide. Yeah, but you can't pay attention to that kind of shit. Spider sure as hell didn't. He graduated from Baruch College with a degree in accounting and promptly set about building an empire. He ran underground gambling parlors all over the five boroughs of New York City, a few in Yonkers, and one or two on Long Island. He made sure not to step on anyone's toes; gladly, even eagerly sharing as much as fifty percent of the profits with either the local Mob families that controlled the territories his clubs were in or with the gangs that ran the remaining territories. They were thrilled to get the cash without taking any of the risk. Because of Spider's largesse, his de facto partners provided protection against robbery and police raids.

"Moe," he once told me, "when you spend your whole childhood trying to not get the shit beat out of you, you get good at figuring out effective survival strategies. After the first time I got held up for my lunch money, I started keeping half the money hidden in my sock. It kept everybody satisfied. I've never forgotten that lesson."

Spider was happy to take his percentage of profits from the clubs and invest them in a wide range of legitimate businesses. Though the corporate structures were thickly layered to hide his interests, Spider Thomas now owned small pieces of two off-shore banks, car dealerships, fast food restaurants, a string of convenience

stores, gas stations, and a chain of laundromats. Laundromats, I liked the irony in that. Spider had turned his legitimate businesses into a money laundering juggernaut. That's what this meeting was about. The Russian mob was known for controlling its own money laundering, but a group of young up-and-comers from Brighton Beach were considering farming out a sizeable chunk of their laundering operations. They weren't of the generation that had spent hard time in Soviet prisons and they weren't particularly interested in American prisons either. They wanted to spread the risk around. That was always Spider's foot in the door, his understanding of risk versus reward.

"You ever play golf, Moe?" Spider asked me a couple of years ago.

"Not much. Why?"

"It's my favorite sport."

Spider was the most unathletic person I'd ever known and I couldn't picture him driving a golf ball more than fifty yards using a Howitzer. "You play?" I asked, trying not to sound completely incredulous.

He laughed. "No, but I love it. Every decision a golfer makes is a calculation of risk versus reward."

I once had a client who compared golf to chess. In his opinion it was the ultimate thinking man's game. I didn't know what it was about golf, but people seemed to see all kinds of deeper truths in it that were lost on me. Maybe I'd take it up someday. Yeah, right after cliff diving and lion hunting with knives.

McGee's Tavern on 7th Avenue in Park Slope had once been an old school Irish pub but was now a bastion of Yuppie-ness. The bar menu featured things like grilled figs and goat cheese on focaccia crisps, and the bar itself offered twenty brands of single malt scotch at prices that would curl your nose hairs. Park Slope was

where people who weren't from Brooklyn lived in Brooklyn
precisely so they might remain apart from the hordes of the great
unwashed. Native Brooklynites like Spider and me and transplants
like the Russians detested Park Slope. The Russians hated it because
it wasn't Brighton Beach and, in this neck of the woods, they stuck
out like circus clowns at a funeral mass. Because both parties
despised the neighborhood, McGee's was deemed a perfect place for
the meet—Brooklyn logic. In spite of McGee's unfortunate turn to
fusion cooking and pricey scotch, the owner was amenable to
renting out his backroom after closing time. He didn't give a shit
about who was renting it or why. For him it was simply a matter of
when the room was needed and how much you were willing to pay
for the privilege of its use.

The idea was that there was to be no muscle at the powwow.
Each party was allowed to bring an unarmed and unaffiliated
second as sort of security blanket. That's where I came in. I was
definitely unaffiliated and, for the only time since I got on the job in
the late '60s, unarmed. I didn't like it, but those were the rules. In a
nod to paradox, the seconds were to arrive first and neither was to
participate in the meeting itself. I suppose that made sense. When
your goal is to discuss the process of turning huge sums of dirty
money into piles of nice clean cash, you don't want any witnesses to
the proceedings. The meeting alone amounted to a criminal
conspiracy under the RICO Act and could earn each party a long bid
in a federal penitentiary.

Neither of the principals had yet arrived, but I'd spotted my
opposite number the moment I walked into the joint. It would have
been tough not to. He was ugly as a rotten peach and big in a very
unflattering way. Fat? He wasn't fat exactly. He was what my mom
used to call husky or chubby, not terms you heard much anymore.
Not very ego affirming and definitely bad for self-esteem. Worse for

his self-esteem was his outfit. In a crimson, double-knit leisure suit, he was about as inconspicuous as a steamed lobster at a white sale. He was fifty if a day and what little hair he had was gray and unkempt. Still, I knew better than to judge him as no threat. Just because he was supposed to be unarmed didn't mean he was and I'd had the piss kicked out of me by some pretty rough motherfuckers who looked like they'd go down in a stiff breeze. I wasn't sure he'd made me right away, but since we were the only two guys left at the bar and the stickman was busy restocking the beer cooler, my guess was he'd figured it out.

I raised my glass of Dewar's to him as a gesture of kinship. He kind of snarled his lip and grunted. He was no threat to Billy Idol, believe me. I shrugged my shoulders, went back to sipping my drink and gnawing on bar mix until the Spider and his potential business partner arrived.

When Spider first approached me about the job, I asked him why he wanted me there.

"You're a Russian Jew. They're Russian Jews," he said as if that explained it all.

"It's not that simple, Spider. It's not like the Masons. We don't have a secret handshake. They're not Russian Jews like I am. First off, I'm a Ukrainian Jew. There's a big difference. When my family lived over there, my *zadeh's* two biggest worries were the foot pedal on his sewing machine breaking and the Cossacks raiding the shtetl. These guys ... that's not how they were raised. Their parents and grandparents were suckled on Stalin and the State. These guys are rough characters."

But it was as if he hadn't heard me. "Shtetl, I like that word."

"Spider, listen—"

"I heard you, don't worry. But they're Jews," he said. "I've grown up with you, surrounded by Jews my whole life."

"Oy, Spider," I said. "These guys aren't Jews the way you know Jews. They pretty much grew up godless, without religion like you know it. I may be as lapsed a Jew as there is, but I'm the chief rabbi of Jerusalem compared to them."

"Moe, the bottom line is I trust you to have my back. You always have, even when it cost you. That's why I want you here."

Argue that.

The Russian arrived first. I'd been told his name was Yuri, not that I believed it was his real name. Whatever his name, he was rather more elegant than his second. Then again, that wasn't saying a whole lot. I'd seen dancing bears who were more elegant than my opposite number. This guy, Spider's counterpart, was in a different league. His gray, chalk-striped suit was Italian with a thread count in the millions and his alligator shoes, also Italian, cost more than the bartender was going to make this week, next week, and the one after that. His shirt was custom made. His yellow power tie was Hermès all the way from Paris and his watch was handmade in the Alps. I wondered if it yodeled every hour on the half hour. He had piano fingers with manicured nails and slicked-back black hair like Pat Riley, but I wasn't dumb enough to think America had softened him up. He had nice white teeth, but a hard mouth and a cold expression that nearly frosted my glass.

"I am Yuri," he said to me. He gave his vicuña topcoat to Dancing Bear, ignoring the man completely.

"I'm Moe." I nodded, not offering my hand. Yuri didn't strike me as a handshaker. "You don't mind if I take a look at your topcoat, do you?"

Yuri smiled, though it didn't exactly thaw my glass. "Very thorough. This reflects well on Spider," he said. "Sergei, give the coat to Mr. Moe."

Sergei. So, Dancing Bear had a name. He handed me the coat. It was lovely and I treated it with respect. It contained no weapon that I could find and I handed it back to Sergei.

"It's clean," I said.

"So, Mr. Moe, to be equitable, would you mind if Sergei were to … what is the phrase?" Yuri pretended not to know. I believed that about as much as I believed his name was Yuri.

"Frisk me. Pat me down."

"Yes, exactly that."

I raised my arms up to shoulder height and spread my legs wide so that Dancing Bear might have full access to the goods. Sergei was even uglier close up and he didn't smell much better than he looked. He didn't seem like much, but, as I suspected, Sergei was a nasty piece of work. I could tell he'd done this a thousand times before. His hands were practiced and strong. I wouldn't have been surprised to find out he'd been a cop somewhere along the way.

"Is not with weapon," he said with a snort, turning to his boss. There was little doubt in my mind that Sergei was simply a flunky and on the regular payroll. I didn't say it aloud, but I thought the choice of a stooge reflected badly on Yuri's judgment. Having a guy's back sometimes meant more than being a tough guy and if Yuri's needs stretched much beyond patting people down, he was shit out of luck with Dancing Bear.

When they were done with me, it was my turn to frisk both of the Russians. Christ, there hadn't been this much feeling up in Brooklyn since Candy DiNardo's parents went on a cruise and she invited everyone in the sophomore class at Lincoln to her house for a make-out party in her basement. That was the night I got my hand under Susan Maestro's bra and touched a hardened nipple for the first time. Man, that was a feeling I would never forget.

"Why you smile like idiot?" Sergei asked.

I was awfully tempted to say something about mirrors and Sergei's familiarity with smiling idiots, but I kept it to myself. "Just thinking about a girl from a long time ago."

"Ah, a sad romantic," said Yuri. "You are Russian?"

"Ukrainian Jew. My people were from outside Kiev."

"Me too, from the Ukraine. Odessa," he said.

"The Black Sea, huh?"

Yuri flashed that smile again, warmer still this time.

"How about Sergei?" I asked. "Odessa too?"

"No. Is Russian born in Chechnya. Strong like bull. Dumb like ox. Loyal like dog."

"Ex-cop?"

"Very good, Mr. Moe. Yes, Sergei was cop in Grozny, but he was greedy. He got caught selling weapons to the Muslims." Yuri wagged his tapered index finger. "Very bad offense. The Muslims will rise up when Soviet Union crumbles. Lucky for him, he saved my brother's life in gulag."

"Loyalty works both ways."

"To a point, yes." Yuri looked at his Swiss watch. "Spider is not late, but ..."

"No," I said, looking at my own. "He will be here exactly on time. It's Spider's way."

As I said it, I realized I had once again underestimated Spider. That I was here as much to put Yuri at ease as I was to act as a second or to provide security. My guess was that Spider knew all along about Yuri being Ukrainian and that once we got talking, Yuri would find out about my heritage. I was meant to be a kind of calling card for Spider, a preview of how he did business. My being here would show his potential partner how thoughtful and rational Spider was, that he considered his choices and acted wisely and in everyone's best interests. My being here would prove more about

Spider's worth than any sales pitch. When he finally walked in, Spider's job would already have been half finished. He would just need to close the deal.

Then there was a sharp rap at the glass door of McGee's and the four of us—the barman, Yuri, Sergei, and me—turned to look. And fuck me if it wasn't the last call girl.

"Let me in," she said, her desperate voice muted by the glass. "Let me in, I forgot my bag. Let me in, please." She kept rapping on the glass with the underside of a thick ring. "I've got my house keys in there. Let me in."

The barman dipped under the service bar and moved to the door. The keys were in the lock, but he turned back to us for a thumbs up or thumbs down.

"Tell the bitch, no." Sergei said. "Go 'way!" He waved at her and shouted.

That did it. She started crying those lonely heart tears and the pounding on the door got louder and more frantic.

"Let her come," Yuri said. "Let her come."

Even as the bartender turned the key, I got that sick feeling in my belly. I didn't know what it was about, but I knew something was wrong. As he pulled the door back to let her in, I went over in my head everything that had happened since I walked into McGee's. The barman dipped back under the service bar. He reached down and came up with a too-large black leather bag. Fuck! That was it, I thought. She didn't have a bag.

"Run," I screamed, as I dove behind a table. "Run!"

But it was way too late for that. The last call girl had already stuck her hand in the bag and come out with a .40 Beretta. Sergei went first, his white shirt dyed red with his own blood to match his crimson leisure suit. Her second shot caught him flush in the face and the back of the rotten peach exploded. Dancing Bear would

dance no more. Then it was Yuri's turn. He too had taken cover behind a table, but with the hollow point ammo she was using, he might as well have hidden behind a wall of papier-mâché. I didn't so much see Yuri go down as I heard it. The last call girl calmly walked over to where he'd fallen, took aim and redecorated McGee's plank flooring with Yuri's viscera.

I peeked over my useless cover to watch her turn the Beretta on her accomplice and blow the barman away. She wouldn't need to waste a second bullet on him. I heard her heels clickety-clack on the floor as she strolled toward me. Funny, I didn't think about my wife Katy or Sarah my daughter. I didn't think about much of anything except Susan Maestro's right nipple hardening to the clumsy touch of my fingers. Not sure if I was breathing, I closed my eyes and waited.

"Better get out of here, Moe, and take this," said the last call girl, pushing an envelope into my right hand. "The cops will be on scene in less than two minutes and my employer won't approve of them finding you still here."

I didn't have to be told twice. I was smart that way.

Ten blocks away, I could still hear the sirens. It sounded like half of the precincts in Brooklyn responded to the call. I pulled to the curb under a street lamp and opened the envelope. There were ten crisp thousand-dollar bills folded into a sheet of lined paper. All the note said was this:

Just golf, Moe—risk versus reward. Hope the money is thanks enough.

Don't worry, you're safe.

I drove to the nearest Catholic church I could find and put the cash, all of it, into the collection box. In spite of his talent for laundering money, Spider wouldn't've been able to get the blood stains off those bills with all the chemicals in the world. He was right

about me being safe, though for months afterwards I paid an awful lot of attention to people walking up behind me on the street. It was silly really. I'd been around long enough to know that if it was coming my way, I would never see it coming.

I never saw Spider again, not alive, anyway. About a year after the thing at McGee's, they found pieces of him in plastic garbage bags in Sheepshead Bay, the Gowanus Canal, and the lake in Prospect Park. Some parts they didn't find at all. Now Humpty Dumpty had someone to keep him company. I went to the funeral but hung back. I wasn't in a reunion with his family type of mood. A man came and sat down in the same pew as me, a few feet to my left. He was very well dressed and appointed and there was something vaguely familiar about him. After a while, I couldn't help but sneak glances at his profile. His face was like a word on the tip of my tongue. I knew it, but I couldn't quite place him. Then he turned to me and spoke in a thick Russian accent.

"You knew this Spider?"

"I did," I said, placing the face. This man looked like an older, rougher version of Yuri. His brother, I thought: the one from the gulag. "Did you know him?" I asked, trying not to lose my breakfast there in church.

He smiled a frostier smile at me than his brother had managed. "Yes, we had business together." He spit on the floor and twice brushed his palms across one another in. "Now business is done."

He stood and left without looking back. I followed his lead and didn't look back.

With Peter Spiegelman

Magic Bullet

By
Reed Farrel Coleman and Peter Spiegelman

May 2001

Darla Vernecki, of Faroe, Texas, had camped out across Sunset Boulevard from the Snake Pit every night of her vacation, video camera in hand, and liter bottle of Mountain Dew at her feet. And the Snake Pit hadn't failed her. Across the river of shiny cars, she'd seen Chili Travers, gliding past the velvet rope with three tall blonds on his arm, Paige Tenbrook in a cloud of cigarette smoke and hand-in-hand with Mary-Kate Passeral, and Vince Lester, in a ragged tee shirt and dark glasses, talking to a black man with big gold teeth.

Darla knew those faces well—Us Weekly, People Magazine and Entertainment Tonight had made them more familiar than her momma's—and she knew their stories too. Chili's coke problems,

Paige's bulimia, Vince's violent romances—they were like scripture
to her, and every second of those limber, nonchalant bodies that she
fixed on tape was a splinter of the true cross—a communion with
something better than herself—something thinner, prettier and
vastly more important. Something she could show her daddy at the
VA when she visited on Sundays, and show the girls at Wal-Mart
when they smirked about how much money she'd spent on her trip.

Chili, Paige, and the rest had made it a good vacation for
Darla—good, but not perfect. Perfect would be Tori. And perfect,
Darla knew, was coming. Rumors had been percolating through the
fans outside The Snake Pit since sundown, and they bubbled more
wildly when the UPN advance men showed up. There was shoving
and bumping, and Darla raised sharp elbows to protect her turf. She
wanted a good shot when Tori appeared, and no one was going to
get in her way. As it happened, no one did.

There were other cameras in the crowd that warm May night,
and footage with clearer views than Darla's, but no one there loved
Tori Sheridan more than she did, and no one kept a tighter focus on
that bland, lovely face. No one else caught Tori's annoyance at the
approaching sirens, or her startled irritation when the man ran by.
And no one else captured that final instant of distilled disbelief—the
fleeting, big-eyed surprise and overwhelming what-the-fuckness
when the bullet hit.

With every stride, the stitch in Jack Voigt's side felt more and more
like someone whacking his ribs with a nine iron. Each breath seared
his lungs, and the more he gasped the less good it did. He'd given
up shouting "Police!" at Willie Moonves' back two blocks ago. He
couldn't spare the air, and Willie wasn't listening.

Already a two-time loser, Willie was the prime suspect in
seven home invasions, three rapes, a carjacking, and the fatal

shooting of a liquor store clerk too slow to open the till. Even with the slickest of lawyers and the second coming of the Simpson jury, Willie had a date with the spike, and while he was bad crazy, Willie wasn't stupid. He knew the score and he wasn't stopping for Jack Voigt, or God, or anyone.

"This place is way beyond over," Tori Sheridan yelled over the noise. Her publicist smiled back stupidly and nodded like a bobblehead. Tori frowned. The VIP Lounge smelled like the bathroom, only not as good, the sofas were sticky, they didn't serve her brand of vodka, and the music sucked. God, who listened to this trip hop crap anymore?

How long since she'd last been to The Snake Pit? A month? Longer? She winced when she thought of all the time she used to spend here and cringed when she recalled that very first time. It was three years ago, the night of the day she'd gotten off the bus from Pekin, Illinois, and she'd stood across Sunset with the rest of the geeks, gawking and fantasizing about what went on behind the black glass doors. The reality, she discovered on later visits, was as glamorous as a box of macaroni and cheese. Tori shook off the memory and reminded herself that tonight was work.

The producers of her show had decided that her twenty-first birthday was the perfect occasion for a coming out party. UPN had announced last week that Tori and Philippe Moya would be starring in Oyster Bay Cove, a new series spun off from the hit teen soap Turtle Bay South, and tonight Philippe would be making a surprise stop at the Pit to give his co-star a birthday present. Of course, his appearance was a surprise only in the Hollywood sense — with paparazzi and camera crews lining the sidewalk, and a squad of PR flacks orchestrating the action. Tori looked at her watch and sighed.

"How much longer? I'm legal and I want to get fucked and fucked up—and neither one is happening here."

"Any minute now," the publicist shouted above the din. "Any minute."

There were sirens in the distance—backup—but Voigt knew they were too far away. The Glock was getting heavy in his hand, and he was getting too old for this shit.

Only once before had Jack drawn his weapon in anger. It was in '92, during the Rodney King riots, though it'd had nothing to do with the riots themselves. He was 36 hours into his shift, and he'd walked into a 7-Eleven for a Snickers and a Coke. He'd walked out again with a separated shoulder and two cracked ribs—pained for sure, but better off than the three *chulos* who exited in bags. He was in uniform back then and knew that that kind of thing was always a possibility. But he'd been a detective for years now, and this—well, this was crap.

Robbery-Homicide detectives didn't sprint through the streets of Hollywood with weapons drawn, panting like hyenas. They didn't skin their palms scaling fences, or shred their khakis coming down again; they didn't bark their shins on fucking dumpsters either. Robbery-Homicide detectives were supposed to think deep thoughts, drink lots of coffee, and kick ass only when the mood took them.

"Shit," he wheezed, as Willie banged a left onto Sunset.

Philippe Moya rolled a perfectly restored, British racing green, 1972 Jaguar XKE convertible to the curb in front of The Snake Pit. Turtle Bay South's producers had decided the Jag would make a fine birthday gift for their newest star, and even better publicity for their new show. And if the press wanted to believe that the car was

actually from Moya, and that there was maybe something going on between the two prettiest under-25 stars in Hollywood that week, then that was best of all. Moya's publicist called her counterpart inside the club and told her to bring Tori out.

"About fucking time," Tori growled, and pushed her publicist less than gently toward the exit. "You won't catch me dead in this shithole again."

Tori Sheridan's handler held open the black glass door.

Sunset was more or less level here, and it gave Voigt a chance to catch his breath. As far as he could tell, that was the only upside to Moonves' choice of escape routes. On a warm Friday night, the boulevard was thick with cars and people—a nightmare obstacle course for chasing a sociopath with a big gun and nothing left to lose. Ahead, Jack saw that the crowds were working against Willie. He was bobbing and weaving through the slow-motion bodies, sometimes stepping off the sidewalk to run in the street. Still, the gap was closing. The sirens were louder now. Jack managed a sprint, and saw car lights glinting on the barrel of Willie's Sig.

Across the street, behind her camera, Darla Vernecki nearly swooned. "Lord Jesus on a stick, that's Philippe Moya in that car! And—oh my god oh my god oh my god—there she is—there's Tori! Oh lord, no one back home's gonna believe it."

Flashes fired around her and all through the crowd by The Snake Pit's door. The racket of shouted questions made her think of startled crows. Darla herself had no questions to shout—just a simple mantra she whispered to herself as she squinted in her camera.

"Over here, Tori. I'm over here."

The sirens were closer, and closing in. Voigt had gained a lot of ground on Willie, and Willie was getting crazy—crazier. He'd given up the bob and weave in favor of a lowered shoulder into whoever was in his path, and he'd take to flashing his Sig and screaming, "Get the fuck out the way!" It was effective, Voigt conceded, but he saw a clot of people up ahead of Willie, blocking the sidewalk and spilling into the street. There were lights flashing in the crowd, and jostling, and the people in the pack were paying no attention to the freight train bearing down. Voigt pumped harder and searched desperately for an extra breath.

Tori Sheridan stepped through the door onto Sunset and stepped into a maelstrom. Cameras flashed like sheet lightning, and a roar of voices followed.

"Happy birthday, Tori!"

"How's it feel to be legal?"

"How're you going to celebrate, Tori?"

"Tori, this way!"

"Tori, turn right."

"Now left, Tori—no, the other left."

"Thanks, Tori—one more."

"And again."

"Now with Philippe, Tori."

"How long've you two been dating?"

"Do you like the new ride?"

"Green's your favorite color, right?"

"Tori, we love you."

"We love you, Tori."

"Hold her hand, Phil."

"Tori ..."

Then the sirens grew louder and the questions stopped and there was another shout. And then worlds collided.

"Police!" Jack Voigt called, and Willie Moonves dropped his head and drove past Tori, straight into the wall of photographers. Cameras flashed and several flew in the air, and bodies fell like dominoes. Screams rose through the crowd. Somewhere a car alarm sounded.

Moonves was down, atop three squirming paparazzi and facing a panicked, scrambling mass that was going nowhere. He levered himself up and wheeled, looking for some daylight, and there—right in front of him—was that fucking jackrabbit cop. Moonves smiled, and raised up the Sig.

Voigt saw Willie and the flashes and heard the bangs all at once. Something shoved him hard in the left shoulder and spun him around. The burn came next, spreading to his neck and down his left arm. He squinted at Moonves—hazy now—and slowly squeezed the trigger. He was careful—just enough pressure for a single shot—and as the Glock kicked up, he felt his knees go soft. Gun smoke was in the air, changing colors under the neon and the strobing cruiser lights, and Voigt heard a shell case ping on the pavement.

The nine-millimeter slug drilled through Willie's sternum, tore across his chest cavity, and buried itself in his shoulder blade. The impact stood him straight for a moment, pushing him half-a-turn to face Tori Sheridan. His eyes opened wide, and in the instant before he fell stone dead, Willie took in the blond hair and blue eyes, the wide mouth and high, firm breasts. He thought for sure he knew her from someplace. Maybe on TV.

Jack Voigt went down at nearly the same instant, the pain in his shoulder blinding, and his head curiously light. He fell fast—like

a puppet without strings—and his gun hand hit the sidewalk hard. There was a bang and a final flash.

Darla had to tell herself to breathe. It was a lot of work, and she had to sit on the curb with her head between her legs to do it. Behind her, through the ringing in her ears, she heard an old woman's voice.

"Harry, what was that noise?"

"Gunshots," Darla heard herself say.

"What? Harry, what did she say?"

"Gunshots. She said gunshots."

"Gunshots?"

It took a cadre of expensive audio engineers from Palo Alto to isolate the sounds of the ricochets from the eleven different video tapes the police collected from the crowd outside The Snake Pit, and an entirely different and even more expensive slew of experts to construct a computer model of the path of the second bullet fired from the Glock.

The model, created from the filtered soundtrack and elements of all eleven videos, showed the bullet as a bright red dot, skipping on the pavement, glancing off the curved hood of the Jaguar, skidding on the mast of a streetlamp, and veering sharply to the right. The little bullet-that-could ended its journey by punching a tiny hole in Tori Sheridan's right cheek, just below the eye, and chewing a jagged tunnel halfway through her brain.

Tori's head snapped back, and she staggered into the black glass doors. The rebound sent her forward again, twisting, onto a pile of paparazzi still tangled on the sidewalk after Willie's crazy charge. Dario Ricks was at the top of the heap and Tori landed in his ample

lap, her face deep in his crotch. Her skirt, caught by a fateful breeze, lifted as she tumbled, to reveal a black La Perla thong and a perfectly smooth, perfectly tanned ass. Every photographer who still held a camera clicked away wildly, and the sky above The Snake Pit was again full of lightning.

Breath came back to Darla in a horrible rush, and she thought her chest would burst. She gulped and gasped, tears streaming down her face. She squeezed her eyes shut and rubbed the heels of her palms against them, but it did no good—those images were seared there, tattooed, as if she'd been staring into the sun. She gulped again, and the Mountain Dew came up in her throat.

When she was empty, Darla stood and wiped her mouth and staggered into the street. She headed toward the doors of The Snake Pit, but a uniformed cop stopped her before she was halfway across Sunset. He pointed back at the spot where she'd stood for five evenings in a row, and at her camera, lying in the gutter and still recording.

Poems

Talking with John Koethe

Hallie Ephron was talking about a glass of milk in a
Hitchcock movie,
a lightbulb glowing inside it.
We're in Wisconsin, so milk is the right answer—
lightbulb or not.
Then I am at a table, signing books, and there's
John Koethe standing tall in front of me.
John is a famous poet
who knew me once when I was not so much
my own self, but more my big brother's brother.
John's presence abrades three decades.
I am twenty again and living absurdly in
Milwaukee.
I am not the mystery writer now.
The memory of my escape from Brooklyn
into Linda's cold, unwelcoming womb is as
present as John or the books (I have yet to write)
on the table.
I am lost again

with a puff of red hair on my bald head and
no gray in my beard.
I am my brother's envious shadow:
Not as smart, not as handsome, not him.
Jules and I go to a burger joint
where they put sticks of butter and oceans of
salt
on the burgers.
The women who fry them are as fat as the butter,
wear white nurses' outfits,
hideous elastic stockings like sausage casings
hold in their legs.
We both miss Brooklyn,
but there is no going back for
Jules.
Going back is all there is and will ever be for
me.

John Koethe is standing in front of me.
We are old men now — gray and unsurprised.
We talk about our children.
I am both fifty-five and twenty in Milwaukee,
I always liked John for himself, not because
Jules liked him.
Jules is a philosopher like John.
John is a poet like me or
me like him,
but like with Jules,
I am not as good as John.
What I remember most about
when John knew me once was

that he slurped his coffee and that he
loved Lou Reed.
We are old men, talking of children,
gray and unsurprised.
Hallie Ephron was speaking of milk.

Slider, part 7

He remembered.
First in the woods outside Kiev,
The bodies-in-waiting, kneeling at the edge of the trench.
Some cried.
Some begged.
None prayed that he could hear.
Mostly they were silent.
Then the
pop pop pop pop pop
of the Lugers and Walthers
and with each bullet
the metal metamorphosis of human beings
into falling lumps of meat.
Then the quicklime
the dirt
more bullets
more bodies
more quicklime.
Layers and layers
like a trifle.

The Sad Wife Trilogy

Jungfrau

Once
we fed ourselves to the other
in careless chunks
across the chasm of night.
Pieces like wedding cake–
 nervous smiles, yellow frosting on her chin,
 crumbs caught in the corners of my moustache.
A photographer shouts, "Hold it! That's it. Perfect! Just like that.
 Smile. No, big smile. Great!"
Flash
I recall
the maitre d' counting heads like the years ahead of us.

Now we wear awkward tilted library books
wedged beneath our chins
where our hearts used to beat.
You must check for a pulse these nights
in the cast iron hum of the oil burner.
We feed our blankets to the center of the bed,

quilts uplifted like great mountain ranges–
 the Andes some nights
 some nights the Alps.
Tonight
the cat sleeps across the Jungfrau.
That means young maiden in German.
I'm pretty sure the cat couldn't care,
looking only for heat trapped on either side of
the mountains
and
maybe pieces of cake.

The Sad Wife

A man stares at the face of his wife in a
photograph.
A man knows her somehow.

A man stares at the face of his watch
imagining gears, sprockets, a mainspring
somehow, even ticking.

There are no mainsprings
behind the face of his wife
nor pictures ticking.

Sleep Now

You roll over to him
miss his unparted lips,
peck him on the chin.
No matter.
Roll over.
Go to sleep
waiting for waves of me
bundled in sad poetry
to roll over.
And I'll be there
waiting too
in waves to
roll over you
and make sad poetry
out of what is left of
you and me.
Roll over.
Sleep now.

Trilogy of My Father

New Orleans

And Betty
watches me
with winter eyes
blue as snowfall
and maybe rain.
Her snowfall says
she knows me
like some weather tired
gypsy
reading my falling father's
tea leaves
in this basement
in New Orleans
not in Spain.

And I said
"Hello"
to Jesus
but I knew

he could not answer.
I read where
his ambition was to be
a soft shoe dancer
not some wounded
wooden
jet plane
married to the runway
by unrelenting failure
and a
cane.

And I kissed
the hands of
Jesus.
Again
there was no
answer.
I did not need one,
Really!
I noticed I was crying
seeing through his

mangled fingers
like Betty
sees through winter
and maybe rain.

Daddy's Other Shoe

Have you seen Daddy's other shoe?
Where did he lose it?
When did he have it last?
Did he leave it inside the cast?
Have you seen Daddy's other shoe?

I remember what it looked like
from the times he'd ride by me
when I was riding my bike.
He'd leave the grocery bags by the hydrant.
One time he was crying.
Have you seen Daddy's other shoe?

He'd call his boys to the curb
to carry his baggage
and bear his legacy.
And without saying
he'd ask, "Do you see me?"
Have you seen Daddy's other shoe?"

I've seen it
At least I thought I did
did you?
Don't "Hi Dad me"
not unless you see it too.
Have you seen Daddy's other shoe?

Or is it that it's fallen
or that it's dropped?
Have you heard it call
calling you to take up his arms
to prop him up
to make him fly?
Or did you turn away?
What did you say?
Did you say

"Have you seen Daddy's other shoe?

I remember he was crying once.

Onion Street

My father teeters with limbo for a leg
his crutches are not wings
he cannot fly.
But he can fly
carried lie cigar ash
blown by an angel
a teetering angel on the head of a pin.
Flying would bury him
crush him, the flying man
under the densities of burning gravity
like a life full of dented cans.

Now I wonder
What waits for me.
Just tears on Onion Street
Onion Street tears.

But I should know
that in Coney Island

the Parachute Jump molders
like the Eiffel Tower of rusty bones,
rusty bones and a halo
for the angel of dented cans.
That it waits
like a reminder
like a cancer
like the cancer that eats his bones
that my time
like his time
is time on Onion Street

Now I wonder
wonder what waits for me.
Tears on Onion Street,
I suspect,
Onion Street tears.

City Kid Poems

Sonnet– City Once Known

Have you not seen the city I once knew
buried beneath years of silent defect,
impatient rust and angry shades of blue?
History's hidden behind its neglect:

The endless sewer to sewer stickball games,
crumbling cement steps worn smooth as slate,
summer Tuesdays' boardwalk firework flames,
my father coming home(always too late).

Soft blacktop leaps to meet a kid's sneaker
rounding first, but dreaming of home at last.
Old tar just hardens, the streets grow bleaker
and bright futures are leveled by the past.

On fall days as shedding trees turn to stone,
my shadows visit this city once known.

Commentary, Sorry

We're all masochists it seems.
Yes, we hate it,
but we're not about to give up boredom for nostalgia.

July is the off month for my sign
always has been
with its autumn-like rhyme
and deja vu nights on Brian's porch,
or instant replays of the boardwalk–
fireworks and such.
Where?
That depended on our mood, I guess.
Never could understand being a man
in July
and when seventeen came to visit
nothing much changed.

Frustration replaced baseball
for we were in love

with Renaissance women
but would have settled on anyone ...
almost anyone
anyone who would have settled on us.
Weekends?
Just longer versions of week nights
without the intermission.

August arrives
but not before
our minds have gone
and Christmas doesn't
really matter.
We make our moves
to see other friends
to do other things
only to realize
we didn't have any others
and that new things are but
poor elaborations of the
originals.

62542152R00168

Made in the USA
Middletown, DE
23 August 2019